# The Fake's Distress

**Also by this author:**

*Bloomington Days: Town and Gown in Middle America*

*Cathedrals of Learning: Great and Ancient Universities of Western Europe*

*Stickmen: Reflections on the Goalie's Eccentric Art*

*B-town Blues*

*Westported*

*Beached*

*A Slew of Clerihews*

*Hewn from Yew: Newry Notables Past and Present*

*The Book of Blaise: A Saint and his Name*

*Footie Doggerel: A Riot of Clerihews and Haikus*


Fiction:

*The Fake's Progress: A Fragmentary Account of the Early Life of Sebastian Conyers*

*The Fake's Regress: Further Fragments from the Life of Sebastian Conyers*

*The Fake's Egress: Yet Further Fragments from the Life of Sebastian Conyers*

*The Fake's Success: Some Remaining Fragments from the Life of Sebastian Conyers*

# The Fake's Distress

## Final Fragments from the Life of Sebastian Conyers

## Blaise Cronin

Copyright © 2023 Blaise Cronin

All rights reserved, including the right to reproduce this book, or portions thereof in any form. No part of this text may be reproduced, transmitted, downloaded, decompiled, reverse engineered, or stored, in any form or introduced into any information storage and retrieval system, in any form or by any means, whether electronic or mechanical without the express written permission of the author.

This is a work of fiction. Names and characters are the product of the author's imagination and any resemblance to actual persons, living or dead, is entirely coincidental.

The views expressed in this work are solely those of the author and do not necessarily reflect the views of the publisher, and the publisher hereby disclaims any responsibility for them.

ISBN: 978-1-6781-8679-1

PublishNation LLC
www.publishnation.net

# CONTENTS

**PART I**

Will Power

Cloud Cover

Manna from Heaven

Mind Games

In Memoriam

Bye George

Nocturnal Gavotte

Killer Cereal

Climate Change

Mirren Image

Close Encounter

Devolution

**PART II**

The Prize Malarky

The Jury's out

Haughty Towers

London's Calling

Spaghetti Conjunction

Sartorial Semiotics

Purge and Progress
Grape and Grope
Famished for Fame
Topic of Cancer
I Love Lucy

**PART III**
In Media Res
Quorate
We Have Lift-off
Setting the Stage
Techno-sex
Taste Buds
Gloves off
Kitchen Cabinet
Turfed out
Ducks in a Row
Christmas Cheer
Prozac Please!

**PART IV**
A Good Read
Phatic Communication
Stalemateyness
Crossed Swords

Table d'Hôte
Fuck Fiction
Fatwa Chance
Bullish
Stage Presence
Fired up

## PART V
Why Me?
Aftershocks
Near Neighbours
A Smile Is Just a Smile
On Reflection
In the Lurch No More
Stop, Start
Metro Man
Screen Time
Clear the Decks
Flight of Fancy

## PART VI
Flying the Flag
Turbulence
The Square Fellow
Saints Alive!

# PART I

# WILL POWER

April came and went and with it, George Parnell Kingsley. That his oldest friend had been named after Ireland's uncrowned king took Sebastian by surprise. Could there have been a family connection of some kind? Not once had the fact been alluded to in conversation or noted in print. Even the most recent media profiles had failed to pick up on the nominal curiosity. Naturally, the writer's demise also came as quite a shock. Death, even when not altogether unexpected, ripples the most assured surfaces. A nurse had given him the news on the last of his futile hospital visits. Four-plus decades of friendship hadn't been enough to get a foot in the door for a farewell peek at his intubated buddy and benefactor. The only person permitted to see George during his three weeks in the ICU had been buxom Jane Kynaston, not, as he had thought initially, a close relative but a distant cousin. It just didn't seem right. Bureaucracy has a way of producing perverse outcomes in its commitment to reasoned equitableness; a case of inflexible rules ruling out common sense. That was how he imagined his departed friend putting it over a disappearing pint in McTigue's.

Like George, Jane had trained initially as an accountant before moving into commercial insurance. Even so, the connective tissue between them was tenuous. Over the years, the pair had rarely spent any time together, but instinct told him she could and would act as next of kin in the event of a medical emergency. Dutiful competency was her redeeming feature, a fact recognized, albeit without much enthusiasm, by both George and her current employers. In speech and manner, she inclined to bossiness. Spinsterhood seemed only to amplify the character trait, one of which she was blithely unaware. At the office, out of earshot, she was known as 'Ober,' having been christened '*Oberführerin*' by a waggish underling with a WWII obsession.

Whether at work or off-duty she eschewed make-up, favoured Playtex underwire bras, and cleaved to functional footwear. That she would be a beneficiary—perhaps even a significant one—of his estate lay within the bounds of possibility, even though she knew virtually nothing about George's friendships or ramified business affairs. He had neither siblings nor dependents and seemed, as best she could tell, to live in contented near isolation. An irregular Christmas card was the most she could expect. He might gift some of his estate to charity but surely family would not be overlooked. In truth, the closest thing to a dependent he had was Sebastian, but Ms Kynaston had been unaware of Sebastian Conyers' existence until their fleeting encounter in the hospital waiting room, after which he had not warranted a second thought. But for the fact that the hotelier was wearing red slacks and sporting hair too long for a man of his years, he might not have registered at all. That sartorial frivolity betokened a skittish personality was one of her fixed notions. George had not uttered a single word following his collapse, whip in hand, at the side of Daisy's bed. His medical condition was for the first fortnight described as stable, little consolation for someone who had suffered a massive stroke and was oscillating between three and four on the Glasgow Coma Scale. Clot dissolving drugs failed to make a difference, as did every other attempted intervention. He went out like a light, with no one present. Indeed, such was the abruptness of the change in his state on the night he expired it would have been tempting to infer the involvement of a nefarious hand. The autopsy eliminated the need for either an inquest or criminal fantasy. George Parnell Kingsley died of natural causes, age 63: intracerebral haemorrhage compounded by the onset of septicaemia. There was no mention of sexual activity, deviant or otherwise, as a possible contributory factor. No one had pulled the plug in the dead of night or tampered with his medication. Shit happens, even in the west of Ireland.

Ms Kynaston's surprise at the news of George's swift demise proved mild compared to the reaction she experienced listening to his will being read out by Arthur Dooley in his paper-strewn office several days later. The gangly solicitor's waxen skin and faintly jaundiced pallor would have made him a perfect specimen for a tableau in Madame Tussauds, she was thinking. Jane's pass-remarkable side had a way of popping up despite her best efforts, like teenage acne. The trait dated from childhood and had not pleased her mother one little bit. It was not a trait shared by Arthur Dooley. Soberly dressed, softly spoken and suspicious of levity, Mr Dooley was an archetypal small-town solicitor whose preference for bland food was daily indulged by his wife of twenty-six years, Patricia Dooley *née* Quinn. She worked part-time in the practice as a bookkeeper. It was Dooley's inherent greyness as much as anything else that had appealed to George. His office may have been a Dickensian fire hazard, but his responsiveness and punctiliousness could not be gainsaid. George did not require big-name legal expertise, not that such could have been found in the small town. Discretion coupled with deliberativeness defined his needs, and Dooley embodied those characteristics. At the time of his death, George was probably the practice's wealthiest and most famous client. His late-life literary achievements would ensure obituaries in the national as well as local press. Nothing, however, in the solicitor's demeanour had changed since the pair's first meeting; neither his approach nor professional fee was influenced by notions of celebrity.

The document that would transform Sebastian's life and simultaneously reduce Jane to apoplexy had been entrusted to a safe pair of hands. She watched as a gilt letter opener released several closely typed sheets of A4 from a manila envelope. First came the deceased's instructions pertaining to burial. Instead of a traditional Irish funeral and rambunctious wake with the embalmed body as cynosure, George requested cremation in Rathboffin, along with a modest memorial service. The event should be secular in nature, the mood upbeat, which did not mean there'd be inebriated attendees stumbling against an open casket or spilling of whisky over the dickied-up stiff. George would exit in low-key fashion, reduced to ashes. As a reflex, Jane tried to imagine her remarks. Should she begin by mentioning how they had once played hide and seek among the lush rhododendrons of Howth Hill or by extolling her distant cousin's recent literary and cinematic successes? A confident if inflectionless voice curtailed her daydreaming. 'The memorial address is to be given by Dr Sebastian Conyers. Others among those present will be invited to speak extemporaneously. A reception is to be held afterwards in McTigue's bar in Ballyhannah, where, with Pádraig's blessing, my ashes will be added to those of the turf fire, said task to be performed by Dr Conyers. A provisional guest list for both events is attached. Additions may be suggested by my friend Dr Conyers and my cousin Ms Kynaston, who will, I trust, make all necessary arrangements for the event jointly, funds being provided to that end.' 'Dr Who?' interrupted Jane. 'Just who is this Dr Conkers?' '*Conyers*,' corrected Dooley, 'Sebastian Conyers, your late cousin's business partner and friend.' It clicked. The fellow in red trousers. 'But I don't know this man. He's not any kind of family relative and I've never once heard his name mentioned by my cousin.' 'Well, Ms Kynaston, I am not really in a position to comment. These are your late cousin's instructions as transmitted to me less than six months ago. The legally binding document from which I am reading was drafted at his request, proof-read and signed by him in my presence. And you can be assured that he was fully compos mentis at the time.' It was as if the absent author had written his will with the express aim of pitting his charmless relative against his tragi-comic chum. George would surely be watching the ensuing farce from the gods. Low-grade mischief of that kind had always appealed to him. Posthumously he would continue to play games; hadn't the draft manuscript of *The Capering Clown*, inspired by the antics of one Sebastian Conyers, already been edited, and provisionally scheduled for publication a year hence? Jane, who had once ordered a Pierrot instead of a Perrier at a book launch in the Shelbourne bar, was beginning to wonder if she knew her cousin at all. Things, already bad, were about to get worse, almost unbearably so for the tweedy spinster.

# CLOUD COVER

The Conyers was full over the May bank holiday weekend, as it had been almost every day since early spring. Forward bookings were robust, cash flow positive and guests by and large of the type that met with management's approbation. It was fair to say that the business had reached cruising altitude quicker than either Sebastian or George could reasonably have expected, given that the country was exiting from a recession. Finding suitable staff in the wake of first Mary's and later Jane's departure had been a challenge. Nor were matters helped by Daisy's sudden flight from the local scene following the ghastly incident; her extensive knowledge of the hospitality industry was no longer on tap. Fortunately, and not for the first time, Carla stepped into the breach, drawing upon her contacts among the migrant worker population. Ana from Lisbon and Isabel from Granada both had prior experience in the hotel sector and were brought up to speed by the Galician gem in next to no time. Their English was more than adequate, their accents charming rather than problematic. It didn't take long for them to realize that the typical Conyers guest not only appreciated but rewarded smiling faces. Good service thus begat even better service: a virtuous circle. The Iberian dream team was how Sebastian referred to his trio of full-time helpers. For the weekend 'Tapas & Tipples' sessions in the bar area Carla had recruited a dark-haired lassie from the heart of the Connemara Gaeltacht. Bilingual Eimear had been speaking Irish since the cradle and her native fluency, once revealed in casual conversation, proved a source of considerable interest for guests, not least those from North America, as few seemed to realize that Irish was a living language, albeit one on life-support.

But a fat, dark cloud had parked itself over hotel following George's hospitalization. As a minority stakeholder in the business, Sebastian was quite right to be worried. The Conyers belonged, in effect, to George and there was no way of knowing what provisions, if any, his friend might have put in place in the event of his death. Sebastian's future could hinge on a whim, on a codicil. The pair had never discussed contingency or transition planning. Of course, wily George knew from experience that the withholding of guarantees would keep his partner on his toes. If everything fell too easily into his lap, Sebastian's commitment to the cause would likely falter. The absence of a safety net ensured sharpness of focus and purpose. But sharpness came at a price: angst. And it was angst as much as sadness that Sebastian was experiencing at that moment. George was gone and there was nothing to be done about that. Grieving was all well and good, but it didn't help run The Conyers. Of immediate concern to Sebastian was the fact that the boutique hotel he had midwifed into being might at any moment be put up for sale or shuttered, leaving him, quite possibly, both homeless and penniless. For several weeks he had been living in limbo. Soon enough, the legal wheels would begin to spin but all he could do for now was wait, ensuring to the best of his ability that his guests were waited upon with the kind of unwavering attention that had become a hallmark of the bijou hotel. The looming black cloud was none of their concern.

The uncertainty surrounding the future of the business could hardly be blamed for the cloud over the relationship between Sebastian and Carla. This was more a wispy cirrus than a cumulonimbus, but a cloud, nonetheless. What might have happened—what the Sebastian of old might have expected to happen—didn't on that fateful night. While sexually aroused George had been flogging beseeching Daisy, Sebastian might as well have been flogging a dead horse. The spontaneous embrace in the street was reprised in front of the spluttering gas fire in Carla's flat. They nuzzled, they squeezed; they hugged, they sighed, without exchanging a word, without taking off their coats, a pair of lost souls providing one another with human warmth on an unseasonably cold March night. Once or twice his lips had drifted over hers, pausing briefly and lightly, warm air emitting in little puffs from their nostrils. Her tongue remained behind gated teeth. His penis scarcely twitched. And then, nothing. They seemed at a loss to know how to proceed, like actors in a studio rehearsal suddenly deprived of their scripts.

Sebastian was exceedingly fond of Carla who happened to be extraordinarily easy on the eye. But he didn't lust after her the way he did so many other women, didn't fantasize about doing the dirty with her. Affection and caring mattered much more to her than seductiveness or sexual gymnastics. Once again, planetary separation: men from Mars, women from Venus. In some respects, she was a potential soul mate, in others his antithesis. For one thing, the judgmentalism he exhibited with such liberality was alien to her. Lookism didn't get a look-in with her. She either didn't notice or chose to disregard people's blemishes. Having worked alongside her at both *Rhopos* and The Conyers he realized that she did not share his libidinous streak. She'd no more consent to a quick panties-around-the-ankles shag atop the reception desk than insult a customer. Her exotic appetites were synonymous with calamari and crustacea.

After a mug of tepid herbal tea and near silence, he had headed back to the hotel, on the way relieving himself against a wall. 'Put a Celtic tiger in your tank,' exhorted the faded graffito. The urgency of his need brought to mind the embarrassing incident on the slopes of Slievemore with Helga. An overactive bladder did not sit comfortably with his self-image. The mere thought of entropy repulsed him. Lying in their respective beds processing the night's events, the pair concluded that their easy-going, working relationship was something to preserve, not jeopardize. A case of morphic resonance, George might have said. They rehearsed their lines for the next day. Simultaneous smiles ceded to warm laughter. Nothing needed to be said. The cloud evaporated and life at The Conyers resumed with habitual smoothness. Sebastian would not be walking down the aisle in Santiago de Compostela any time soon. Carla deep-froze her private fantasy. She felt genuine affection for a man old enough to be her father and wayward enough to be her younger brother. For all his fecklessness and occasional insensitivities, he was hard to dislike. Sebastian Conyers possessed a raffish charm, while his almost unerring ability to land on his feet was worthy of a Cirque du Soleil acrobat. She couldn't decide whether that was down to talent or luck. If nothing else, his mercurial nature made her smile.

# MANNA FROM HEAVEN

Patricia Dooley's lipstick popped against the mayonnaise walls. It would be a stretch to describe the forty-eight-year-old with the ready smile as vivacious, but she possessed enough vim to have more than a handful of silent admirers about town. The Dooleys made for an odd-looking couple, confirmation of the adage that opposites attract. She had taken a shine to Sebastian the first time George and he had met with her husband to discuss the old bank building purchase. Polished and dapper was how she described the town's newest hotelier to her friends in the community gardening group. He carried himself well and spoke with easy authority. The long swept-back locks further distinguished him from her husband, not to mention the entire over-fifty male population of Rathboffin. She was taken with his flamboyance, but no more than that. Her private thoughts, though, were not the kind that would have engendered a confessional blush. Menopause had drained the last scintilla of sexuality from a placid marriage. Sebastian, eyes scanning her bosom, was wondering if she was still up for it when Lurch, as George—a teenage fan of *The Addams Family*—had baptized the lugubrious solicitor, emerged from his lair, extended a bony hand, and ushered him in.

The call had come much sooner than he'd expected, but his head was already full of gyring what-if scenarios. On the surface he appeared relaxed and in good spirits. He hadn't burdened Carla with his concerns, instead regaled her with mirthful stories about his old friend. How on earth could he and her father have been an item when George's life up to that point was ostensibly one of exemplary celibacy? They'd probably never know. For the previous forty-eight hours a slow-churning dread had disrupted Sebastian's bowel movements. What if George had died intestate? Would everything go to the officious relative, or would his friend's assets be distributed across multiple persons unknown, or perhaps bequeathed to a worthy cause? If he did leave a will, what if any provision had been made in respect of the hotel? He had known George for more than forty years, but he also knew that his chum, ultimately, was not for knowing. He had revelled in his inscrutability, relying on a combination of disarming affability and slickness of wit to give people if not a false at least a carefully curated sense of who and what he was: a man with as many layers as an onion. The ever-ready, lopsided grin that had won so many over would flash no more. Sadness, genuine if fleeting, weighed down on an unsettled tummy as the orphaned hotelier waited to be informed of his fate. He recalled one of the glib exhortations he had used with his life-coaching clients: 'Uncertainty is the mother of self-discovery.' It provided little consolation. Imparting wisdom was easier than acting on it.

Having dispensed with the niceties, Dooley pulled from a desk drawer the document he had opened in front of Jane Kynaston the previous afternoon. He read from it in the same monotonous voice, beginning with the late writer's instructions pertaining to both the cremation and memorial events. The first round went to Sebastian. He, not Kynaston, would deliver the eulogy. Round two also, definitively so. Ownership of the hotel would be transferred in its entirety to him, debt-free, with no mention whatsoever of the distant cousin. Not so much as a linen cupboard for Ms Kynaston. Lurch delivered the information in deadpan fashion, as if mildly autistic. He was issuing mere words; Sebastian was hearing celestial sounds. It seemed inconceivable that things could get any better, but they did. The writer's award-winning, architect-designed house and all chattels associated therewith were now Sebastian's, as was the Audi sedan. His innards were churning again, but with excitement. When, he wondered, had his friend drafted the will? Had it been revised or was it in its original form? Could he conceivably have experienced a premonition of some kind? There'd be no solving the mystery.

George's impenetrability would follow him to the grave, just as he would have wished. Having won the lottery literally a year or so earlier, Sebastian was now winning it figuratively. Even in a third-rate novel, such a convenient coincidence would stretch credulity.

The glad tidings rolled on. Sebastian would also be receiving a lump sum of one hundred thousand euros, no strings attached; Ms Kynaston twenty thousand; Mateo Delgado twenty and one Jenny Lamb also twenty; various worthy causes more modest amounts. That was the knock-out punch. Whether Jane had heard any of what was said subsequently is unclear. The previous day her face had turned the colour of an over-ripe peach and she was quaking visibly in her chair such that Mr Dooley feared she might have a seizure. It was not so much that she had an expectation of inheritance, rather the indignity of being trumped by this Johnny-come-lately. Storming out of the office past a startled Patricia Dooley, she was Lyssa incarnate. More was to come. George's net worth was far greater than either one had imagined. Yes, he had inherited a small fortune; yes, he had managed his assets with judiciousness, and yes, he had made good money from his book deals and movie adaptations, but just how much took Sebastian's breath away. There was, however, one condition attached to the will. Sebastian would undertake to organize a biannual literary prize in Rathboffin. Of course, the condition was not the kind that could be enforced legally, or not without difficulty, so better that it be described as a request, a *quid pro quo*.

A separate document described in greater detail what George envisaged, the financial aspects and what would be required of Sebastian in his future role as director of the Parnell Prize, said role to be performed while he continued to manage The Conyers. He chuckled on hearing the choice of name. The endowment's current market value, Lurch informed him, exceeded €7 million and was spread across a diversified portfolio of stocks and bonds, in a fashion that was neither unduly conservative nor foolishly aggressive. It would continue to be managed by Fay & Florin, an investment firm in the capital. They would have ultimate veto on expenditures. The principal, naturally, was not to be touched but even in a stagnant economy the dividends accruing would be sufficient to underwrite something quite special. Better still, the coffers of the Parnell Prize would be boosted as downstream earnings from multiple media platforms poured in. The Croesus from Kilkenny would be leaving his mark, in more ways than one. Most of what Mr Dooley said thereafter went unheard as Sebastian's mind switched into overdrive. They would reconvene in a day or two, review George's appended instructions and discuss the mechanics of implementation to ensure compliance with both the spirit and procedural minutiae of the will. Sebastian wafted out of the office past a tea-sipping Mrs Dooley, floated down Church Lane and breezed into The Conyers where he scooped up an astonished Carla and spun her around dervish-like beneath the portrait of St Sebastian. 'There is a God. And his name is George. *Arriba Jorge!*' That evening guests seated in the bar and lounge areas were surprised to find both the debonair manager and his gracious assistant replenishing complimentary glasses of Prosecco with rare conviviality. The dark cloud had passed; Peter Pan was back on cloud nine.

# MIND GAMES

From her bedroom she thought she could discern the cone of Croagh Patrick in the hazy May sunshine. Perhaps it was a chimera. True, she had been a distant relative but not as distant as the dictates of George's will seemed to imply. Hadn't she, on hearing of his sudden incapacitation, without hesitation, taken leave from her job in Dublin, packed for an indeterminate absence and motored across the country to be at his side? It seemed the natural, the right thing to do. She would be compensated for her good deed, but neither in the manner nor to the extent that she deemed appropriate. What she had felt in the moment was what she would continue to feel: insulted. It was rank injustice, nothing less. What on earth had inspired her cousin, a sensible career accountant, to lavish his money on a fop like Conyers, basically cede control of his estate to an unknown quantity?

Jane belonged to the population of women who gripped the steering wheel in the one and eleven position while also hunching forward. Her body language seemed to suggest that she was looking for the road, as if it somehow might not be in front of her or, alternatively, might at any second dematerialize. That afternoon, on leaving Dooley's office, she could be seen clutching the wheel of her Ford Focus with such tightness that her knuckles resembled blanched hazelnuts. Cars honked; she seethed, oblivious to the traffic around her. It was a minor miracle that she reached the Slievemore Hotel carpark unscathed. Jane, never one for 'the drink,' nor the kind of woman who felt comfortable sitting alone in a public bar, needed a snifter. The Polish barman pored a large, leggy brandy into a preposterous balloon glass while making an abortive attempt to engage his visibly agitated customer in small talk. 'Put it on room 406, please,' was all she said before taking the glass and heading up to her bedroom, the very same one in which Sebastian had so heroically defended Aoife from the giant spider. If only hotel rooms could talk.

Jane and the fop arranged to meet the next afternoon in Keenan's. It would not have been her choice of rendezvous. Sebastian, wearing his faded Levi's and a suede blouson, looked to her mind like a superannuated pop singer. She entered through the lounge bar door, upholstered in tweed. Her begrudging handshake felt as limp as his penis. Sebastian ordered a glass of red wine, the house Malbec. She might have known. His type couldn't keep away from the stuff. The tartness of the coffee caused her face to scrunch up like that of a petulant child. Having emerged as undisputed *victor ludorum*, Sebastian could afford to be magnanimous. That infuriated her even more, which, of course, was his intention. George must have enjoyed imagining how the pair's first face-to-face encounter would play out. What a smug twerp, probably one of those dubious homosexual types, she thought, watching as he swirled his wine with D4 pretentiousness. Ms Kynaston belonged to the generation that had yet to become comfortable with the appellation gay. Moreover, she was just the kind of person who, had she known about conversion therapy, would have deemed it a laudable solution. Could it have been that her late cousin—strait-laced and grey-suited during the entirety of his Dublin days—had been sexually involved with, or perish the thought, in an open relationship with this fellow? Had George's move from the metropolis to the rain-drenched west raddled his brain? She didn't want to think about it but could not prevent herself. Sebastian guessed where her thoughts were going and rather enjoyed it.

Passive aggression gradually gave way to sullen acceptance. He would grant her time to deliver remarks and accepted the few additional names she proposed inviting, though doubted that many would make the trek west. She seemed not to know any members of their Trinity circle and, unsurprisingly, was clueless about the publishing and entertainment spheres that had become George's late-life milieu. She looked blank as he read out George's list of invitees.

It was dawning on her that she really did know next to nothing about her late relative. He almost felt sorry for the frump across the table from him. They'd meet for the last time at the cremation ceremony. When her inheritance finally came through, it would pay for a new Ford Focus and a hiking holiday in northern Spain. It had long been a dream of hers to walk the Camino de Santiago. Whether the satisfaction she felt on completing the pilgrimage would have been tarnished by the knowledge that her late cousin had once shacked up in historic Santiago de Compostela with the leather-clad photographer Mateo Delgado must remain a matter of conjecture.

Sebastian tarried in Keenan's. The surge of euphoria he first felt on learning that he was effectively set up for life had not faded and would not for some time. Both he and Carla had woken up with debilitating hangovers the night after the reading of the will. Yet, as he sat in the darkened interior enjoying that special mid-afternoon pub atmosphere, his still woozy head began to fill with images and sounds of George, pint in hand, expatiating on subjects about which he was knowledgeable and others about which he knew next to nothing. Often, it was his mastery of the Socratic technique that fooled the casual listener. Penetrating questions, the hallmark of a good barrister, were all too easily construed as evidence of deep domain knowledge. The unmindful listener was having the wool pulled over his eyes by a master carder. When it came to forensic questioning, George had few equals. Lacing his remarks with quicksilver wit, he further convinced anyone in earshot that he must know whereof he spoke. On his day, he could be formidable, as eavesdropping regulars at McTigue's had come to realize. His jovial fireside presence there would be missed. From here on in, Sebastian was bowling alone.

# IN MEMORIAM

A cane-handled umbrella shielded Carla and Sebastian from the worst of the cloudburst. May was showing its temperamental side, further incontrovertible evidence of climate change, if you believed Connaught's Cassandras. Jane, unfortunately, was caught short and arrived at the ceremony bearing a more than passing resemblance to the proverbial rat. An odoriferous rat, given how tweed interacts with water. He counted roughly sixty people scattered around the low-lit room, most talking in hushed tones. It was altogether un-wake like, rather too reverential. Music played, not loudly enough for his liking. Voices rose as he amped up the decibel level; the room coming to death-affirming life. A knot of stylishly dressed individuals caught his attention: publishing and movie production types, he guessed. Unbeknownst to him, several had checked in early at The Conyers, leaving their luggage at the front desk with Carla. There was no sign of Carol. Time, in her case, had not been a great healer. Decades on, and still her loathing for him had not diminished, which was a great shame as Sebastian liked the idea of being on good terms with his ex. Wasn't that the 'done' thing these days? Overall, a sartorially mixed bag, with most attendees plumping for sub fusc. He recognized a few local faces, including the irrepressible Claude, who would be catering the follow-on event at McTigue's—Pádraig's toasties might not cut it. Out of the corner of his eye, Sebastian watched the old goat make a bee line for one of the media types, an ash blonde in her forties. Rebuffed but unruffled, he headed straight for Carla, who, of course, had his number.

A blown-up, black-and-white photo of the deceased writer, the same one that had been used on the dustjacket of *The Galician Octopus*, occupied pride of place at the front of the room. It stood next to a pedestal bearing a small urn, across from a wooden dais and lectern. A stately Paschal candle glowed off to one side where the undertaker maintained a discrete, watchful presence. The deceased's instructions had provided no guidance as regards music, so Sebastian and Jane, after a spot of wrangling, had come up with a selection best described as idiosyncratic. She had not the foggiest idea about her cousin's tastes, or indeed whether music had ever mattered to him, but felt that a hymn or two and maybe 'Amazing Grace' would be fitting. Sebastian knew his friend had little interest in any kind of music other than C&W. The playlist opened with a set of Galician folk tunes featuring the bagpipes, which was what greeted the guests. Only a handful could have known that the traditional pipes were a nod to the occasion when Mateo, on the lash with George, had charmed the regulars at McTigue's and exhibited, with unforgettable exuberance, his love of Spanish-Celtic music. After the last set of attendee remarks came Merle Haggard's 'The Bottle Let Me Down.' Classics by Johnny Cash, Loretta Lynn and Tammy Wynette rounded out the selection, to the evident astonishment of the ash blonde and her cosmopolitan companions. Sebastian couldn't resist a little mischief.

It would have been in character for George to have written his own obituary or monody, not that anything to that effect was mentioned by Mr Dooley. Quite possibly a draft languished in a desk drawer or on a computer hard drive back at the house. By now people had taken their seats, and Sebastian, having called the proceedings to order, paused the music. He eschewed the small lapel microphone, gripped the sides of the lectern with his hands. He was noteless. A quondam lecturer on the international stage, Castletownmorris's Dr Conyers knew that an audience of sixty did not warrant amplification. He would grab and hold the room's attention. His eyes raked the rows of seats: Carla, Claude, the media mavens, sober types from the Dublin accounting world and, striding into the room at the very last minute, clad in his signature black leather, Galicia's most famous photographer. Carla had said that her father was hoping to make it. That should guarantee a lively send-off in McTigue's, thought Sebastian.

Foregoing a conventional introduction, he launched straight into his remarks. 'If George ever prayed, which I sincerely doubt, he would have prayed for there to be no God, for no God could condone evil and human suffering, not to mention the abomination that is Sharia law. But, then again, he could never have done that because to do so would have been to acknowledge, first, the possibility of the existence of a deity, whether benign or malign, and second, to concede that prayer might somehow be able to influence the tide of human affairs. George, my friends, was an unreconstructed atheist, who never gave Pascal's famous wager the time of day. "Agnosticism is a posh word for waffle." "Only fools bet against reality." "Eternity is a long-winded eulogy."' That got an immediate if decorous laugh. '"Hungry for meaning? Try sliced pantheism." "You pay a premium for prudentialism." Those were the kinds of things he'd come out with at the drop of a hat or a sip of Jameson. Did I say *a* sip?' Another sliver of laughter. 'Dear not so old George was a man of substance, in every sense, a chubby, cuddly chameleon; an impish puppeteer with an unsurpassable ability to make us believe that what we saw was what we were getting. Let me put it another way: there was a George for every occasion, for every friend. His talent was to be able to keep all the plates spinning, all the Georges in order, all of us happy in our comforting delusion. We, each of us here today, believed we were his best friend because he allowed us, encouraged us to believe such. And, of course, we wanted it to be the case. With that wit, supple intellect, and a grin more winsome than gormless, how could we not have been seduced? Who doesn't want to be in the orbit of, not to mention sit next to the sociometric star? I first met him at Trinity in the sixties, drank my way around Dublin with him, from the Bailey to the Stag's Head, from Davy Byrnes to McDaid's. I might never have escaped the clutches of Mother Church but for him. More to the point, had he not set aside his abacus in favour of a quill, some of you might never have heard of or met the man we are gathered here today to remember. Almost singlehandedly, he has put Ballyhannah on the map, convinced a generation of local Leaving Cert students that popular fiction constitutes a meaningful and possibly lucrative career path.' That aside earned a titter or two from the local contingent.

Sebastian stopped to drink from an at-hand glass and read the room. Jane, sitting in the front row, looked almost as uncomfortable as she did peevish. Carla wore a sad smile. Mateo fiddled with the extremities of his hedge-like moustache. Claude was leering at a woman two rows in front of him. The ash blonde may or may not have been paying attention. Rather than reminisce further, Sebastian switched gears. 'George won't just live on in our memories. There will be a tangible legacy in the form of the soon-to-be launched Parnell Foundation and Prize.' Another strategic pause. 'Raise a hand if you knew that Parnell was our friend's middle name?' Not one person did. The announcement about the prize caused a ripple. The ash blonde looked up, now attentive. Sebastian explained in a few words that the endowment would be used to fund a literary prize. 'Thanks to George Parnell Kingsley's generosity, the media spotlight will be directed west.' The hotelier skipped over his future role in the foundation. No need to show one's hand too soon. He had learned that by observing George, a master of the tease.

Jane did her level best under the circumstances, but her clothes were still damp, so too her hair. What she said was well-meaning, the sentiments clichéd: a childhood memory or two to justify her presence and a few remarks about his last days in the hospital. The rest was all leather or prunella, adding nothing to the known bones of George's life. She was relieved to get back to her seat. Sebastian invited others to step forward. Heads turned; eyes scanned the room. Who'd go first? Surely there was at least one windbag, one self-promoter desperate to attain the podium, someone with an untrumpable story. A former president of the Institute of Chartered Accountants in Ireland testified to George's professional and indeed personal qualities, in a manner that was as inoffensive as it was insipid. A home-grown luvvie who played a supporting role in the screen adaptation of *The Actuary's Miscalculation* injected an element of distasteful campness into the proceedings, using George as a pretext to talk about himself and his burgeoning career. The C-lister was followed by the ash blonde, who introduced herself as George's publisher. It was she, Annabel Hyde, who had taken a punt on the unknown writer, she who had helped negotiate the movie rights for both books, and it was her company, Constitution Press, that would be bringing out *The Capering Clown*. Ms Hyde spoke in effusive fashion of the writer's talents, lauding his speed and clarity of thought. With a smile, she acknowledged that he did indeed have an extraordinary ability to make everyone feel they were special, the way Seamus Heaney and Bill Clinton did. 'His cussed charm,' were her exact words. Sebastian's gaze didn't deviate for one second. Nor did Claude's. The professional lives of the publisher and foundation director seemed destined to intersect. Matters of rights and royalties would require attention in the months and years to come. To Sebastian's surprise, Señor Delgado chose to remain silent and so, with 'Amazing Grace' playing in the background, Sebastian announced that a coach was waiting to take one and all to McTigue's, where their friend would be guaranteed a warm send-off.

# BYE GEORGE

A spanking new Mercedes-Benz bus, emblazoned with the logo of Kavanagh Coaches, pulled up outside the funeral home. Seán Óg was at the wheel, proud as punch. 'Bring her back in one piece, lad,' was all his father had said as he handed over the keys of his fleet's flagship. Sebastian rounded up the attendees and shooed them on board as if they were dallying sheep. A few chose to travel by car; most didn't. There was alcohol to be taken, after all. The media people, mobile phones in hand, settled in at the rear, preferring to keep to themselves. Accountants of all stripes co-located in the mid-section. Locals gravitated towards other locals; Trinity men brayed back old times. All in all, it was a perfectly natural process of social sorting: the Clapham omnibus as sediment jar. Claude, an outlier, looked for an attractive, unaccompanied female to lit upon, but in the melee ended up beside Jane. She would certainly not have been his first choice. Up front Sebastian; George next to him in a simple pewter urn. Carla and her father occupied the seat behind, talking nineteen to the dozen.

As they were heading along the coast road a patch-eyed collie darted in front of the bus, causing the driver to break sharply. A screech of tires, a dull thud, several audible gasps from the rear and the faint sound of metal against metal. The dog was dead, the vehicle undented. George, already dead, spilled forth as his pewter container bounced over the steel-capped steps of the bus. Sebastian, with Carla's help, retrieved as much as possible of his flaky friend from the floor. 'Holy Mary, Mother of God,' gasped one of the locals on seeing what had happen. Once a shaken Seán Óg had sorted matters out with the dog owner, the bus resumed its journey and conversation reignited. The urn remained clamped between Sebastian's thighs. It was the closest George had ever got to his friend's private parts. In seats eighteen and nineteen, Claude's touchy-feely behaviour, which came as naturally to him as mooing does to a cow, had elicited a hissing rebuke from his frumpish neighbour. It was a harbinger of things to come.

In rural Ireland, death is serious business, notwithstanding the fun and games associated with wakes. Saying goodbye, whether to a loved one, relative or friend of long-standing, calls for something more than weekday attire. Pádraig, stiff in his best bib and tucker, looked as if he was going to a wedding or christening. That morning he had applied both razor and gel to sterling effect. George would not have recognized the man who had pulled more pints than Don Juan had ladies. The lounge area had been commandeered for the memorial event, with regulars corralled in the public bar. Padráig's wife and sister-in-law had just finished setting out the cold buffet, a colourful array of meat, fish, vegetable, cheese and sinful desserts provided by *Chez Claude*. An open bar would loosen tongues, elicit, no doubt, incautious reminiscences about the departed one. Standing by the smouldering, all-weather turf fire, the sometime professor of information systems cleared his throat and with a stentorian 'Ladies and gentlemen' brought the room to near stillness. He had toyed with the idea of an urn pun or two ('Farewell to our not so *urnest* friend...Time for me to *urn* my keep') but thought the better of it in light of the on-board spillage. Ghoulish humour had always appealed to George but might not meet with the unqualified approval of the assembled group. Never had Sebastian seen him snap or lose his temper. His chum seemed preternaturally unperturbable.

'Time to raise a glass to our departed friend, to send him on his way across the Styx.' With that he removed the lid of the casket and sprinkled the contents over the glowing sods of turf. 'Ashes to ashes, no alien tears,' he added, sotto voce, before draining his glass. And that was it. Soft words were exchanged among the various clumps of guests. Awkwardness accelerated consumption, which in turn relaxed inhibitions. In no time at all, the lounge bar was a-buzz. Without asking, Padráig activated the music system. The room filled with jauntily melancholic tunes that fitted both the occasion and mood. Before you could say platinum print in Galician, Mateo had burst into song. A few of the locals joined in; the accountancy tribe watched with mild envy; the sophisticates exchanged knowing glances. But Mateo, tumbler of whisky in hand, was not for stopping. His infectiousness proved hard to resist. As did the haunting 'Theme from Harry's Game.' The combination cracked any remaining resistance. Sebastian watched the last traces of superciliousness evaporate in the media corner. The camp producer was swaying side to side, his left arm draped around an androgynous creature with an enigmatic, elfish smile. Sebastian had failed to notice him/her up to that point. Even Annabel Hyde was humming along, eyes closed; so, too, her designer-stubbled companions. Jane may have been the only hold-out.

As the clock ticked down, the merriment ramped up. George was all but forgotten, mournfulness giving way to raucousness. One or two of the locals were by now well oiled. A few of the suited accountants had loosened their ties and their tongues. Mateo remained a pulsing presence, a pollinator of bonhomie across social lines, impossible to either ignore or dislike. The Dubliners had taken over from Clannad and flushed faces were general around the room. Soon it would be time for Seán Óg to ferry the rackety group back to Rathboffin. But not before 'the incident.' No alcohol-powered gathering, be it wake or wedding, was going to conclude without at least one guest threatening to maim another for some slight or other, whether real or imagined. It could have been predicted. And it would have been much worse but for the timely intervention of the experienced landlord. As soon as the rubicund accountant delivered his first imprecation at Claude, Padráig was on the spot, like a referee preventing handbags between opposing soccer players. 'But he put his greasy hand all over my wife,' thundered the husband of the alleged victim. A blousy head nodded in conspiring agreement. Claude, per usual, had taken the kind of liberties that sex pests argue are nothing more than spontaneous signs of genuine human warmth and friendliness. The affronted husband was straining at the leash; gobby Claude, a master of histrionics, protested with flailing arms that he had never been so insulted in his entire life. Padráig, with a peremptory 'Out!', steered the frothing Frenchman to the door, pushed him into the street. 'Don't let me see your fecking face in here ever again.' Whether he knew of Claude's reputation, had witnessed the incident himself or simply didn't like foreigners was impossible to tell. The ejected chef installed himself at the back of the bus where he maintained a low profile for the duration of the evening, muttering away to himself in French.

An authoritative if anachronistic 'Time gentlemen, please' from Padráig signalled that Seán Óg's patience was about to expire. Sebastian dashed to the loo, not wanting to get caught short on the way back to Rathboffin. Imagine the embarrassment if he had to ask the driver to pull over. 'Bloody bladder,' he muttered to himself, not for the first time. 'Micturition as *momento mori*,' now there's a good title for a paper, the former academic thought to himself. The mood on the bus was subdued. Even Mateo seemed to have run out of steam. Or perhaps it was because everyone was now remembering the specific reason for the outing. George Parnell Kingsley seemed to have slipped from the collective mind over the past few hours. Aimlessly running his finger over the etched name on the urn and thinking about the last time they had occupied the fireside nook; Sebastian hadn't noticed the elf slip in beside him. A pair of oval eyes angled up. She—for it was in fact a 'she'—had near translucent, unlined skin. But the nose ring! Why did some young people want to look like livestock? Not what might be considered a conventional beauty, but captivating; vulnerable yet infused with self-assurance. Such were his first impressions of 'Middlesex,' as he would surely have baptized her had he been talking to George. She wore a zippered black jacket with black top and black jeans. Messy bed hair and a hard-to-decipher fine-line tattoo on her neck completed the look. 'Jenny. Jenny Lamb. I should have introduced myself earlier. I'm with Constitution Press, which is how I came to know our mutual friend. I worked with George quite a bit over the last few years.' Her comments were delivered in a fluted, adolescent voice that reinforced the aura of vulnerability.

What Sebastian didn't know was that his late friend had taken to calling Jenny, who had a background in cinema and print publishing, his right hand. They had been near constant companions during the making of both *The Actuary's Miscalculation* and *The Galician Octopus*, working together on the screenplays. George had requested her involvement on both projects and Annabel was happy to oblige; anything to keep her star author happy. She was convinced that he could go on to become another Stephen King but also knew that the literati viewed his popular fiction with condescension. 'A storyteller, not a writer,' as a *Telegraph* reviewer put it, with a dismissiveness born of canonical certitude. George Kingsley was never going to nab a Man Booker, but his sales figures were already off the charts. Some of the money rolling into Constitution's coffers would be used to subsidize young authors whose work might not otherwise see the light of day. Annabel wouldn't hear a word against the great Parnell.

'He was, as you well know, an unusual man. Devilishly clever but not at all overbearing. Old enough to be my father but young at heart. Oops! It sounds like I'm delivering a eulogy,' said she with a light laugh. His brain had been working overtime. So, that's who she is! George had named her a beneficiary in his will: same amount as Jane. Sebastian was intrigued. What might the 'right hand' know about his friend that he didn't? Yet another layer to the onion that just kept on peeling. George may have been committed to the flames, but he was still a presence. Hours later, in bed coaxing his slumbering manhood into rigidity, Sebastian had an 'aha' moment as he visualized the minimalist tattoo on Jenny's neck. It comprised three lower-case letters, g, p, k.—his friend's initials. Over the years, he had put up with more than his fair share of teasing about his libidinous nature and amorous calamities. By rights it should have been the other way around. All along he had made the lazy assumption that G.P.K. was celibate if not in fact asexual. But then came the out-of-the-blue affair with Mateo and now the titivating possibility that something might have transpired between him and this androgynous elf. Chameleon Kingsley should have been his name. What other secrets had George kept to himself? He thought of Churchill's famous 'riddle wrapped in a mystery inside an enigma' quote about Russia and didn't know whether to laugh or fume—exactly what his friend would have wanted.

Most of the passengers alighted on Sligo Street, the remainder outside the stylishly illuminated Conyers. 'You're staying here too, are you?' Ms Hyde enquired of Sebastian as the media covey snaked through the foyer. They had scarcely exchanged a word all evening, though every so often each had glanced in the other's direction. 'Yes, I often do.' 'Well, it seems refreshingly different, I have to say. Not what one expects in this part of the world. A colleague in Dublin recommended it to me. Told me to look out for a large portrait of St Sebastian. We once published a fictional biography of the saint, so I have something of a soft spot for him.' She was edging towards chattiness. 'As do I,' responded Sebastian, 'not least, I suppose, because we share a name. The painting used to hang in a convent. I picked it up at auction.' '*You* did?' A quizzical look crossed her face. He smiled. 'Actually, it's my hotel.' Only a month or two earlier what he had just said would have constituted a lie. Now, though, he was both manager and owner He proposed a nightcap. She hesitated. 'Just a quick one and I'll introduce you to my namesake.' 'In that case, why not?' She would welcome additional information about the literary prize he had alluded to at the funeral home. It had not for one moment occurred to her that the well-spoken hotelier—clearly not a local judging by his accent—might also be the director designate of the Parnell Prize.

# NOCTURNAL GAVOTTE

Drinks in hand, they plopped into a pair of bucket chairs next to the marble fireplace, overseen by the sanguinary saint. Just why was this English fellow running a boutique hotel in the west of Ireland? And what explained his close friendship with the most successful author on Constitution's books? More to the point, why she had been kept in the dark about George's desire to establish a literary award? It would make sense for any writer planning to endow a posthumous prize to at least inform, if not discuss the idea with his publisher. She was coming to realize what Sebastian—and most recently Jane Kynaston—already knew, that there was more to George Kingsley than met the eye. Their mutual friend had taken a perplexing delight in partitioning his life, ensuring that nobody knew the whole story. And for no reason other than the glorious gratuitousness of it all.

Figuring that the emotionality of the day coupled with incautious alcohol consumption would work to her advantage, she waited for him to divulge a few titbits. But Ms Hyde was no more immune to the effects of alcohol and a long day in strange surroundings than he. Thus, after a hiccupping start, two encapsulated life stories began to reel out, chapter by interleaving chapter. She'd married the president of Constitution Press when based in New York, but after their divorce relocated to London to head up the UK arm of the business. It had been an amicable break-up, a welcome return to her birthplace. Constitution published both literary and popular fiction, quite different from her previous experience with Cambridge University Press. She, for her part, was surprised to learn that the Irish-born hotelier and former owner of *Rhopos* had at one time pursued an academic career. She had never heard of either the Grubb School of Business or Groverdale, Iowa. Just as well, thought Sebastian. Stories about sexual harassment, discredited or not, should be treated like sleeping dogs. Although some of the hotel's early promotional literature had alluded to the writer's involvement in the business, it seemed to come as a complete shock to Annabel to discover that The Conyers was a joint venture between him and George. 'And what about Jenny Lamb?' asked Sebastian, switching tack. 'What about her?' came the parry. She could tell where he wanted to go but would make him work and wait. It was well after midnight before she revealed that George and Jenny—previously known to her family, friends, and colleagues as Jeremy—had indeed established a bond: a very special relationship, was how she phrased it. He probed a little further but failed to elicit the hoped-for confirmation. Salaciousness continued to be the spice of Sebastian's life. Even after all these years, society gossip and celebrity news remained part of his daily diet. He was just as likely to be seen reading the *Sun* or *Tatler* as the *Spectator* or *Guardian*. Defying ready pigeonholing appealed to him.

Next, conversation turned to the Parnell Prize. Constitution's own authors had won an impressive number of literary awards. In the last decade alone, Annabel's better-known names had appeared on quite a few long- and shortlists on both sides of the Atlantic. Major successes included a National Book Award and a Pulitzer in the US and in the UK a Costa and Man Booker. A win or even just making the shortlist boosted sales and authorial egos in near equal measure. Naturally, her established writers had their sights set on the International Dublin City Award, worth €100,000, almost as much as some writers make in a lifetime. 'There's hardly a month goes by without another gong being announced,' Annabel cautioned. 'Remember Gore Vidal's snarky observation that there are more literary prizes than authors? I confess I'm curious to know what our friend George has, or had, in mind. There are so many genres and sub-genres, it's a really crowded space. Making a new prize stand out is going to take some effort and imagination. The monetary value matters, of course, but prestige matters even more, and prestige must be earned. It's not something that can be bought or acquired overnight. One really need some big names, people like Ian McEwan or Edna O'Brien, to confer prestige. But getting those luminaries involved will be almost impossible unless you have literary connections or can offer them ridiculous sums of money. For obvious reasons, I favour prizes that allow publishers to submit multiple works and don't impose too many constraints. Selfish, I know. That's the one drawback of the Dublin Award. Nominations are made by libraries. Anyway, who's going to run the Parnell? Will it be for fiction or non-fiction, age-limited or not, national or international, first-timers or all-comers? How much is the pot? Will there be an organizing committee, a panel of judges, an award ceremony, media coverage? Who'll appoint the committee members?'

She had warmed to her subject, the questions now tumbling out in haphazard sequence. Sebastian, listing in his chair like a Galway hooker at low tide, was drained. 'Perhaps we can chat some more tomorrow,' she suggested apologetically. 'No, no, my fault entirely. Almost dozed off. Been a long and strange day,' he countered, rendering himself upright. Tired though he was, he wasn't so tired that he couldn't turn somnolence to his advantage. 'Tell you what. I'll fill you in on the details tomorrow afternoon, including my future role, if you like. I could certainly use some advice. Better still, I'll take you to Ballyhannah and show you George's house.' They agreed to meet up in the foyer at four. He didn't mention that he'd be making a dinner reservation for two at *Chez Claude*. With that, they stood up. A handshake seemed absurdly formal at this point, but a hug of any kind was too American and open to misinterpretation. A peck on the cheek might not be a breach of etiquette, but which cheek first? He went to the left, she, simultaneously, to the right. Their temples connected. Giggles. Next time he went to the right, she the left. Same result, though noses instead of temples. Third time they both headed left, and their lips brushed together. 'Oh, I'm, er...' 'No, no...' Air kissing might have been a safer bet, but the gesture was as phony as a politician's promise. After a sheepish laugh they retired for the night,

Sebastian with a smudge of brick-red lipstick on his mouth. His sanctified namesake would have been amused by the vignette that had just played out beneath him.

# KILLER CEREAL

Jenny, the first to appear for breakfast, was complimenting Isabel on the summer berry parfait with yoghurt and granola. Exquisitely layered in tapered crystal, it would not have looked out of place in a *cordon bleu* cookery book. Digging her spoon into the dish seemed like an act of vandalism. 'Are you from Spain, by any chance?' 'Yes, Granada,' came the semi-automatic response. Guests loved to know where the genial, dark-eyed waitress was from, why she was in Ireland, if she had a boyfriend. They meant well, but occasionally it could feel intrusive. Her day began at six and a long list of tasks required her attention. Being an *amuse-bouche* for the leisured class was not part of the job description. She'd think, I'm here to prepare and serve breakfast, not regale you with my life story. But the great majority of visitors meant well, and transgressions were rare. In any case, their compliments, not to mention tips provided ample compensation. And, truth be told, she was at times no less inquisitive herself. Like many Spaniards, Isabel could be a right chatterbox. She believed the same to be true of the Irish. Some conversations just felt so natural, she'd forget that she was waitressing.

From across the room, she had mistaken the early riser for a man—the gait, the shoulders, something didn't seem quite right. Not that it mattered a jot. Isabel was as accepting as her boss was judgmental. In no time, the pair were gabbing away, with Jenny dusting down her O-level Spanish. Several scenes from *The Galician Octopus* had been filmed on location in Grenada where the crew had spent the evenings listening to *Flamenco puro* in the Albaicín neighbourhood. 'I was born there,' squealed Isabel with delight. 'My parents still live there. I miss them so much.' A jolt of homesickness shot through her. Merely hearing names like Alhambra or Albaicín could induce a Pavlovian response. Funny how our past walks alongside us wherever we go, like a stray that won't be shaken off. With the arrival of Tim, an executive producer, Isabel withdrew, but Jenny would make a point of seeking out her new friend later that morning to say '*Adiós.*' Once, in her Jeremy days, (s)he'd had a crush on a sixth former who looked a lot like the waitress. Rita had been his last girlfriend before transitioning.

When Annabel joined the group, the topic of conversation turned from berries to business. How best could they leverage the news of George's death to create a pre-publication buzz around *The Capering Clown*? 'Sounds callous talking like this so soon after his death, but business is business,' said Annabel, brushing aside croissant crumbs with a monogrammed linen napkin. 'The monetization of sentimentality, I remember my ex calling it once. And in any case, why on earth would our late friend object? The more sales we generate, the more money flows into the foundation, boosting the endowment. I can assure you, if George's ghost were sitting here now, he'd exhort us to exploit his misfortune mercilessly, not only in terms of book sales but also spinoffs, merchandising and media rights.' Heads nodded in synchronized agreement.

Jenny would be uploading a major feature on the writer and his life to the Constitution website. She planned to follow that with a promotional blitz around his two earlier books to coincide with the expected flurry of obituaries. 'Go for it,' was all Annabel said, aware that her junior colleague probably knew more about their prize asset than most people ever would. To her credit, Jenny had divulged little about her close friendship with George to her boss, much less to other colleagues. Discretion worthy of an earlier era thought Annabel. Tim, all 3mm stubble and deliverables, was in the process of arranging preliminary meetings with a slew of film production companies and potential backers. 'George's BAFTA nomination for *The Galician Octopus* has strengthened our bargaining position. There'll be a bidding war for the rights to *Clown*, mark my words.' He was as confident as he sounded, a consequence of having the letters MBA after his name. 'Pity there isn't an award for recently deceased authors,' joked Annabel. It still rankled that her best-selling writer was deemed insufficiently highbrow, somehow lacking in literary merit: popular but not prestigious, as dismissive *LRB* and *TLS* readers would have it. And therein lay the problem for Annabel and Constitution Press. While awards for literary fiction were ten a penny, there existed scarcely any for writers like George Kingsley. What was needed was something along the lines of the People's Choice Awards in the US, but for writers. Her George would wipe the floor with the literary lions.

The prestige economy—to use the kind of terminology once employed on a routine basis by Sebastian in his academic career—held definite views on what counted, whether in the realm of science or the arts. Popular taste was one thing, consecrated taste another. Neither book sales nor raw citation data told the whole story—nor penis size he would likely have added. Such crude indicators of impact or import had to be treated with caution: quantity did not always equate with quality. As the old saw goes, 'Not everything that counts can be counted, and not everything that can be counted counts.' Imagine, for instance, judging the musico-historical significance of Beethoven by logging downloads or number of LPs sold. Those in the know knew what was best. All men may be equal, but not all men have equally good taste; only a select few attain connoisseurship. Whether George could have, or believed he could have, written critically acclaimed literary fiction would never be known. 'Speaking of which,' continued Annabel, 'I wonder what our departed friend had in mind for his Parnell Prize. It may be something that could work to our advantage; if nothing else, another platform to showcase our products. I should know more by this evening after my meeting with the Conyers chap. Haven't quite figured him out yet, but he is rather good company.' Neither of her colleagues knew that she had been conversing with the hotelier until late the previous night. 'I gather he was a professor at one time; worked in the US, but now owns and operates this place. More to him than meets the eye, I suspect. Possessed of a needy charm.' And with that they headed back up to their respective rooms for a morning of emails and phone calls.

# CLIMATE CHANGE

Imagine, if you will, all the elements of a perfect summer's day rolled up into one joyous confection, each one—temperature, sunlight, barometric pressure, windspeed, luminosity—tweaked to perfection. That was the afternoon Sebastian and Annabel headed for Ballyhannah. Weather of such sublimity displaced every other topic of conversation. For a brief—and it would be brief—moment the world's worries were put on the backburner, chores forgotten. And what a great leveller, what a source of national single-mindedness it could be. On meeting, everyone drew upon a common repertoire of meteorological salutations, no matter their age, class, or gender. The beauty of the day seemed to drive out pettiness and mean spiritedness. Enmities were put on the long finger. Sebastian found himself mouthing Beethoven's *'Alle Menschen werden Brüder'* as he strolled, stylish in navy-blue linen suit, into the hotel to pick up Annabel. 'Not bad, not bad at all,' she thought to herself. He had height, a presence about him, helped by the hair, even if it was of its time. She'd deduct a few points for the nose, but other than that he scored highly.

Sebastian was in buoyant, adrenalin-fuelled mood. George had put a tiger in his tank. What better way to spend a glorious afternoon than cruising along the coast road with a member of the chattering classes at his side, one who had more than a touch of Helen Mirren about her. He was not the first to have noticed the similarities, which began with, but went beyond, amplitude of bosom. There was no denying Annabel took pleasure in the casual comparison and would do so once again that evening. They drove through the village, past McTigue's. His hand rested on the gear stick, his pinkie ring making a soft clicking sound against the chrome detailing each time he changed gears. No wedding ring, she observed. Once all the paperwork was sorted out, the property would be Sebastian's along with the converted barn that had been his base for a couple of years.

The terms cottage and barn had thrown Annabel. She'd imagined, as one does when in Connaught, a white thatched structure with an outlying shed, used perhaps for storing hay or stabling a donkey. Her surprise was visible. The cottage proved to be a prize-winning, architect-designed house with an Audi parked in front, while the so-called barn would have seemed as luxurious to a cow as Versailles to a tenement dweller. 'Wow!' said the publisher, or maybe it was 'Gosh!' Sebastian was too busy comparing his traveling companion with his mental model of the comely thespian. 'What a wonderful retreat for a writer. And the view. My goodness! It's simply stunning.' The wild Atlantic was as smooth as an infinity pool, the surrounding mountains and headlands blue tinged and ruggedly three-dimensional. The late afternoon air was perfumed with the scents of countless native plants. A single ridge of high pressure could transform Ireland beyond belief, justifying the marketing hyperbole. 'This would give Big Sur a run for its money. What writer would not want to be holed up here? They'd have no excuse not to produce a masterpiece.' Like so many before her, Annabel had forgotten, or never been introduced to, the first law of Celtic climatology: it can't last. 'For every day like this,' chided Sebastian, 'we have to endure weeks of unrelenting gales and unforgiving rain. I'm not sure you'd be quite so taken if you were standing here in mid-February. Ballyhannah is a million miles from London, in every sense. Trust me, I know.'

He unlocked the front door, picking up a mound of mail as he led her into the open-plan kitchen. Apart from a little dust and the faintest whiff of mustiness, the fitted cabinetry and sleek appliances looked as if they had just stepped out of a showroom catalogue. Another 'Wow!' She'd spent too long in the States. This time it was triggered by the Connemara marble island, the green veined patterning of which made him think of snot. She was caressing the gleaming surface with the palm of her ringless hand, making 180 degree sweeps like a windscreen wiper. As she leaned forward, he caught sight of her cleavage and coal-black bra. It surely was too blatant a move for it to have been intentional. Without a word, he yanked open the enormous fridge, starkly empty but for wine and beer. The Chablis gave up its cork with a fart-like retort. 'To George. To Constitution Press. To the Parnell Prize.' They clinked glasses. 'And to you,' she added with a hint of a wink, before asking, 'What will become of this place?' The question had been anticipated. There seemed no reason to fudge. 'Part of my inheritance,' he replied, adding with palpable disingenuousness, 'Can't imagine why. Never hoped for anything. Never once thought about him dying, come to think of it. Anyway, the good thing is I won't be living over the shop any longer. Working and sleeping at The Conyers is not something I'd recommend.' Annabel was even more intrigued. First George's 'special relationship' with Jenny, the right hand formerly known as Jeremy, now this. How many 'special' friends did George have? What else might emerge? He had still to bring up the subject of the foundation and prize, not, of course, that there was any rush. This was a day to be savoured to the maximum.

Glasses in hand they walked to the edge of the cliff, less than fifty yards from the back of the house, watching the gulls swoop and glide over the motionless water. Nature was in its pomp, Sebastian in the pink, like a monarch surveying his realm. He showed her the barn with the kitchen table at which he had drafted the business plan for The Conyers. 'Adorable,' was her one-word assessment of the residence. They set up a table and chairs on the neglected patio, brought out the chilled Chablis and a packet of unopened crackers. Weeds had sprung up between the dark-red bricks covered with their tufts of moss, like ill-fitting wigs. In the distance a shimmering horizon, high above a flocculent cloud or two, all around the reassuring buzz of workaholic bees. Annabel, head back, eyes closed, was soaking up the sun's rays, relaxed in way she hadn't been for some time. She was aware of a moist warmth. In his recliner chair, Sebastian was rolling the wine from one side of his mouth to the other. 'Crisp, summery, lots of minerality. Would have sold well at *Rhopos*. Come to think of it, we may well have flogged it to George at some point, not that the blighter could tell a Fumé from a Fuissé.' He had used that line before and would again. She dismissed her kitchen island fantasy, reengaged with her host. He had mentioned *Rhopos* during their late-night chat, but she had not properly grasped that the business involved art *and* wine. No one, she was beginning to think, was quite what they seemed in this remote corner of Ireland. 'Tell me more,' she asked, her curiosity genuine. By the time he had recounted the rise and fall of *Rhopos*, the bottle was drained. A second was tempting, but ill-advised, given that days like this brought out the boys in blue with their killjoy breathalysers. After almost two hours, the conversation had still not come around to what was to have been the unofficial business of the day. 'Listen, why don't we head back to Rathboffin and talk at length about the Parnell thing over dinner? I'd appreciate your advice.' It seemed as if he was reluctant to divulge details. She really didn't have an option, but nor did she mind.

They returned to the hotel and freshened up before walking the short distance to *Chez Claude*. The setting sun burned with an apocalyptical brightness; a massive orb of molten gold suspended in the dimming sky by an invisible thread. 'Sebastian, *mon ami*, your favourite table is ready and waiting,' purred Claude, his eyes fixed on the Mirren-esque embonpoint. Sebastian caught her playful frown. He had planned the dinner; he had planned the entire day. Claude escorted them to the corner table and, per custom, seated Annabel—the very same Annabel who had rebuffed him at the memorial service—with exaggerated courtesy, his hand one minute on her shoulder, the next resting with apparent innocuousness on her hip. He sailed close to the wind, she thought. There followed a theatrical enumeration of the evening's specials along with wine suggestions, before the caricaturable patron launched into a tirade about a *lourdaud* called Pawdreeg. Annabel looked blank at first. Sebastian expressed sympathy for the restaurateur's unpardonable treatment at the hands of Mr McTigue the previous day, nodding his agreement with each successive expression of outrage directed at the over-zealous pub owner. Diplomacy was essential to survival in small-town Ireland. Then the tirade ended, as quickly as it had begun, like a sun shower.

# MIRREN IMAGE

Their arrival had attracted some glances from fellow diners. The establishment was full, a loquacious assemblage of loyal townies and seasonal trade. By local standards they made a striking couple. In Foxrock or Sandymount they would have blended in without causing heads to turn. Sebastian was wearing the same acceptably crumpled linen suit, partnered with a clean white shirt while his companion had plumped for a lantern sleeve, tie-front print dress that revealed more than the local parish priest would have deemed decent. Throughout the course of the evening, Claude's gaze wouldn't once meet Annabel's. It was as if her nipples were her eyes. She was used to it, and, presumably, had she found such behaviour off-putting, could have chosen to expose less pectoral flesh. Ms Hyde made no secret of the fact; she dressed for herself *and* for effect. The result was sexy, in that French way, without being sluttish. What professional woman did not appreciate the leverage provided by cleavage? Dowdiness might not have mattered when selling limited appeal academic tomes, but with trade publishing it could be downright disadvantageous. Fact of life, she'd have said, with a shrug. It was absurd to pretend otherwise. Men were men, after all—except, of course, when they were Jenny. Sebastian, too, dressed both for himself and effect, preferring, however, to achieve effect without either over-exposing his chest or wearing Medallion man jewellery. For males of his stripe and vintage, a signet ring and cufflinks defined the bounds of decorative acceptability; everything else was trumpery.

They skipped starters and went straight to the *confit de canard*. Claude persuaded them to order a zesty Juliénas from a vineyard he knew personally: something to do with his brother's in-laws or his in-law's brother. It proved a more than passable partner for the duck. The old goat certainly knew his stuff but not where to draw the line. He'd be lucky if he made it to retirement without facing a sexual harassment or assault charge. Cultural norms were changing, in the west of Ireland as elsewhere. Like ethnic jokes, dirty old men were no longer considered a laughing matter. If you were a fan of Les Dawson or Benny Hill, you might not want to advertise the fact. Sebastian, though, continued to have a soft spot for the ageing roué, and, indeed, Messrs Dawson and Hill. Before long, even casual innuendo would be enough to land a chap in hot water, he reckoned. It was a topic that had engaged (and enraged) George as much as it had him, living as they did in a purportedly modern country where the publication or utterance of blasphemous matter defamatory of any religion constituted a criminal offence. Imagine being hauled before the Beak for mouthing something as innocuous as, 'Joseph prayed for a blow job from the Virgin Mary.' The only possible grounds for prosecution would be sub-par humour.

Elements of modern Ireland were stuck in the Middle Ages, like a critter in quicksand. No wonder Muslim nations around the world lauded the country's blasphemy law and encouraged its emulation. Of course, all things are relative. In Ireland, you might receive a fine or spend a few weeks in the slammer for insulting or telling an off-colour joke about the Prophet Muhammed, but in Saudi Arabia your head would be on the chopping block in the blink of an eye, assuming your eyes hadn't already been gouged out. Sebastian, having spent time there, knew just how dangerous any misstep or slip of the tongue could be. That particular constitutional absurdity was one of the very few things that had ever caused George to lose his temper. Implacable was the only way to describe his opposition to the gagging of free speech, especially when it came to the subject of religion. Since there was no Supreme Being—whether God, Allah or any other—it was doubly offensive to grant protected status to speech pertaining to fantastical entities. If mockery of God and his bearded prophets was taboo, then, logically, so was mockery of banshees, fairies, and leprechauns. Too bloody bad if people's feelings are hurt. It's not as if proselytizing Christians and Muslims hadn't hurt more than just feelings over the centuries. You didn't need an LLB to know that poor taste was no basis for poor law. He could hear the words coming out of his departed friend's mouth with icy fluency. In fact, shortly before his death, George had revealed to Sebastian that an idea for a book was forming in his mind, a psycho-sexual crime story based around Asian grooming gangs in the north of England. Annabel may or may not have been aware.

Discussion of Claude, naturally, and the weather, just as naturally, filled the first few minutes as they mindlessly fingered the artisanal bread and acquainted themselves with the wine. Whether she found his Paddy joke ('How can Irish people tell it is summer? The rain gets warmer.') as funny as her laugh suggested mattered not. It was the prelude to, 'I have to say, I really do like that dress.' Before she could acknowledge the compliment—which in a different context would have constituted a far from imaginative chat-up line—came the follow-up. 'Has anyone ever told you look like Helen Mirren?' She could have replied with a playful roll of the eyes or a laconic yes, as had Daisy when, in the very same restaurant, Sebastian had remarked how much she resembled Chrissy Hinde of the Pretenders. 'Oh, really?' was all his guest said. The ball was back in his court. But he was experienced at this game and without hesitating lobbed 'like a *young* Helen Mirren' her way, stressing the young. The smile stretched to her molars. 'Have you read her autobiography, by any chance? Wonderful book. She has Russian aristocratic roots. Just wish she had published it with us. I've long been an admirer of hers, both for her acting and the way she lives life to the full. Quite a woman!' He raised his glass. 'To Helen Hyde. Or do I mean Annabel Mirren?' The afternoon had been spent in effortless conviviality and the evening seemed set to follow suit, Claude's vaudevillian interruptions notwithstanding. 'Is he always like this?' she asked, amused more than exasperated. 'It's the price we pay. Think of it as a cover charge,' quipped Sebastian.

A wide-ranging conversation, at times flirty, at others serious-minded, allowed them to establish their bona fides, though once again there was scant discussion of the Parnell Prize. The wine helped, not that either had been unrelaxed after their afternoon in the sun. Any last remaining traces of tentativeness on either of their parts would be washed away by the port. Annabel, although enjoying their interactions, sensed that her new friend was still more interested in finding out as much as he could about her than divulging information. The bait had been dangling for too long. 'So, what about the prize? Is it a state secret?' she joshed. Another Americanism. Why did every second sentence in the New World have to begin with a redundant 'so'? It bugged him, had from the very beginning. Perhaps he was too nit-picking, too much of a prescriptivist. Still, it came across as condescending, in much the same way as Americans' drawled use of the passive-aggressive 'whatever' did. Both made him want to reach for his blunderbuss. Either one would have earned him a clip around the ear during his school days. Just why was a conjunction being dragooned into service to do what an interjection could do? The regrettable trend had spread, virus-like, from the US to the UK and even Ireland. He'd first noticed it in the States, where it seemed to have been the preserve of nerds and computer geeks. No surprise there, of course, but to hear a publisher kick off a sentence in such fashion was the thin end of a wordy wedge. He kept his views on matters of transatlantic language usage—especially anthimeria or the verbing of nouns—to himself, instead answering her question with good grace and directness.

The prize would be awarded biannually. 'The intriguing thing is that our late friend, mischievous as ever, has decreed that the award shall be for a work of literary fiction. Straight away he's setting the moggy among the pigeons, having been a writer of popular fiction himself. I suppose that means John Banville could be nominated for his high-brow fiction, but not for his detective stories under the pseudonym Benjamin Black. I don't want to go into specifics regarding the size of his bequest, so please treat what I'm going to say next as confidential,' continued Sebastian. 'I think that the prize could, initially, be worth let's say, seventy to seventy-five thousand.' He overlooked her three-letter exclamation, a palindrome beloved of Americans. 'But how do you decide who is and isn't a writer of literary fiction?' The question was not unexpected. 'You, the publishers, will make that decision for us.' 'Are there any other stipulations attached to the prizes?' she asked, intrigued to be in at the birth of what could conceivably become a significant event on the cultural calendar, one, moreover, that would be of potential interest to Constitution Press. She was warming to the unconventional hotelier.

Beneath the table, a penis, now Bratwurst-like in both girth and length, was demanding attention the way a bothersome mosquito bite does. He brushed aside her offer to go Dutch, joking that only dykes should pay. It was the kind of remark that would have been blue-pencilled by even the most junior Constitution editorial assistant or greeted with indignant silence if uttered at the Christmas party by the office Neanderthal. But wasn't this a social as opposed to a work dinner? She released a cautious smile, then a guffaw. Horniness didn't give a fuck about political correctness. Peacocks had bright plumage, long-haired hoteliers red trousers, and for good reason. It was promiscuity, not courtly love that made the world go round. And sex sold books: just ask Jackie Collins or Jilly Cooper. How liberating not to have to worry every minute of every day about what one said, how one reacted to the comments of others. People shouldn't be pilloried for puerile humour, especially if they are picking up the tab. The truth was, blokeishness had never discommoded Annabel, an admission that would have shocked her female colleagues. His offer of a nightcap back at the hotel was accepted; it would either accelerate or delay the inevitable. But first Sebastian had to extricate his dinner companion from the grip of the French octopus whose hands were everywhere they should not have been. Annabel chose to see the funny side of things and the pair departed without threatening legal action against the incorrigible restaurateur.

# CLOSE ENCOUNTER

The night sky was cloudless and twinkly, the full moon like a gossamer communion wafer. He draped his arm around her shoulder, scooped her in. They drifted along the deserted street towards Church Lane, her head angled against his neck, young lovers with a combined age of more than a hundred. Where would it happen? Her room? His, wherever that was? A broom cupboard? The erotic charge she had felt in the restaurant and earlier in the day had lost none of its potency. Annabel's erogenous zones signalled in unequivocal fashion that she was up for it—evidence-based self-assessment, to use the jargon *du jour*. Sebastian couldn't indulge his fantasies for fear of a bulge reappearing down below. The 'where' question also engaged him. Would she risk using her room or would the best bet be his personal quarters off behind the registration desk? Would any of the day's guests, more specifically any of her work colleagues, still be hanging around in the lounge area? The idea of a knee trembler in the car park behind the hotel did occur to him, but he thought the better of it. The ground floor loo was also a possibility, though less than appetizing. Ah, the paradox of choice.

The ground floor area was quiet, mostly unlit but for the soft glow emitting from the mirrored, back-lit bar and a pair of dimmed sconces near the fireplace illuminating St Sebastian's pierced torso. No one was afoot. A muted chime from the tall clock in the alcove next to the staircase announced midnight. On the counter a few dirty glasses waited to greet Isabel. Their heart rates had increased. Annabel's armpits were damp. Sebastian slipped behind the bar, pulled down a bottle of Courvoisier from the topmost shelf. Just as he was at full stretch, she came at him, a tempest of pheromones. The brandy flew from his hand and executed a perfect somersault before landing amid the liqueur bottles arrayed on the glass shelf below. An expensive shattering sound ruptured the ground-floor silence. Oblivious, they clenched one another like a pair of wrestlers. Hands roamed, groins grinded, tongues darted. A ravenous physicality consumed them. He heaved her onto the bar-top, a rheumatic Nureyev coming to grips with a full-figured Fonteyn. The top of her dress was bunched around her waist, her bra hanging loose by one strap. Fully *en pointe*, he cupped a plump breast with his left hand, sucked on the other with leech-like tenacity, the nipple stiff inside his grateful maw. His right hand was lodged high up her dress, tugging at silk panties. Osculatory slurps counterpointed throaty moans. His nose and lips were soon smeared with her juices.

With a movement that was as ungainly as it was efficient, he clambered onto the narrow countertop, then with elephantine clumsiness onto her near naked body. She tugged at his belt and flies as they slithered hither and tither. The trouble with hot sex is that there are just too many hillocks and declivities to explore. Absolutely every anatomical element excites, but one doesn't have the hands, tongues, and dicks to do all that needs doing. It is at once exhilarating and frustrating. Sebastian felt like a child granted free rein in toyshop. And, of course, the greater the arousal, the greater the risk of *ejaculatio praecox*. It's alright for women, he'd think; they can orgasm until the cows come home, whereas once we've shot our load, that's pretty much it—not that he belonged to the 'Wham! Bam! Thank you, Mam' fraternity. At that moment he was expending almost as much energy trying not to come as endeavouring to maximize his (and presumably her) pleasure. A wiser man might have given some thought to the geometry of flat surfaces. The four-foot-tall countertop was narrow, its surface highly polished. As he struggled to insert his porcine-pink pecker into her quivering pussy, his foot brushed against the dirty glasses sending them in a fatal tailspin to the marble floor. Undeterred, he pressed on, pushed in deeper and deeper, thrusting with all the delicacy of a high-quality stallion. Suddenly, they were airborne, descending in what felt like slow motion. He landed first, flat on his back, with a thud that sounded almost as sore as it felt. Her chin hit his nose; a jutting knee numbed his gonads, sent lightning bolts of pain along his spine. He absorbed her fall. The groans she was hearing were not groans of pleasure. He had departed the counter-top before coming and his dick, unharmed, had in an instant shrunk to the size of a shy cocktail sausage. His left upper thigh was stinging, and a wet patch had formed around it. Pain may have rocked Daisy's boat, but it was anything but an anaphrodisiac as far as Sebastian was concerned. He would not be rising phoenix-like that night. 'My God! Is that blood?' gasped a near breathless Annabel. 'The broken glasses.' He felt as if he had wrestled with a grizzly. She looked as if she had walked through a wind tunnel. As they struggled to their feet, they heard the front door open and the sound of footsteps coming through the foyer. 'Sebastian! Quick!' They scrambled on all fours across the room like a pair of mountain gorillas. From behind an armchair next to the fireplace and beneath the saint's unwavering gaze they could make out two figures: Jenny and her stubbled colleague. They were chatting, but in appropriately subdued tones. To the distressed couple's relief, they headed straight for the staircase. Annabel emitted a long, slow 'Phew!' as she wrapped her arms around the wounded hotelier. 'I'm fine, just fine,' he protested. 'I'll clean up in my bathroom.' Passion had retired for the night and Annabel followed suit. It seemed the right thing to do. Sebastian slept fitfully, his dreams populated with Dalí-esque images of morphing breasts and gaily coloured bottles raining down from cerulean skies.

At an unearthly hour a persistent knocking rescued him from a dream in which his head was being devoured by an omnivorous vagina. It was Isabel, a picture of Spanish agitation and outrage. Someone has smashed the beautiful bar and hurled broken glass all over the place. Worse still, there was a trail of blood. '*Madre mia!*' she yowled, more than once. 'Some people in this country are worse than animals.' Had the cut not been concealed by his bathrobe, who knows in what direction her thoughts might have headed. Once he had pacified his distraught dream team member, he'd need to concoct a plausible explanation before Carla showed up for work. And all he had wanted was an uncomplicated fuck with a stacked publisher.

# DEVOLUTION

Sebastian was seated by the turf fire staring at the foam atop his slow-drawn pint of Guinness wondering where the ashes of his friend might have ended up after the grate had been swept clean. A waste disposal site? Tossed over the cliff into the sea? Added to Tabby's litter tray? A month had passed since the festive send-off, and this was his first time back on the premises. Pádraig had greeted him with uncharacteristic warmth; emotional effusiveness was typically not a trait that served a publican well. 'So, it's back here now you are?' came the question that required no answer. The conductivity of small-town social networks was something else, Sebastian had come to realize. Only three days earlier McHale's van had hauled his relatively few chattels from The Conyers to George's house, yet probably everyone in the village already knew the name and age of their new neighbour, not that he would have been an unfamiliar face around the village. He and George might have been 'blow-ins' but they had been accepted, granted *de facto* resident status by those who mattered most, without going out of their way to ingratiate themselves with the locals. Flashing the cash or false bonhomie didn't cut it in this part of the world, which isn't to say that the odd lace curtain didn't still twitch or that the occasional tut-tut wasn't heard. But once an alpha male such as Pádraig signalled approval, that was that: the tribe got in line.

    Sebastian had entered the post-euphoria phase, not that he was taking his good fortune for granted. The glow had dimmed, not faded. Now, though, it made sense to think about normalizing his affairs, stabilizing his heretofore rickety life. On paper, he no longer needed to worry financially. The hotel, which he owned outright, was trading successfully and Carla was administrative reliability itself. He had also inherited a mortgage-free house and refurbished barn in a stunning location. His bank balance was in the rudest of good health thanks to the €100K lump-sum George had left him. For the first time in his sixty-plus years, he could claim to be both cash and asset rich. It had neither been planned nor worked on, certainly not expected. All it had required was for his oldest friend to frenziedly lash the bare back of a strapped down woman who bore a more than passing resemblance to a famous rocker.

George's generosity was spectacular. He had set up his friend for life, albeit earlier than he likely imagined would be the case. And what had he asked for in return? That Sebastian institute and oversee a biannual literary award in Rathboffin. As *quids pro quo* went, it was the deal of the century—a presumably non-legally enforceable condition. What true friend would not wish to honour such a request? George, he suspected, knew exactly what he was doing. He was, after all, giving away most of his fortune to someone who served as the model for the temerarious lead character in *The Capering Clown*, someone for whom common-sense sometimes seemed anathema. He was testing his friend's metal, setting him a moral challenge. Sebastian remembered Moore's Paradox: 'It is raining, but I do not believe it is raining.' Had his clear-thinking friend thought of it too? Did he imagine that Sebastian would argue that it was not illogical for him to concede that honouring his friend's wishes was the right thing to do while also claiming that he did not believe it was the right thing to do? A case of using to logic to have one's cake and eat it? With George, one never quite knew what his intentions were. He enjoyed playing with people even if—especially if—they didn't realize they were being played with. Pressed on the subject, Sebastian might have described his friend's behaviour as manipulativeness without malice. George may have been calculating and gnomic, but never sadistic.

The conversations with Annabel had provided Sebastian with a glimpse into the world of literary awards. Despite the farcical end to their evening, the pair had parted on the best of terms. Email addresses were exchanged. They would resume where they had left off next time their paths crossed. He intended to draw more fully on her knowledge and experience once he began to apply himself with due seriousness to the task set him by George. The learning curve would be steep, just as it had been when launching The Conyers. To be sure, the hotel would continue to occupy much of his time, but he also knew that, operationally, he could rely on Carla and her small team. It came to him in the shower as he was preparing to move into George's house. It was so obvious he was puzzled why he had not thought of it sooner. A strategy was evolving. One evening when the lounge area was quiet, he invited Carla to join him for a drink by the fireplace. 'While on duty?' she asked with a quizzical look. As was his, if not the Spanish way, there'd be no beating about the bush. 'How would you like to be manager of The Conyers? I'll increase your salary by twenty percent.' Her eyes widened. He hadn't finished. 'You can move into my quarters here, which will save you having to pay rent in town.' Her eyes were very wide now. 'And there's one other thing. George's black Audi is yours, to keep.' It was physically impossible for her eyes to widen further. It was the happiest, most natural smile he had seen in ages. She knew he wasn't joking. Now it was her turn to win the lottery. He extended his flute. They clinked. Still not a word. Couldn't find the right one. A tear slipped down her cheek. 'Oh Sebastian!' She desperately wanted to hug him. He knew not to mix business with pleasure—in her case at least.

Some elaboration was in order. Her new title was not merely honorific; it implied executive authority. 'Think of me as the CEO, responsible for setting goals and overall strategy, and you as the COO, responsible for overseeing general operations on a day-to-day basis.' 'What, Sebastian, is a C-O-O?' 'Sorry, sorry. Chief Operations Officer.' '*Claro*,' came the reply. Her tummy was churning with excitement, her head dizzy trying to absorb what he had just said. She couldn't wait to tell her father that she was going to be *Directora de Operaciones* at The Conyers. For the next hour or so, he explained what the role entailed, outlining with concrete examples the extent of her executive and budgetary authority. She wasn't flying solo, but her hands would be on the controls. Responsibility for hiring, scheduling, remunerating and firing staff now rested with her. Selecting suppliers, negotiating with vendors, determining menus, devising guest polices, managing reservations and such like; all these were now part of her bailiwick. 'Bale-y-week?' He smiled, clarified. Carla was trying to take it all in, thrilled rather than fazed by the prospect. She had never taken a business course, studied hospitality management, or read a single paragraph on employment legislation, yet here she was, poised to assume the role of manager of the region's most acclaimed boutique hotel. News of the appointment, Sebastian assured her, would be sent to all the local papers and the industry press. He was true to his word. Two weeks later she was able to send clippings from several publications to a proud parent in Galicia.

# PART II

# THE PRIZE MALARKY

By January of the New Year Carla had shed any doubts she might have harboured about her suitability for the role of COO. Combining affability with self-assurance, she had introduced several modest changes: flexible check-out times, which improved 'the guest experience,' and more stylish uniforms for the dream team, a move designed to boost worker morale, not that worker morale had been a problem. On the infrequent occasions when a guest became truculent, she exhibited an enviable ability to deescalate situations and mollify the disgruntled party. Month by month Sebastian was delegating responsibility for tasks that previously had either bored or irritated him. She did not feel taken advantage of; rather saw the extra workload as an indicator of his trust in her, a measure of her abilities. From the outset, he had made it clear that as COO she could at any time bring on board an assistant, either part- or full-time, should her newfound responsibilities prove too onerous. The granting of latitude to the conscientious was always a safe bet, he reckoned: something to be seen as a compliment rather than a pretext to exploit another's good nature. Personal experience had taught him that living on the premises made it almost impossible to disengage; it really was a case of being on call 24/7. Burn-out was in neither of their interests.

Even though The Conyers lacked a full-service restaurant, it had been booked solid over the Christmas and New Year period. By mid-January Sebastian felt ready to devote the bulk of his energies to establishing the Parnell Prize in accord with his late friend's wishes, the goal being to award the first prize in early 2013, which would allow a lead time of more than a year. It was an ambitious goal, given that he knew diddly squat about literary prizes and had no connections whatsoever to the world of trade books. On the other hand, he had experience of both the mechanics and economics of scholarly publishing: the sluggish process from manuscript submission through peer review and subsequent editing to final release. And hadn't he on a couple of occasions served as a judge on a 'Best Paper' panel? Almost invariably these activities were performed behind the scenes, out of the public eye. Peer review came in two guises, single- or double-blind: either the author was unaware of the reviewer's identity or neither the reviewer nor the author was aware of the other's identity. A literary prize was very different; here the unstated aim was to maximize attention; judges were chosen because of their celebrity or literary eminence. As a rule, the greater the buzz around a book prize, the more books would be sold. And a judicious leak about fractiousness among the selection committee or a dollop of scandal didn't hurt, on the basis that all publicity is good publicity. Sebastian could still remember the brouhaha that followed Marxist John Berger's denunciation of the Booker corporation as a colonialist organization in his 1971 winner's acceptance speech. Biting the hand that fed you, fed public outcry: priceless publicity for free.

In academe things are different. With few exceptions, authors make do with symbolic capital, what Dr Joe Bloggs would call peer recognition. Savvy members of the academic tribe can exploit their stockpile of symbolic capital to engineer a pay rise, negotiate a counteroffer or secure a position at a more prestigious institution. For this lucky minority, symbolic capital can indeed be converted into hard currency; the vast majority, however, make do with intangible rewards. A prestigious literary prize, on the other hand, delivers both pecuniary and symbolic rewards: the winner walks off with cash and kudos, bankable kudos at that—a bigger advance for the next book. The real value of the Nobel Prize in Literature is not so much the generous cash award as the almost incalculable reputational gain that accompanies it: laureates become gods overnight, demonstrating how symbolic capital can, in exceptional cases, exercise a dramatic multiplier effect.

The problem facing Sebastian was simple yet complex: how to establish instant credibility for the Parnell Prize. Had he chosen to launch a scholarly journal in his former field, he would have faced the same challenge, been confronted by the same questions. Why would any career-minded scholar choose to publish in a brand-new journal, one that no one had ever heard of? Journal prestige was earned over time by the publishing of top-notch research submitted by reputable authors. But to attract top-notch submissions from reputable authors in the first instance, a journal needed to have prestige—the old chicken and egg conundrum. So, for a start-up journal to break into a crowded market would, at the very least, require an editor and editorial board of unusual distinction. Which, in turn, raises the question: why would eminent scholars throw in their lot with an unknown journal? The literary version of that question had been pinballing around Sebastian's head for some time. True, the size of the Parnell Prize would automatically attract media attention and, no doubt, submissions from publishers would be forthcoming, but to build sustainable cultural legitimacy it would almost certainly need to be associated with a distinguished panel of judges. Recruiting big names to the awards committee and dishing out eye-watering prizes might be enough to get the venture off the ground, but there could be no guarantees. Ultimately, the credibility of the Parnell would—or should—be determined by the intrinsic quality of the prize-winning work. He certainly didn't want it to become the literary equivalent of the Al-Gaddafi International Prize for Human Rights.

# THE JURY'S OUT

George's instructions matched precision with concision. The prize would be awarded for a previously unpublished work of long-form literary fiction written in the English language by a writer under the age of thirty-five, born on the island of Ireland. That automatically excluded the would-be Joyces and Becketts who had moved to the country in search of bog-scented inspiration and now felt themselves to be more Irish than the Irish. It also kept at bay all those Irish Americans who had acquired a green passport on granny's coattails and for whom creative writing was a lifestyle choice to be inflicted on others. George had always been of the mind that Irishness was not something that could be acquired osmotically whether by relocating in mid-life to the Burren or by filling out citizenship forms. Self-published work was ineligible, which at a stroke ruled out countless self-imagined geniuses. Nor could authors self-nominate. Works were to be submitted by *bona fide* publishers, no more than two per company, and appraised by a committee, to be appointed and chaired by the director of the Parnell Prize. Only books published in the preceding twelve months were admissible. The cash value of the prize would be determined biannually by the director in consultation with Fay & Florin, the Dublin-based firm responsible for the stewardship of the foundation's assets. Such, then, was the framework within which Sebastian would operate. It afforded him appreciable organizational latitude. Rathboffin would host the award ceremony.

The view from the cottage window was the same as from the barn, the worktable of superior quality. Beyond, the indefatigable Atlantic pressed against shore and headland. Last time it had been a business plan for a boutique hotel, this time it would be a procedural template for a literary prize. Developing multi-year budget projections for a start-up business called for painstaking analysis and detailed calculations. In comparison, setting up a book prize would be a walk in the park. Even so, careful project planning was called for. For the first time since George's demise Sebastian began to systematize the steps involved in establishing and running the prize. He needed to nail down the sequence of tasks and their interdependence, from announcement through submissions-winnowing to jury formation and the award ceremony. As a brand-new event on the cultural calendar, getting the word out to key constituencies and stakeholders was of paramount importance. He would have to hire a marketing and PR outfit to build awareness, give serious thought to issues of branding and graphic design as well as cross-platform promotion and advertising. They'd need to target relevant arts and tourist organizations, trade publications such as *The Bookseller* as well as *The Author*. National and international media coverage would be a *sine qua non*. The promotional effort would be heavily front-loaded, starting as they were from a base of zero. Once the prize was established, press coverage could pretty much be guaranteed in successive years. Each of these steps had significant budgetary entailments. It was clear that the foundation would have to earmark funds for pump-priming activities in addition to recurrent outgoings. He'd need to agree policies and procedures with Fay & Florin, including expenditure ceilings.

Sebastian fiddled with his electronic calendar, experimenting with different timelines. Provisionally, it made sense to close registration by end of September, allowing the selection committee time to sift through the submissions before drawing up a short list by early December. He was not in favour of announcing a long list followed by a short list, since there might not be that many works to consider, given the stringency of the submission guidelines. February would be a good time to announce the winner, a way, too, of brightening up the dreariest month. The award ceremony itself would be another significant line in the expenditure budget. While Rathboffin would be a comparatively cheap location compared with Dublin, remoteness constituted a challenge: would people be prepared to travel to the west of Ireland in the middle of winter for a brand-new book award? And then there was the all-important matter of the selection committee and the non-trivial matter of honoraria. If the judges were literary A-listers, they'd not come cheap. As for evaluation criteria, he opposed any kind of box ticking: if the 'I-know-it-when-I-see-it' approach to quality assessment worked for the Swedish Academy, it would work for the Parnell. His initial thinking was four judges. Although he would be a non-voting member, as chair he'd reserve the right to cast the deciding vote in event of a split decision.

Dr Sebastian Conyers may once have been something of a name in the world of information systems, but he had neither standing nor presence in the literary world. Not only that; he lacked connections. He could not think of a single writer of note in his circle of friends and acquaintances. Nor did he know anyone in the book trade, with one exception. Time for a pow wow with Annabel. But before heading to London he'd visit the investment firm overseeing the endowment. Up until then there had been no contact whatsoever between the two parties. All he knew was their name, courtesy of Lurch. He needed to present his preliminary cost estimates for launching the prize, brand-building and such like along with tentative estimates of the fixed administrative costs, which encompassed everything from remunerating the judges to underwriting the award ceremony. It had quickly become clear to Sebastian that the prize money constituted the tip of an iceberg. He was going to need guidance on what he could reasonably expect to draw down from the endowment for the inaugural and subsequent years. But first, he'd be requesting that Fay & Florin open a checking account in his name. Nothing could happen until that detail had been attended to. Working pro bono was one thing, digging into one's own pocket another.

# HAUGHTY TOWERS

A gossamer fog hung over the land as the X5 sped eastwards. Time was he'd have switched stations the moment he heard the voice. But Lyric FM's king of the gab had, bit by bit, won him over. You'd pivot from Bach to Bono, then be subjected to a clunker of a pun or a shaggy dog story. 'Marty in the Morning' served up quirky musical sandwiches thick with banter, irresistible if at times indigestible. There really was no stopping Mr Whelan, as his game guests quickly came to appreciate. The man was as Irish as Kerrygold, more craic than a line of coke. 'Christ! I've gone native,' Sebastian muttered to himself, barrelling down the outside lane, flashing at more observant drivers. He shot past Mullingar, then Leixlip until the inevitable traffic jam took the wind out of his sails. You'd never see the like in Rathboffin. He parked in Henry Street and headed on foot for Docklands, the collar of his beige overcoat turned up. The air was sharp but laced with intimations of imminent warmth. A wan sun hung over the Wicklow mountains; all around, tardy commuters and bleary-eyed students, scuttling towards early retirement or bright futures. Overhead and along the river walls, ornery gulls, more garrulous than Marty himself. There was a good feel to the day. Winter light had a way of putting things in perspective.

The Docklands of his undergraduate days had vanished. There wasn't a stevedore or strumpet to be seen. Generations of grit and grime had been replaced by steel, glass and concrete. 'Silicon Docks,' they called it. Who could have imagined that Dublin would become one of Europe's leading financial centres? His destination was a gleaming glass behemoth with an atrium designed as much to intimidate as impress. Sebastian strode up to a sleek semi-circular desk and asked for Fay & Florin. A heavily made-up young lady with a passion for Botox responded in rote fashion: 'Seventh floor. Do you have an appointment?' She pointed to a ledger and the name Dr S. Conyers joined that day's list of visitors to this post-modern temple of Mammon. The lift rose noiselessly and came to a judder-less stop. A disembodied Mancunian voice announced the floor and the silver door peeled aside to reveal a matrix of glass-lined corridors. He stepped out and headed for a carefully coiffed middle-aged lady sitting beneath a sign with the words 'Fay & Florin.' 'Conyers, Sebastian Conyers. To see Mr Fay.' 'He's expecting you. Follow me, please.' From the conference suite he could see Anna Livia Plurabelle heading seawards and amused himself by eyeballing a high-flying seagull. Gavin Fay was in his late forties, with a healthy complexion and a fine head of wiry hair. He had the build of a collegiate rugby player and a handshake to match. His suit was tailored, his shirt collar cut-away; had probably attended Belvedere or Clongowes, networked his way into a good starter job and spent the next decade putting in the long hours that would secure him a Victorian villa in south Dublin and a corner office with panoramic views of the city. His wife might want to do something about the ear fuzz.

'Shocking news about our friend. So unexpected.' 'Indeed. Absolutely awful. Had you known him for long?' enquired Sebastian. It emerged that Gavin and George had met professionally almost two decades earlier. 'I was working in the accountancy world at the time, before moving over into the investment side of things. That's where we got to know one another. He was, as I'm sure you'll agree, one of a kind, as amusing as he was smart. I was still a junior partner here when he asked us to manage his portfolio. George inherited quite a sum and was himself a very astute investor, but he didn't want to be distracted by the financial stuff. Trust me, he would have made a darn good day trader if the writing hadn't hooked him. Between ourselves, he made a tidy sum during the recession. And, of course, with the book deals and spin-offs, his net worth grew significantly, and will continue to for some time. Anyway, the strange thing is that it was only a year or so ago that he first outlined his thinking behind the Parnell Foundation. It was to be established after his death and so, having gone over the usual procedural matters with him, I sort of pushed it to the back of my mind never for one moment imagining we might lose him so soon.' With that he switched tack. 'And when did you first meet him, Dr Conyers?' Gavin listened as Sebastian explained how they had been together at Trinity in the sixties and how after decades he had wound up in the west.' 'Well, it's clear he thought highly of you, Dr Conyers. As you probably know, I received a copy of George's will from his solicitor.'

Having dispensed with the niceties, the pair, now on first name terms, got down to business. Gavin opened a folder and handed Sebastian a set of papers festooned with pie charts, graphs and tables. 'The bottom line, Dr Conyers, is that the endowment is in good health. I would describe the portfolio as moderately conservative and judiciously diversified, reflecting George's wishes. At of close of business yesterday, the value of his investments was just north of €8 million. If you look at this chart you can see that average annual rate of return for the last decade has been around the three and a half percent mark. Our job, not that I need to tell you, is to ensure that the endowment is managed in such a way as to generate sufficient interest income to fund the prize to the level and in the manner that George envisaged, and, indeed, you would wish.' With that, Sebastian pulled out several sheets of his own from the leather document bag at his side. 'This is a detailed expenditure budget for years one, two and three. As you can see, there are several significant one-time costs involved in getting the venture off the ground, things such as branding, advertising, and promotion. It won't surprise you to hear that the administrative costs are almost as much, if not more, than the proposed prize money.' Gavin liked numbers and as a result revised his initial assessment of his visitor, whom he had marked down as an airy-fairy gallery director or festival organizer. By the time he left, they had agreed to proceed with the prize valued for year one at €75,000. Over time, as operating expenses regularized and the endowment yielded higher returns, it could be ratcheted up. Ten minutes later, they shook hands, committing to say in regular contact. The Botox-ed girl in the atrium ignored his friendly 'goodbye.' It brought it home to him; he was an old geezer in his sixties as far as her generation was concerned, invisible if not risible. There wasn't a hope in hell of any young woman giving him so much as a sideways glance, never mind a blow job. As he walked out into the street, an avian screech was followed by a fat splat sound. Another inch and he would have been flying to London accessorized with creamy white seagull poop.

Terminal one was busy, over-run by shorts-wearing optimists dragging beribboned roller bags bought the previous week in Argos. He went straight to the Aer Lingus check-in desk, where he enquired, with politeness but faint hope, if there was any possibility of an upgrade. 'Let me just see what I can do, Sir,' chirped a young man with a foppish fringe and a tan that could either have been a perk of the job or from a bottle. His fingers danced a merry jig over the grubby keyboard for what seemed like minutes. 'Would 2A suit?' he asked with a genuineness that could scarcely have been insincere. 'Absolutely! How very kind of you.' Unlike the bitch in Docklands, the youth smiled, pleased to have been able to oblige. Life would be so much more fun if I were gay, Sebastian thought, as he headed for the security line along with the sun-seekers. Instead of looking for it, it would come looking for me. Then he remembered Annabel and their unfinished business. All was not lost. Two G&Ts later the green-liveried jetliner was making its measured approach into perpetually congested Heathrow.

# LONDON'S CALLING

Sebastian pulled down his matching weekend and document bags from the overhead bin; waited for the jet bridge to sucker-kiss the fuselage. The trolley dolly granted him a standard-issue smile as he exited with the brisk purposefulness of the self-important. It reminded him of old times. He weaved through the thronged terminal like a slalom champion. Funny how one's energy level ramps up automatically on arriving in a major metropolis. The Heathrow Express lived up to its name, the tube its reputation. It was a stuttering, over-heated rattle from Paddington to Holborn, but at least he managed to miss the worst of the evening commute. After checking in, a leisurely five-minute walk took him from the Bonnington, his frill-less base for the next two days, to leafless Bloomsbury Square. Constitution Press occupied a single-fronted Georgian townhouse with a red door topped with an ornate fanlight window. A brass plaque gleamed. In the spacious reception area with its egg and dart cornicing he encountered a selection of recent titles and a blue-stocking graduate protected by a modular desk. Annabel's office was on the third floor. As he ascended the last flight of stairs, he saw a tailored wool suit framed by the doorway. The skirt stopped just above the knee, his eyes didn't: the top three buttons of her blouse were open. With an easy smile and a kiss on both cheeks she ushered him into the office. From its large sash windows, he could make out the square and its gardens in the gloaming.

 Annabel had probably spent longer than usual in front of the mirror that morning, understandably so. She had a dinner date, teen-like nerves, too. Having warmed to the hotelier in Rathboffin, the dial had not yet begun to move towards cool. Rather to her surprise he had parked himself in her thoughts. Their aborted coupling in The Conyers had frustrated her just as much as it had him. After all, hadn't she been celibate for the best part of six months? She felt neither regret nor embarrassment, just plain old frustration. While shaving her legs in the shower, the idea of office sex had come to mind. Judging by what she saw on TV and movies it was a common enough occurrence these days, risky perhaps but by no stretch of the popular imagination a degenerate act. If they could screw on a bar, then, surely, they could manage a quickie on her mahogany partner's desk with its green leather writing surface. Even if they were to roll off, it would be onto glass-free carpet rather than bruising marble. Sebastian, not that she had any idea, was very familiar with the challenges of workplace shagging, both above and below desk, on both sides of the Atlantic. His expertise would come in handy.

Catch-up conversation sparked as easily as a Californian wildfire. They looked out the blindless windows; she pointed out a few landmarks that he wasn't altogether sure he could see in the dark. 'Silly me,' she said, 'I completely forgot that you used to live here.' Naturally, he inspected her bookshelves, cast a glance over the draft manuscripts stacked next to a silver drinks tray. Survivors or soon-to-be victims of the weekly editorial cull? Her large desk was clear, except for an Apple workstation and laptop. Behind it hung an etching of Addison. After the last shouted 'Good night, Annabel' had drifted up the stairwell, she said, 'It's just us now. Jenny and two other colleagues are attending a book fair in Edinburgh. I'll be joining them later in the week. By the way, I've booked a table for seven-thirty in a nearby trattoria. Nothing remotely fancy, I assure you. We can stay here until then if you like.' After a second or two's pause, she asked, 'How about a drink in the meantime? Gin, Scotch...?' 'Sounds perfect. I'll have a G&T,' he said, the effect of his two in-flight beverages having worn off; hers, consumed an hour earlier, hadn't. She poured a generous tumbler of Beefeater and added a splash of flat tonic water. 'No ice, I'm afraid' she added with an apologetic raising of the eyebrows. A clink, a tilt of Waterford crystal, a deep, satisfying swallow. 'Has your leg recovered?' she asked, not that she didn't know the answer. Not that he didn't know she did. There was unfinished business to attend to. Another big swig. Lights out. Take two. Action.

They lay side by side on the leather, partially clothed, sweat-smeared. Her face was flushed, his knob droopy and gooey. At first Sebastian had become entangled in his trousers but managed to extract one leg thus affording him sufficient freedom of movement to complete the act he had initiated all that time ago in The Conyers. As he humped, she kneaded his buttocks, steering and at times slowing his pelvic thrusts. It was hard on his right knee, harder still on his tense, outstretched arms, but that was a small price to pay. Cautiously he rotated her to one side, then engineered her into the doggie position. Sebastian set to, first with lapping tongue then eager-beaver penis. His ejaculatory cry cum grunt, delayed for as long as was humanly possible, would likely have been audible in the reception area. To sustain the pleasure, he had had to distract himself. If he didn't think about climate change or how to spell 'chiaroscurist,' he'd have released his load with indecent haste. That for him was the great paradox of high-performance sex. He was continually amazed how male porn stars could keep at it for so long, thrusting robotically, neither draining their seed before the scripted money shot nor keeling over from psycho-physical exhaustion. He didn't know her age, her father's name, or her favourite colour. But if you needed a detailed description of her pudenda, no problem. It had always intrigued him how effortlessly bodily intimacy could be achieved with virtual strangers—at certain privileged moments, of course. Normally, we're mortified to discover an undone zipper or an exposed nipple, but such inhibitions fly out the window once we're aroused. He experienced no sense of shame when flapping his penis in front of Annabel but would have cringed had either his father or George ever caught sight of it pointing at a urinal. It didn't make sense, but sexual arousal engendered senselessness.

# SPAGHETTI CONJUNCTION

Caruso was buzzing, packed with a mix of locals and passing tourist trade. Bloomsbury's mansion flats were home to many of the regulars, known by sight if not name to the long-serving staff, all black and white and cheery *'Ciao bellas.'* Annabel was a non-local regular, lunch mostly, whose looks ensured a corner banquette and the kind of service the nearby table of Texans soon realized would not be coming their way. But wouldn't the same have happened in reverse in Austin, they might like to ask themselves? Spaghetti carbonara for her, Bolognese for him; a bottle of Barbera d'Alba for both. Watching them—animated and clearly at ease though they were with one another—it probably would not have occurred to anyone present, certainly not the Texan contingent, that the mature couple seated on the red velvet had just fucked their brains out atop an antique desk in a nearby office. Before leaving Constitution Press, they had abluted, separately, in the tiny William Morris-wallpapered loo on the ground floor. Best not to bring one's own fish and cheese to the restaurant.

They both knew the drill. Exchange bodily fluids, carry on like adults. There'd be no dewy-eyed, lovey-dovey nonsense, no whispered sweet nothings over the tiramisu. They'd shag again, should an opportunity present itself, but certainly weren't embarking on a relationship, weren't about to fall in love. They were fuck buddies, who not only fancied one another but had recognized potential utility in the other—a compound mutuality of interests, tacitly understood. This time, Sebastian did open up about the prize, and a biggie it was, she acknowledged. He described the terms and conditions as laid down by George along with the gist of that morning's conversation with Gavin. 'Hmm. A max of two submissions per publisher. Irish born *and* under thirty-five. Narrows the field considerably. Well, our friend has stayed close to his roots, I'll grant you that. I suppose it provides an opportunity for small Irish presses to showcase the next Colm Tóibín or Maeve Binchy.' As Annabel spoke, she was trying to remember who in her stable fulfilled the criteria. The Parnell Prize was now firmly on her radar. 'Four judges, with you, let me guess, casting the deciding vote, if need be,' she chuckled. 'Well, seventy-five thousand will get you a ton of media attention, but have you given any thought as to the composition of the jury? That'll be important. I suspect it'll determine to what extent the high priests of the literary establishment sit up and take notice.'

Her role, she intuited, was to provide him with an *entrée*. 'Look,' interjected Sebastian, 'I'll be honest with you. I've read enough of the canon to be able to bluff my way through a Belsize Park dinner party, or at least the first course, but am I a regular reader of the *London Review of Books*, *The Paris Review* and the like? Nope. Put it this way. I'm more a Melvyn Bragg than a Lionel Trilling man. I might be familiar with the names of some of those appearing on the Man Booker shortlist in any given year, but I'd be lying if I said I planned to read their work. How can I put it? I've ploughed through *Ulysses* but understood only parts of it. I've dozed off reading Proust. I am ignorant of contemporary Japanese fiction, have no time for postmodern conceits and Stanley Fish leaves me cold.' He thought the Fish bit was funny, but she remained expressionless. 'I confess I adore Edna O'Brien but couldn't give a fig about Maya Angelou. And I'm not persuaded that McEwan is all he imagines himself to be. In short, I am woefully under-qualified for the role I am assuming.' 'But you'll perform it anyway,' she laughed. 'Of course. Unless we end up with a hung jury, there'll be no need for me to read the submissions, at least not until we get to the shortlist. If it does come down to tie between two titles, then, naturally, I'll step into the breach.' 'Or award the prize jointly,' she ventured. 'And how much are you planning to pay your judges?' He leaned across the table and laid his hand atop hers. 'Actually, I was hoping you'd help me out there.'

She took a careless sip of her wine. 'It's not something I've ever done myself, but I know quite a few people who have. I'd say £4-5,000 would be the going rate, though the amount of work, the numbers of hours readers need to put in, bears no relation whatsoever to the level of remuneration. But people do it for a variety of reasons, vanity being one. The key thing is, will big, or biggish names hitch their wagon to a prize that no one has ever heard of?' That was the $64,000 question to which he was about to propose a €10,000 solution. 'Generous,' she granted, 'Might just be enough to persuade a couple of luminaries. When you think about it, from an author's point of view, especially one specializing in literary as opposed to popular fiction, that's a hefty royalty check. Of course, they don't all have to be writers themselves. You might consider a literary critic or well-known reviewer from one of the broadsheets, or an academic studying contemporary fiction. Might I be right in thinking you'd like me to suggest a few names?'

Between fork-loads of fiddly spaghetti, names emerged, some more serious contenders than others. By dessert, though, he had the beginnings of his very own short list. Nic Langdale, whom she had met the previous year in Frankfurt, wrote for one of the Sunday heavyweights and taught creative writing courses in both Scotland and the States. His first novel had been short-listed two major prizes but that early promise awaited confirmation. A couple of snippy critics had him marked down as a six-day wonder. He'd prove them wrong. Two further reasons recommended Nic: first, he was a familiar face on TV; second, he had gone through a fractious divorce following a fling with one of his postgraduate students. Mrs Langdale had not greeted the revelation with the kind of compassion her husband had hoped for, indeed expected. Instead, she leaked the story to the *Daily Mail* and filed for divorce with a promptness that astonished him. Previous dalliances had been forgiven. The old 'You are the tree trunk, they are mere branches,' no longer worked its magic. A check for €10,000 was, therefore, not something the philanderer would likely turn his nose up at, given that he was now living in rented accommodation. From his perspective, it would also be a way of getting his name back into the limelight, this time for the right reasons.

Annabel's second suggestion was her lunchtime companion for the next day, one of Constitution's most respected authors. Hardly a coincidence, he thought. Amelia Carlyle, who had been with company almost her entire career, had published nine novels, several of which had been in contention for literary awards. On two or three occasions, she had come very close, but a major prize still eluded her. Just turned sixty, Ms Carlyle was in her literary prime, widely respected for the pellucidity of her prose and the sensitive incorporation of serious social issues into her fiction. Her work would likely not have appealed to Sebastian: much too earnest. But Amelia's name would help confer legitimacy on the Parnell. It was agreed that she and Sebastian should meet the next day in Annabel's office following the ladies' lunch date. Among her other suggestions, two stuck out: Con Digman, the Ulster-born Slutsky Professor of English Literature at Cavendish College, and Tina Harrington, a literary critic and editor-in-chief of *Prismatics*, a quarterly magazine that wouldn't be found dead in a hospital waiting room. He would contact them once he had nailed down Nic and Amelia.

There was a tussle over the bill, resolved by a toss of the coin, which set Constitution back by the equivalent of half a dozen hardback sales. He accompanied her to Holborn station, where they kissed without either ostentation or passion. Passing through the automatic ticket barrier, she gave a breezy wave, then disappeared down the clattering escalator. If he could persuade Amelia to become a member of the jury, the remaining pieces should fall into place, was his thinking. And if Amelia could be persuaded to throw her hat into the ring, Constitution Press would be well positioned to ensure that its authors were at the table, was Annabel's thinking. She did wonder if there might be a perceived conflict of interest in the event of a tie and Amelia were to lobby on behalf of a fellow Constitution author.

Sebastian had also given the matter cursory thought but decided that it would be absurd to question the ethics of a jury member selected by himself, especially one with impeccable credentials. As she headed towards Putney and he back to his hotel, they were of one mind: both the sex and the dinner had exceeded expectations.

# SARTORIAL SEMIOTICS

Amelia read him quicker than a sentence in *Thomas the Tank Engine*. Savile Row tailoring, or Dublin's equivalent; broken-in brown brogues; round-faced pinkie ring, heirloom probably. Comfortable in himself. Appearances mattered in her book, but an excessive interest in one's appearance was not healthy. The long hair was a mite too carefully coiffed. A man and his mane, hmm? She'd be chary of working with a narcissist. Still, he had greeted her with courteousness, taking her hand with the requisite blend of pressure and sensitivity, holding it for just the right amount of time. She considered herself a connoisseur of handshakes. His was *à point*. And, he had looked her straight in the eye while proffering a fail-safe 'How do you do?' The follow-up, though, sounded rehearsed: 'It's a pleasure to meet you. Annabel has spoken highly of you, as, indeed, did my late friend, George Kingsley, a great admirer of your work.' The last part came as news to Annabel.

Although Amelia had not read any of George's books, she welcomed flattery. In truth, George had never even mentioned her name to Sebastian. Writers had that in common with career academics: kudos compensated for the lack of monetary rewards. Amelia had forged a successful career as a novelist but could hardly be described as well-off. There wasn't a hedge fund manager or Harley Street surgeon in the background to eliminate financial worry. A writer's income could be as unpredictable as the Irish weather. Home was an idyllic if modest cottage near Rye and her car lived in perpetual fear of the MOT test. The daily challenge to populate the page with words remained a lonely pursuit. No surprise, then, that the occasional pat on the back lifted one's spirits. True, the proliferation of literary prizes and the attendant scandals invited cynicism, but the year-round circus, for all its absurdities, did boost book sales and put bread on garret tables. Not to be discounted: that was her initial assessment of the Parnell Prize director. If the hair raised a red flag, the manner and bearing did at least suggest a public-school background. Having detected a couple of aberrant 'o' and 'a' sounds she did wonder if he might possibly be Anglo-Irish and not, as Annabel had assumed, English: for Sebastian negotiating vowels had always been like walking through a phonetic minefield. Upper middle class Irish Catholic, possibly? English educated? If so, she'd put her money on a Jesuitical establishment like Stonyhurst. 'Give me a child until he is seven years old, and I will show you the man.' Schools like had shaped people like her father. Castletownmorris Grammar School had helped misshape Sebastian Conyers.

Sebastian liked what he saw, most particularly the high cheek bones and jaw line. No spring chicken, but no sign of a turkey neck either. Concealed under a cashmere sweater, breasts that chose not to seek the limelight. Her skirt was calf-length, leaving yet more to the imagination. She, too, wore a gold pinkie ring, her only jewellery apart from the princess pearl necklace. Amelia's nape-length hair, silver-grey and full-bodied, was swept up and back, disdainful of product. A pair of piercing blue eyes, framed by a symmetrical countenance, radiated intelligence. Probably vegetarian or pescatarian. With her unblemished and almost make-up free skin, she looked like the chatelaine of a great house or an Ivy League professor of Art History, though sounding rather more like the former than the latter. If you needed someone to play the role of a viscountess in a BBC period drama, she was ready-made for the part. Sebastian was visualizing her naked, fantasy lorgnette in hand, stooping to regard his erect penis, all the while wondering if her prose was as fastidious as her appearance, if her writerly imagination could have stretched to someone like him bare ass fucking someone like Annabel on an office desk? He might have been surprised to know the answer.

Once again Sebastian caught himself on, to use a colloquialism from his schooldays. No sooner had he shaken hands with a stranger than the sexual fantasizing kicked off. He didn't have to try to mentally undress a woman; it happened immediately, involuntarily. It was as easy as downloading a software app. To describe this as a talent might be pushing things, but if you were a male living in Afghanistan or Saudi Arabia on the look-out for a wife, you'd have to say it was an Allah-given gift. Beauty, they say, lies in the eye of the beholder but that struck Sebastian as a cop-out. He lived in the phenomenal world, wanted to see for himself, required empirical evidence. On occasion, he'd had been described as a womanizer but, to his credit, never a perv. Kinkiness was an acquired taste; one he had committed no time to acquiring. Even George, it appeared, had gone further down that path than he. From his time in the States, Sebastian knew he'd be classed as a sex addict and no doubt encouraged to enter a 12-steps program with other hapless souls who either wanked themselves silly watching too much porn or indulged in multiple, simultaneous extra-marital affairs. Neither of those pastimes struck him as being in the same league as a heroin addict shooting up with a dirty needle in a doss house. In any case, once socially unacceptable behaviour was labelled an addiction, the offender had his get-out-of-jail card. A few weeks or months in rehab, a contrite, preferably lachrymose, public apology and you were good to go, all sins forgiven—the American way. The process resembled a slow-motion, drive-through confessional. Under no circumstances would Sebastian consider engaging in such self-abnegation. Neither coercion nor perversion had ever been part of his make-up. His sins—if sins they were—belonged to the venial variety, sins against the Catholic and feminist catechisms. He adored women, loved sex. Since when did natural instincts warrant demonization and proscription? Although he thought of it as a rhetorical question, it was one to which he could have provided an historically accurate answer, if pressed.

Amelia had been briefed by her long-time publisher. Since the prize was for Irish writers, that automatically ruled her out of contention. Being on the jury was thus in no way prejudicial to her own interests, but potentially beneficial to Constitution's. The prize money was eye-watering, the proposed honorarium generous. And it would give her a platform, remind readers of her existence. But what would she be getting herself into? There was a credibility issue. She had never heard of Sebastian Conyers and wondered whether a manifest outsider lacking familiarity with the literary world would be able to organize such an award. Earlier, over lunch Annabel had explained the terms of the bequest and the guidelines for administering the Parnell Prize. Quite unusual and possibly risky, they both agreed. 'But what if it does establish a foothold and becomes a talked-about date in the calendar and you've spurned the opportunity to be in at the birth?' Amelia listened to her publisher but, innately cautiousness, wanted to hear from the stallion's mouth. Always happy to talk about himself, Sebastian gave her a brief account of his professorial life and his unexpected post-retirement career as a boutique hotelier. It seemed sensible to use the word 'post-retirement' rather than burden Ms Carlyle with the lurid details surrounding his abrupt departure from Iowa Central University. 'Most of my reading over the years has been academically focused: arid, technical, formulaic stuff, to be honest. All the attributes that would automatically doom a submission for the Parnell. My job is to stay in the background, let the judges do the reading and adjudicating. The only time I could envisage sticking my oar in would be in the event of a tie.' At this point Amelia was wondering what the *TLS* or *New Statesman* might make of a hotelier at the helm one of the biggest literary awards in the world. Very Irish, she thought to herself. She hoped, for his sake, that he had the hide of an elephant and the organizational skills of Busby Berkeley.

Turning towards Annabel, Sebastian addressed the matter of jury composition. They mentioned some of the names under consideration before asking Amelia for her thoughts and suggestions. 'It being an

Irish prize for Irish fiction by Irish writers, I really do think you have to have at least one home-grown name of note on the panel. The only problem might be if they were young and had recently published work of their own that was eligible for consideration. That, I suppose, will depend on the timeframe within which submissions are to be considered. In any case, someone like Anne Enright or Edna O'Brien would be perfect. Either one would provide instant legitimacy.' After a slight clearing of the throat, she continued. 'And, of course, there is the matter of politics, with a small 'p.' Jurors are rarely without ego and usually hold firm views on what does and does not constitute literary excellence. You may find managing the interpersonal dynamics of the award committee a challenge at times. Without wishing to overstep the mark, I am not altogether sure that Tina Harrington would be my first choice. Smart though she is, one does find her stridency and showboating hard to swallow. In my opinion, she is the just sort of person likely to disturb jury harmony.' Annabel remained silent. Sebastian had no view, having never heard of Ms Harrington until the previous evening. Amelia, however, had not forgotten the *Prismatics* editor's review of her last novel: 'A self-styled stylist who wishes she were Susan Sontag.' That had stuck in the chatelaine's refined craw. What goes around, comes around, she reminded herself. Even Amelia could see the value of an occasional cliché. Without much further discussion she accepted Sebastian's gracious, still informal offer, as much to stymie her crop-haired rival's prospects as to bulk up her checking account.

It was already five and dark. Sebastian offered to walk Amelia to her car, several blocks away. She would drive across town to Kensington and spend the night there with friends. 'Oh, I insist. Need to stretch my legs.' The soignée writer stepped out with a briskness that surprised him. 'Your friend, Mr Kingsley, must have been an interesting man. And you say he never once raised the topic of the Parnell Prize with you. Yet, here you are, its anointed director. A most unusual set of circumstances, I have to say; most unusual…and all the more interesting for that.' She smiled for the first time as she extended her hand. 'And where,' she enquired opening the car door, 'will the award ceremony be held?' 'Rathboffin in County Mayo,' came the reply. 'Oh, how…how exotic,' that being the first word that sprang to mind. She reprised the smile and, exhibiting paparazzi-proof technique, ducked into the compact car revealing nothing. The secretary was on her way out just as Sebastian arrived back at Bloomsbury Square. He loped up the stairs two or three at a time, knocked and entered Annabel's office. 'Well, done, Dr Conyers' she said. 'I can tell Amelia likes you.' 'Well, if she does, she doesn't show it.' 'Trust me,' was all Annabel said as she turned off the lights. It may have lasted longer than one of Jacques Chirac's legendary three-minutes-including-shower sessions, but there sure as hell was no standing on ceremony, no holding back. On the return flight to Dublin, the best moments of possibly the best desk-top sex of his life played on repeat. He could have rogered the trolley never mind the dolly behind it.

# PURGE AND PROGRESS

February and March passed quickly. Sebastian had been busy refurbishing his new abode, disposing of George's chattels and personal effects, everything from clothes to body grooming materials. Casting aside a close friend's belongings could all too easily feel like casting aside the friend. The situation demanded a certain delicacy, as every grieving relative knew. Dealing with George's unexpectedly large collection of knick-knacks was hardest. What did one do with a slightly chipped diecast JCB, or a pillowcase imprinted with the smiling face of the Monkees' Davy Jones? Except for the writer's personal papers, everything, from kitsch to carpets, was consigned to two jumbo-sized skips. He couldn't be bothered sifting through the accumulated clutter, trying to figure out what if anything might tempt a charity-shop customer or local house clearer. Eviction orders were also served on the over-sized leather sofa, the mahogany dining table and matching chairs along with the bulk of the wall art. And so it was that, on a miserable Monday morning, the last remaining traces of George Parnell Kingsley were hauled away to a landfill site deep in the Connaught countryside. The following week, a sleek white pantechnicon arrived from Dublin with replacement furniture more in tune with the style of the renovated cottage. Now, at last it could breathe. So, too, the house's new occupant after what had been a hectic, life-altering few months.

Although Sebastian had relinquished many of his duties as owner/manager of The Conyers, he remained both observant and engaged. He pored over the weekly reservations and revenue data, compared monthly and quarterly trend lines, looking for any warning signs of potential difficulties ahead or early indicators of opportunities to be capitalized on. Responsibility for day-to-day operations rested with Carla, and she embraced her enlarged portfolio with exemplary thoroughness. In addition, the green-eyed COO had enrolled in an online hospitality management course—a paper qualification might come in handy at some point in the future. Following an otherwise complimentary review in the *Irish Times*, they decided to address the hotel's lack of a full-service restaurant by moving to seven-days-a-week tapas. Installing a fully equipped kitchen for a twelve-room hotel made little economic sense and there were no immediate plans for expansion. With Sebastian's blessing, she had hired a half-time technical assistant to help with website development and nascent social media. The battle for hearts and minds was being waged these days as much in silico as in vivo. She remembered a smiling Sebastian saying something to that effect the previous year and having to go online to find out exactly what he meant. Declan was big into computer gaming but not, he pre-emptively assured them, on company time. The young fellow ticked many of the classic geek boxes, looks-wise as much as in terms of social skills—which was either a recommendation or not. He was the sort of person who'd wallow in MUD if he didn't have a real job. Since Declan would not be interfacing with guests, he seemed like a more than decent fit for the role. His skill set, Sebastian realized, might come in handy once it came time to promote the Parnell Prize, even though he intended to hire a Dublin-based PR outfit for marketing and advertising. If Declan proved himself, the half-time job might be made full-time. Wisely, Carla had let it be known to the lad that Sebastian was a former professor of information systems. There'd be no pulling the wool over the boss's eyes.

Though unfamiliar with the phrase 'not resting on one's laurels,' Carla understood it intuitively. By nature, the newly appointed manager was a doer with what her course manual described as a strong service orientation: in fact, she was one hundred per cent customer-facing never mind customer-centric without ever having heard or seen the terms. Living on the premises might not have been to everyone's liking but she had customized the space to make it a reflection of herself, decorating the small rooms with a set of abstract prints she had made a few years earlier along with several of her father's landscape photos. For now, living on the job posed no real challenges: quite the opposite, it enabled her to save for a mortgage deposit. Maybe it was all too good to be true, but it certainly didn't feel that way, especially when behind the wheel of her spotless Audi. Sebastian had set her life on a trajectory that she could simply not have imagined. And hadn't the *Rathboffin Chronicle* run a profile of her the previous week in its popular 'My Day' series? She'd been stopped in the street after that by friendly locals whom she didn't know. No clouds lurked on the horizon, but every so often she experienced a twinge of sadness. Her feelings for Sebastian persisted.

# GRAPE AND GROPE

It took several voice messages before the writer picked up. 'Yeah. Sebastian *who*?' The raspiness suggested a smoker or a hangover victim. In this instance both were correct. Nic Langdale, a two-packs-a-day man, had never lost his teenage fondness for the bottle: a drained Bulgarian red sat beside the phone, next to a clump of unopened bills. Some six months earlier, he had proposed a celebratory drink with his creative writing students after the last of the seminar's no-holds-barred, in-class critiques. The one drink had become several, then many. Wrap-up sessions—to use his terminology—had a habit of going off-piste. Sometimes he'd strike lucky, get his end away: Nic's idea of the perfect evening. On that fateful night, shortly before four in the morning, having experienced perfection with a bipolar lesbian from Inverness, he stumbled through the front door of his terraced house, slipped on the hall rug, and fell against a console table bearing a large Imari bowl. With a household-waking crash the bowl became a colourful mosaic on the parquet floor. The resultant vomit added little to the ad hoc tessellation.

That wasn't the first rollicking evening to have ended insalubriously at 23 Kitchener Lane, but it would be the last. Such escapades could be relied upon to furnish raw material that served a novelist well. And, of course, that was an excuse the reprobate had resorted to more than once. Wasn't it his job to make the reader feel the characters' emotions, experience vicariously life's highs and lows? He had once described himself to a splenetic Mrs Langdale as a plein air painter who used words instead of oils, an artist who spurned life drawing in favour of life itself. Like Constable or van Gogh, he needed to be out in the world to reach his full potential, to do justice to his craft: no atelier, no cork-lined room, no monastic cell for him. 'If I've lived the experiences I'm describing, there's no way on earth the reader can feel short-changed. Think of it as a quest for ecological validity.' 'Eco validity my foot!' snapped Mrs Langdale, accustomed to his self-serving justifications. 'If you need to screw a twenty-something to produce a convincing literary account of screwing, then perhaps I should hit you over the head with a mallet so that you can better describe for your pathetic readers the sensation of pain.' She continued without interruption in this vein for some considerable time before expressing her unalloyed disgust for him. A florid expression of personal loathing had become a familiar refrain on such nights. While hardly music to his ears, it usually heralded the final movement of her symphonic outrage. This, however, would prove to be the terminal tirade. He received his marching orders, and they would not be rescinded. Next morning, clear-headed Helen Langdale instituted divorce proceedings before heading to Camden Passage in search of a replacement bowl. 'Try painting that with words,' she muttered to herself more than once. Mrs Langdale had just ensured that her husband would have a plentiful supply of fresh material to fuel his literary genius.

Since his defenestration, Nic's daily consumption of alcohol had increased in inverse proportion to his novelistic output. Regrettably, the muse had buggered off. To fill the creative void and make ends meet, he'd taken to cranking out a 'Writer's Life' column in a popular weekly and reviewing for a couple of middle-brow papers, all in addition to his regular contributions to more up-market titles. Now, so many new books were coming his way that he wouldn't have the time to get on with the stalled novella even if the muse were to return. Sebastian explained that he'd been given his name and number by Annabel Hyde. That anchored Mr Langdale's attention. It also conferred credibility on the voice at the other end of the line. 'A literary prize, you say. In Ireland. Hoping to unearth another McGahern, are we?' The voice was stimulant-rough but not lacking in sophistication, well suited to TV and radio. 'How much did you say?'

Nic wondered if he had misheard at first. His head was clearing, fast. Sebastian trotted out the spiel that Amelia had heard, and others soon would. No surprise, then, that almost the very next question raised by Nic related to the proposed fee and—rather greedy thought Sebastian—expenses. 'How many judges?' he asked. 'Any names I'd know?' His love of gossip matched his competitive streak. 'Amelia Carlyle? I might have bloody known. Hasn't yet nailed a biggie for herself so goes for the next best thing, dishing them out. Two peas in a pod, we are.' A hearty laugh filled Sebastian's ear. 'Count me in.'

# FAMISHED FOR FAME

Cavendish College dated from 1690; Con Digman from 1960. Named after its benefactor, the college was firmly established as one of the UK's premier institutions of higher education, both academically and socially, on a par with Durham University or St Andrews. Digman, originally from Bangor in Northern Ireland, had won a scholarship to Cambridge where he read English and stayed on to complete his doctorate. The grammar school *wunderkind* rose swiftly up the greasy pole, to the delight of his mentors and the sniffs of his occasional detractors, moving from a junior research fellowship at a lesser Cambridge college to first a readership and then, in startlingly short order, to the Slutsky Chair of English Literature at Cavendish: English, he gathered, had not been Slutsky's mother tongue. Con's reputation was made on the back of his monumental reinterpretation of the Irish Famine, *Hunger in Words*, a study based on a vast and diverse collection of contemporaneous source material. While the ambitious author did not set out with an ideological axe to grind, he succeeded—through painstaking comparative textual analysis and the novel application of automated stylometric techniques to his corpus—in revealing the limitations of existing theories that purported to account for the aetiology and preventability of the famine, a famine that profoundly affected or ended the lives of millions—and, over time, gave rise to almost as many books and articles. Political scientists and historians were going to have to think again. Many of Con's findings made for uncomfortable reading and not a few shibboleths were demolished by the evidence he had amassed and analysed with such panache.

Digman had originally intended to submit the manuscript to Cavendish College Press but decided instead to go with Constitution.

He had first met Annabel during her CUP days and been impressed. 'We'll make this one of the top-selling non-fiction titles of the year,' she assured him. 'If the public will buy Hawking's *A Brief History of Time* like it's an Agatha Christie mystery, *Hunger in Words* should be a blockbuster.' His trust in her was rewarded. Of course, nothing was more likely to cause dyspepsia among Con's fellow dons than broad critical acclaim combined with financial success. Obscurantists didn't do mass appeal and Digman's appeal was proving massive. Worse, he had exhibited dangerous interdisciplinary tendencies. Naturally, popularisers—never mind disciplinary strays—were considered fair game at high table but the 'Con Man,' as his claret-supping denigrators called him behind his back, took their feigned compliments and playful digs in his stride. Happy as a stylite atop the greasy pole, he could afford to. Moreover, being a son of the benighted province, he had a skin that was as thick as his accent and a talent for repartee that belied his Presbyterian upbringing. The accent, it should be said, did him no harm whatsoever when lecturing in North America: female graduate students, and even a few males, were known to go weak at the knees just listening to him. Political correctness—as quondam Professor Conyers knew to his cost—had already blighted the academic landscape in the US and was now infecting the UK. Even the old goats at high table could see that the writing was on the wall, and you didn't need to be a runic expert to read the message. Not that the Slutsky professor would ever dream of risking his reputation, given the prevailing climate; not, mind you, that he had ever felt tempted to play the student field. Con was at one with Grace, his librarian wife, and indeed the world. His solid upbringing had stood him in good stead.

Talent more than ambition had seen the boy from Bangor rise to the top. And talent, he believed, was a God-given gift. The Decalogue pretty much defined Con's value system: conservative liberalism his political outlook. It had been a relief to escape the structural sectarianism of the red-handed province, not that he, like everyone else, hadn't learned the syntax of survival, from decoding accents to reading physiognomies. As a result of that unsparing upbringing, he had determined to judge people on merit, not externalities. Neither identity politics nor affirmative action seemed the way forward: a case of Gresham's Law of social engineering more likely. When immersing himself in the political history of the Great Hunger he had been struck by the widespread, reflexive vilification of the Irish peasant class as feckless drunks and illiterate idlers. Dismissing entire populations as essentially sub-human nurtured insentience and legitimized hatred. Labelling, as he put it in his inaugural professorial lecture at Cavendish, is the first step in the process of othering, an indispensable tool of totalitarian regimes. At the same time, he felt it his duty, wherever possible, to seek out and develop talented students from ethnic minority backgrounds: encouragement without either condescension or traducing of standards characterized his approach. There were times when talent fell between the cracks. He felt a moral imperative to rescue some of those who might otherwise be overlooked. And so, in his Skype conversation with Sebastian, Con hoped that the four-person jury would include what he did not describe specifically as a person of colour. He felt strongly, as an Irishman—and he expressed his delight that the Parnell Prize was not restricted to those born in the twenty-six counties—that the jury should reflect the New Ireland and the important contributions the ethnically diverse younger generation was making to the literature of the land. 'I'm not for a moment proposing a quota or anything like that, but you may like to consider adding a name from what I'm calling the Celtic New Wave in my forthcoming anthology. If you like, I can send you brief bios of a few writers who bring an insider-outsider or, if you prefer, a bi-cultural perspective to their work.' The offer was accepted with mild reservations.

It seemed to Sebastian that his compatriot was probably less interested in the honorarium than being able to subtly shape public perceptions about emergent Irish writers, names that lay just beyond the literary pale. The prize would provide him with an opportunity to move his agenda forward. Thanks to Annabel, he now had three names in the bag and three others coming in an email from the Slutsky Professor. He'd look the trio up online before deciding whether to make an approach. Con signed off with a friendly 'Look forward to meeting you in the flesh.'

# TOPIC OF CANCER

Halima Getachew fled the Marxist-Leninist paradise that was Ethiopia in the late seventies at the age of twenty. Two years later, after a harrowing odyssey, she wound up in Ireland, in Galway. There, following multiple wrestling bouts with state bureaucracy, she succeeded in matriculating as a student in a local further education college, determined to complete the pharmacy degree she had begun in Addis Ababa. The transition was tough, and not only in terms of climate and language. She experienced an almost debilitating sense of deracination, exacerbated by the imprisonment and subsequent death in prison of her father. Just looking at a map of the world brought home to her how far the Horn of Africa was from the west of Ireland. She had not seen her mother once since leaving Addis and would not again: a broken-hearted Nuru Getachew followed her incarcerated husband to an early grave. Six months after graduating, Halima married Peter O'Hare, an easy-going fellow student and Galway native. Their only child, Nyala Getachew-O'Hare, was born nine months later.

Her arrival into the world helped ameliorate Halima's homesickness. From the very first moment that bloodied, dark-skinned Nyala emerged squalling from the womb she was swaddled and coddled, enveloped in Amharic sweet nothings. The mother-child bond was fierce, strengthened by their private communications, not that Peter was ever meant to be, or in fact felt excluded. Hearing the language of her kinfolk spoken with precocious fluency by her daughter would bring tears to Halima's eyes. The words she taught her child were impermeable vessels transporting sights and sounds, stories, and songs from one continent, one generation to the next. In the young girl's mind, conversation became equated with unconditional love while words seemed to her to possess near alchemical properties. It came as no surprise to her parents that she exhibited from her primary school days an exceptional facility for language, both spoken and written; not even Irish flummoxed her. Her précis and essays were gilded with stars. By her early teens she was a member of the school's senior debating team, as remarkable to members of the audience for her natural beauty as her fleetness of thought. She sparkled her way through Oxbridge, taking a first-class honours degree in Comparative Literature. Her world was starting to look a lot like an oyster.

Yet, it was back in Galway, less than a mile from the family home, that Nyala would accept a teaching position in a convent school. Her university friends had assumed she'd move up and on rather than backwards, failing to grasp that she marched to the beat of her own kebero. The day job would cover the rent and allow her sufficient freedom to pursue what she knew from an early age was to be her avocation. Remaining close to her parents, in particular her mother, also played a part in her decision. Friendship came naturally to her, but so, too, did emotional distance, as Fenland swain after swain had soon learned. By her early twenties she had already published several short stories and a first novel, one that many felt deserving of a prize. It was her follow-up book, however, that made literati on both sides of the Irish Sea sit up and take notice. The ethereal beauty, with genes sourced from somewhere between the Equator and the Tropic of Cancer, had produced an auto-fictional gem, *Ireopia*, that raised a flock of eyebrows around her hometown and beyond, not that novel was either gratuitously sensational or strident in tone. Its success enabled her to move to a half-time teaching position, devote more time to her craft.

A country shaped for centuries by emigration was being rapidly reshaped by immigration, struggling to absorb an influx of guest workers, economic migrants and asylum seekers from all over the world. Even by the time Nyala was growing up, the thawb, burka and dashiki had all established a presence in Ireland's major cities and towns, exotic to behold but unsettling for some. In her traditional white dress, worn on special occasions, she contributed in her own graceful way to the shifting sartorial landscape. Ireland of the hundred thousand welcomes, she had come to appreciate, was prone to hyperbole if not hypocrisy. The young writer may have been but one data point in the global demographic convulsion but her nuanced recounting of growing up in a bi-racial family touched many a reader. For every heartfelt welcome there existed a counterbalancing squint of suspicion, sometimes more: it might be a snide aside or racial slur, on rare occasions the threat or actuality of physical violence. She neither laughed nor cried when confronted by a group of ululating youths one Saturday afternoon in Eyre Square. Their 'Paki, Paki, Paki' taunts caused some head-turning from passers-by but provoked no righteous intervention. There was ignorance, and then there was ignorance. These pasty-faced dimwits need to pay more attention in Geography class, was her first thought. And where did they think their great, great aunt Lucy came from? In the face of bigotry, even the finest debating skills were about as effective as a peashooter against armour. The reality of contemporary Ireland was at odds with the self-congratulatory rhetoric emanating from Leinster House and Donnybrook; for every overt instance of racism there were two or three of the covert variety, the kind that could never be proven in court but nonetheless cut to the quick.

More than once, Nyala had been told to go back where she came from. Her 'I'm there already' induced either a look of perplexity or a sheepish grin. Despite such moments, she conceded that a Panglossian attitude to immigration was irresponsible. The complexity of the so-called immigration question demanded something more than either a head-in-the-sand or pie-in-the-sky approach; something more, too, than yet louder banging of the nativist drum by the ever-fearful. In media interviews, she had—to some people's surprise—acknowledged that if Ireland were to become a truly multicultural society, then, indeed, there was a sense in which it could be said that it was no longer Ireland, at least not the Ireland of popular imagination, history books, fiction, movies, or tourist brochures. Instead, it would begin to resemble a scaled-down New York or London, just another post-ethnic, polyglot melting pot. Nyala had made a good faith effort to understand and reflect the nativist's viewpoint. Paradoxically, by trying to become what it believed it should be, Ireland would over time cease to be what it had been. Its defining characteristics would be erased; Irishness, the racial construct postulated by Seán Ó'Faoláin, would be obliterated. That was the complicated reality—the core contradiction—addressed with both bravery and intelligence in *Ireopia*. It was to the author's credit that readers of her book were divided as to whether it was pro- or anti-immigration.

# I LOVE LUCY

The drive from Ballyhannah to Galway took Sebastian half an hour, finding a parking spot almost as long again. He scurried across the swift-flowing Corrib and headed for Claddagh Coffee, relying on Nyala's emailed directions. The granite-grey river reminded him of Jack B Yeats's 'The Liffey Swim;' of his Trinity days; of that city's fluid class divide, and of George. It had started to rain, a stealth drizzle. You'd be soaking in no time. A peculiarly Irish form of precipitation, he thought, shielding his hair with the otherwise useless *Rathboffin Chronicle*. She wasn't the only non-Caucasian on the premises, but Nyala stood out with her cappuccino colouring, high cheekbones, and big eyes. Ethiopians invariably did; sculpted, both the men and women. It was a generalization of the no-longer-acceptable variety but warranted by Sebastian's personal experiences. Funny how in a world enamoured of evidence-based this and that, the blindingly obvious couldn't be stated when it came to physical characteristics. Although obesity was on the rise, no one should ever be described as fat, certainly not in the States, where fatness had been normalized. He recalled a shoeshine girl in Washington's Regan National Airport whose features he'd never forgotten. She was as far from fat as Dublin was from Djibouti. Instantly smitten, he'd sat down on the elevated seat to have his tasselled loafers buffed, forgetting they were suede. His doubly absurd tip was as lavish as the Ethiopian smile was radiant. In less than sixty seconds they'd made one another's day. Where, he sometimes asked himself, was she now and what had she made of her life? A mail-order catalogue model, harried mother, neurosurgeon, sex slave? Sooner rather than later, that mega-watt smile would have catapulted her into another world, for good or ill.

Nyala greeted him in friendly fashion, but not with the kind of smile that shone shoes. He was slightly damp and sticky. If photogenic perfection existed, it was standing a couple of feet away. For a maddening few seconds, he could feel his face heat up. The Sebastian of old had resurfaced, at precisely the wrong but entirely predictable time. How could she not be aware? What a fucking pain! He looked away to mask both his annoyance and neo-adolescent nervousness. She had, of course, noticed. Novelists have a way of noticing things. Nyala smiled, inwardly. On the table in front of her an unopened paperback and what looked like homework assignments awaiting the dreaded red pen. 'Marking?' he asked in an effort to naturalize the moment. Teacher gave a slight nod of the head. Struggling ever so slightly, he followed up with, 'Can I get you something?' praying she'd agree so that he could head up to the counter and regain his composure. With her Ethiopian background, she'd know a thing or two about coffee, he assumed. 'Just tea, thank you.'

Sebastian delivered his pitch, the one that had netted Amelia, Nic, and Con. She thought she'd heard the name George Kingsley but not read anything by him. What had prompted his friend to fund a prize for literary fiction, specifically Irish fiction? How had he come upon her name? Was she not perhaps too young to be a judge? They moved on to discuss the parameters of the award, timeline, composition of the jury. She had still not once mentioned money. Between questions she sipped her tea, cupping the mug with both hands, occasionally blowing a feathery breath onto the golden-brown surface. In the background, the Gaggia machine went through its full repertoire of hisses and gurgles and the rain, no longer half-hearted, slapped against the plate glass window. How could dark-skinned people live in such a wretched climate? It was a question he knew he was not at liberty to ask, inoffensive though it was. She had yet to remove her full-length black overcoat. 'It's very kind of you to think of me and, of course, I am grateful to Con for his recommendation. Do you mind if I sleep on it before deciding?' 'Of course, but don't you, er, wouldn't you like to know what the honorarium is?' A nod and a mere quarter-smile. She certainly knew how to work the dimmer switch.

'I'm curious,' she began, just as he was expecting her to up and leave, 'how you see your role in all of this. Was it an idea that you and Mr Kingsley had been working on together?' Her questions were polite if direct, like a forehand struck with minimal back-lift, the kinds of question that it made good sense to ask. 'Have you worked in publishing or the media, by any chance?' If Helen of Troy's was the face that launched a thousand ships, he could only imagine the armada Hyala's might send down the slipway. Sebastian was like a hare in headlights. It was those eyes. Milk ponds with hazel nuts; adhesive they were. He wondered if he might perhaps be drooling, unawares. Natural beauty was a fearsome thing, more so when wielded without preening or predatory intent. She could so easily have weaponized her looks. That she displayed not an iota of coquettishness the whole time they spoke made her even more irresistible in his eyes. As he feared, his blushing had not gone unnoticed. Nor his near drooling. He might look like and endeavour to come across as a man of the world, but there was an underlying vulnerability if not innocence to him. She liked her knights to have chinks in their armour, not that he could have guessed. The conversation moved along more easily, sustained by a second cup of tea. On separating she extended a hand and once more adjusted the dimmer switch. It was a smile that sent him skipping back to his car.

# PART III

# IN MEDIA RES

Bristling with a panoply of communication devices—landline, mobile phones, workstation, laptop, printer and even a fax machine—the kitchen island now served as central command. Scattered folders, draft brochures and promotional mock-ups covered most of the rest of the marble surface. Sebastian had commissioned Byrne & McNally of Dublin, a respected ad agency, to create an integrated marketing and advertising campaign around the prize. When they met for the first time in Ballsbridge, Brendan Byrne's initial questions each began with the same word: why? It was a technique that had served him well since childhood. 'Why Parnell? Why not the Kingsley Prize after the man himself? Why exclude popular fiction since that's what he wrote, made him famous? Why hold the award ceremony in the middle of winter on the edge of the Atlantic in a place most people have never heard of?'

Byrne's surgical probes provided the reassurance Sebastian had been hoping for. 'Indeed, Mr Byrne These very questions are the reason we're having this conversation. Your job, I suppose, is to render their asking unnecessary.' It wasn't meant to sound rude but could easily have come across that way. Byrne, though, had seen and heard it all before. Bluntness and impatience were occupational hazards in the fast-paced media world, where all that glittered was indeed gold—albeit of the lamé or leaf variety. 'Although,' continued Sebastian, 'there are some big money literary prizes, none, to the best of my knowledge, targets under-thirty-fives, more specifically, under-thirty-fives from the island of Ireland who write serious novels. Just imagine the impact of a €75,000 cash award on a struggling writer, trying day in day out to make ends meet. It could have a transformative effect, result in a work, or works of genius being produced that might otherwise never see the light of day. I don't need to tell you that Ireland punches well above its weight in the international literary stakes. I see the Parnell as a way of unearthing another heavyweight, someone on a par with William Trevor or John McGahern.' Sebastian would surely have cringed had he heard a playback of his remarks. But he was not for stopping. 'And as for Rathboffin, didn't Joyce, Synge and Yeats, to name but three, all have significant ties to the west of Ireland? It may be rural and remote but it's undeniably romantic, powerfully so. How can I put it? if tiny Hay-on-Wye can be 'The Woodstock of the Mind' why can't Rathboffin be the...well, I'll leave that bit to you. Anyway, I have no doubt you'll come up with the perfect pitch, the ideal way to frame the Parnell Prize, differentiating it from other awards.'

Brendan Byrne had been twiddling a pencil between the fingers of his left hand, very occasionally jotting down a word or phrase in his moleskin notebook. He found it best to let clients hold forth until they ran out of steam, having revealed the limits of their knowledgeability. It had quickly become apparent that Conyers understood the branding challenge and, unlike many other first-time clients, was conversant with the concepts and terminology of creative marketing. 'But it's not just Yeats and his ilk. George Kingsley himself headed west to find his muse,' began Byrne. 'Maybe your late friend wasn't a writer of high-brow fiction, but he nonetheless discovered or invented his literary self in the west. Clearly, as you say, the magic, the beauty of Connaught should be part of any promotional campaign. Call it literary geography or literary tourism if you will. The west is to artists and writers as, oh I don't know, Giverny was to Monet or the Lake District to Wordsworth. Turn a perceived disadvantage into an actual advantage. That is step one. Step two is to leverage Ireland's extraordinary literary heritage, evidenced by the disproportionate number of novelists, poets and playwrights produced here. Our aim should be to position the Parnell Prize as a continuation of that tradition, intentionally designed to widen the talent pipeline.

Importantly, to my mind, it should not be a case of winner takes all. We're going to shine the spotlight as widely as possible, highlighting all the authors who make the shortlist. Just being among the final three, four or five will give new names welcome publicity, provide encouragement to publishers, large and small. Another key part of the messaging will be the selection committee. They will play a big part in shaping public perceptions of the prize's credibility. Come up with names no one has heard of, and the media won't give you the time of day. In short: the bigger the names, the easier it is to get attention. Perhaps you can't land a megastar, but if the jurors have interesting personal backgrounds, literary standing and, better still, media salience, that should do the trick. Not sure I can help much in that regard, but I'm interested to know who you have in mind as we'll be needing potted bios, headshots, links to websites, media clips, videos and so on. The sooner we can get some or all of them in front of the camera on air talking about the prize, the better. Between now and the inaugural prize ceremony we need to have a controlled stream of media releases and follow-ups. We'll also want to get the tourist industry people behind us, have them understand that it'll be a boost for the region, in particular for the local hospitality industry. Then there's the literary establishment, and not just the *Dublin Review of Books* and *Irish Times*. We'll want to place the news releases and updates as widely as possibly to ensure that publishers, critics, writers and self-anointed arbiters of taste are aware of developments. Later, we'll need to put our heads together and plan the February award ceremony. We really need to ensure media coverage of that on, for instance, *RTÉ News* and possibly *Nationwide* and, ideally, on UK networks and beyond. I take it you already have somewhere in mind for the event.'

Sebastian mentioned that he hoped to secure the Rathboffin town hall but had yet to decide on things like format and running time. He did, though, reveal the names of the four jurors, following up with a few sentences about each one. 'Not bad at all,' was Byrne's reaction.

'I've seen Getachew whatshername interviewed on TV. She's as clever and articulate as she is telegenic. *The Hungry Stones* I have heard of but not, I confess, read. Can't say I know much if anything about the author. At least he's Irish. The Amelia lady is new to me, but Nic Langdale I am well aware of. He certainly has a media presence, for one reason or another, and that's ideal for our purposes. Seems to me that you've assembled an interesting quartet with, I imagine, quite a diversity of viewpoints. For the first year at least, I'd recommend steering clear of scandals, engineered or otherwise. I know that a feuding selection committee makes for good copy, but I think you'll want to bed down the award before inviting controversy. And while on the subject of personalities, we're going to have to give some thought as to how we present you. After all, you are the public face of the Parnell and it's to you the media will turn for information. They'll want to know why someone who was once an academic in the US became a hotelier in the west of Ireland before assuming the directorship of the Parnell Foundation and Prize. It's an unconventional trajectory. Now, I'll be honest with you, I'm one of those who reserves the title doctor for people with medical qualifications, but, having said that, I would encourage you not to discourage people from addressing you as doctor. Adds a certain cachet. In any case, don't be surprised if some of the papers dig around for a backstory. If there are any skeletons in your cupboard, I can guarantee they'll be rattled.'

# QUORATE

By 2012 more than 30 million people worldwide were using Skype. Yet only two members of the Parnell jury knew of the peer-to-peer communication software and only one, Con Digman, was a user. On first hearing the term, Amelia thought pier-to-pier had something to do with sailing. This was where Declan proved his worth. In less than two weeks he had the quartet connected to and proficient in the app, ready for Sebastian to host the first online meeting of the selection committee from his cottage. He had no intention of paying travel or accommodation expenses if he could avoid it: George's beneficence was not to be squandered on boondoggling. It had taken considerable back-and-forth to have all four sign and return their memoranda of agreement, supply him with bios and provide publication-worthy mug shots. Sebastian, as a former department chair, was familiar with the saying that leading faculty was like herding cats, but this lot is bloody feral was how he put it, rather incautiously, to his geekish assistant.

Now, at last, they could push ahead with the business at hand. Or so he naively thought. Writers have egos, which is unsurprising. If you expect people to read what you write, it follows that you must have a healthy regard if not for yourself as a person, then at least for your literary talents. In most fields of artistic endeavour, self-belief is a necessary if far from sufficient basis for success. Regrettably, though, some authors have massively inflated egos, creating difficulties for those in their orbit. Nic Langdale, possessed of a mouth that seemed to lack a shut setting, was one such. Even before Sebastian had raised the first substantive item on his agenda, Nic's over-sized ego was on full show. The familiar TV face was discoursing on literary excellence. 'Limpid prose, deftness of dialog, none of that shit really matters.' The sound of an uncontainable belch was heard simultaneously by the ladies in Galway and Rye. 'Great writing grabs you by the short and curlies,' he banged on, the lunchtime drink having evidently morphed into a bottle. 'In art historical terms it's the difference between Basquiat and Poussin.' The Slutsky Professor of Comparative could hardly believe what he was hearing. All foam no beer, was his immediate assessment of his co-juror. 'And in literary terms, that would be what, Nic? We are, are we not, awarding a book rather than a painting prize?' Con's dig was ignored by Mr Langdale who continued to pontificate with volubility about privileging ballsy writers who grappled with meaty issues like incest and paedophilia. 'Give me socially relevant writing, writing that doesn't just disappear up its own butthole.' 'So much for *l'arse pour l'arse*,' shot back Con, in quite uncharacteristic fashion.

Meanwhile, Amelia, who had been known on occasion to exhibit passive-aggressive tendencies, was stiffening in her chair, beneath a reproduction of Poussin's 'A Dance to the Music of Time.' Ginny, the sleekest of Abyssinians, perched as usual on the desk next to the computer screen, sensed that not all was well with her genteel owner. 'Am I to take it, Mr Langdale, that we are to close our eyes to all forms of literature other than agitprop and social realism, that we are to go down a path as nullifying as that taken by the Turner Prize, valorising turgidity and pretentiousness above all else?' Sebastian could see where this was going. Had they all been in the same physical space, the potential for fisticuffs would have been real. Hyala had still not uttered a word, but her wide eyes were even wider than usual. 'Ladies and gentlemen,' came an ever so slightly peeved if authoritative male voice from the west of Ireland, 'might I suggest we leave the ideological arm wrestling until we actually have a book or two in front of us?' No one spoke, though Hyala smiled. 'We do seem to have got the hay wain in front of the horse, do we not?' he continued. 'I'm all for agonism, but since we're going to have to work closely together for the next six months or so, let's hold off, at least for now. Instead, why don't we go around the virtual room and, in time honoured fashion, properly introduce ourselves before settling down to the business of the day. Frightfully conventional, I know, but probably for the best. There are several nitty gritty matters that require our attention before we can even begin to think about the serious stuff.' For a moment Nic almost felt contrite. The quartet was about to discover that the chairman of the jury was no push-over.

They may not have galloped through the agenda, but with Sebastian exhibiting the skills he had used to such good effect at the Grubb School of Business the meeting came to a more than satisfactory conclusion without further acrimony or grandstanding. Whether his announcement that they would be receiving half of their honorarium in advance played a part is hard to tell; it would certainly have pleased Nic Langdale. Over the course of an hour or so a by now thoroughly relaxed Sebastian brought his team up to speed with the plan of action devised by Byrne & McNally, encouraging them to respond to any and all requests from the PR people and, of course, from the media. The more visibility they could generate through their own actions, the more authors, publishers and the general public would take note. 'You,' he said, 'are the public face of the Parnell. Its credibility, in the literary world, stems from you, not from the cash prize, certainly not from me. As of now, I have no idea how many submissions we can expect, whether dozens, scores, or hundreds. Surely, there cannot be that many Irish-born writers under the age of thirty-five who will have published a prize-worthy novel in the last twelve months, can there?' Amelia was the first to speak. 'Prize-worthy, no. But what publishing house will spurn the opportunity to submit when there is next to no cost involved and no downside? Let's hope, though, that the numbers are manageable. Since we don't have a platoon of behind-the-scenes readers triaging for us, it's all down to us. I mean, what are we to do if, say, we each receive seventy-five new titles to be read in a matter of a couple of months?' She probably knew the answer, but it was Con Digman said what needed to be said with an assurance born of two decades of peer-reviewing scholarly journal articles and producing full-length book reviews. 'Trash tends to announce itself very early in. If you're still cold after five pages, I doubt you'll ever be won over. Each of us, as well as writing, reads for a living. I'm confident we can quickly discount the manifestly frivolous, patently mediocre and calamitously ambitious in a matter of minutes. My guess is that given, for the sake of argument, fifty books to evaluate we'd independently identify the same ten or so that possess some merit. It's once we whittle those down to four or five that the serious jousting begins. That's when we read and re-read the final short-list, lay out our stalls, earn our money. So, I don't think we should worry too much about being overwhelmed, though the postman may well be.' No one demurred; Sebastian moved on to the next item. By the end, Amelia wondered if he managed his hotel as efficiently and effectively as he did meetings.

# WE HAVE LIFT-OFF

A hectic couple of months ensued. There were moments when Sebastian felt like a pawn in the grip of a chess master. Brendan Byrne and his team were relentless in securing interviews with a broad spectrum of media outlets, both in Ireland and the UK. He soon became a dab hand at delivering what his former B-school colleagues used to refer to without blushing as an elevator pitch and learned to deflect questions away from himself to the purpose of the prize. 'Can you tell us how it is that a hotelier is running a literary award?' was almost as common as 'And what was the nature of your friendship with the late Mr Kingsley?' One radio interviewer had come dangerously close to implying that he and his good friend had been in a relationship. That was swiftly knocked on the head and post-interview the boor reminded of the country's slander laws. Fortunately, the tabloids gave literary prizes a wide berth, so muckraking did not become an issue; not that the rakers would have unearthed anything, unless, that is, their grubbing had taken them to Groverdale, Iowa.

At some point in almost every exchange he'd be asked why the Parnell Prize—the choice of name itself guaranteeing a question—was for literary fiction when George Kingsley was known exclusively for publishing works of popular fiction. 'Just make something up,' had been Brendan's blunt advice and so he did. Following the publication of *The Capering Clown*, George, he would say, had planned to take his writing in a different direction. Sebastian cringed at his own phrasing, but it worked a treat, the claim being, of course, unfalsifiable. Predictably, there'd be questions about the composition of the jury, whether it should have been all-Irish, whether it was diverse enough. The first question was so silly he'd typically ignore it and the second he'd swat aside by noting both the gender balance and the inclusion of a mixed-race individual. His wanted to say that it was diversity of viewpoints not skin colour or chromosome pairings that mattered. The growing obsession with identity politics resulted in near identical questions being asked over and over. The laziest journalists would send him a list to be answered which at least allowed him to, in the language of his handlers, stay on message. Advertisements were strategically placed in the literary press and a barrage of announcements and follow-ups sent out by Byrne & McNally to publishers in major English-language speaking countries. The company also initiated contact with cultural and tourist organizations throughout Ireland, not just the Connaught region. All queries relating to procedures and policies were directed away from Sebastian to the PR company and handled in-house. Printed copies of each nominated book were mailed directly to the jurors by the publishers. All in all, the early indicators of interest were encouraging. People in the know were beginning to talk about the new kid on the block. Word had it that one or two of the established awards were less than pleased by the advent of such a rich prize, not so secret in their desire to see it fail. Annabel proved a reliable source of trade news and gossip.

At the local level, there was work to be done. One of Sebastian's first tasks was to drum up local support and book the Rathboffin town hall for the award ceremony. To that end, he secured a slot on the monthly meeting of the town council. Most members either knew or had heard of him. As owner of *Rhopos* and manager of The Conyers he had quite naturally established a presence, even if he was not tight with any of the elected members. Once a blow-in always a blow-in was the mindset among the multi-generational families but Conyers, to his credit, had done little to cause upset, apart, perhaps, from exhibiting a surfeit of sartorial flamboyance and episodic pomposity. Having been granted a fifteen-minute speaking slot, he was able to deliver his polished elevator pitch all the while underscoring the considerable tourist benefits to the town of hosting such a prestigious award. Almost certainly there would be an influx of journalists and interested other parties. It might not be the Puck Fair or the Rose of Tralee, but the Parnell Prize would help put Rathboffin on the map and provide a shot in the arm for the local hospitality industry. There was unanimity in the council chamber, a most unusual occurrence. Even the pernickety Shinners overlooked his imperialist accent. Not only was there a vote of thanks from the chairman but an assurance that the normal rental and associated staffing costs of hiring the town hall would be waived. Better still, the council would launch a complementary promotional campaign of its own.

Time was passing quickly. The jurors were steeling themselves to slog through the more than seventy books that met the submission criteria. Sebastian had given them a firm date for the first cull. At that point they'd each come up with their top-ten list, after which they'd have three weeks to arrive at their final four. The winner would be selected at a face-to-face meeting on the eve of the award ceremony. Their contracts required that the name of the winner not be divulged to anyone prior to the public announcement. It was, Sebastian stressed, imperative that absolute secrecy be observed. A leak of any kind, by any one of them would have a deflating effect on the entire proceedings. Sustaining suspense was mission-critical, as he almost put it before realizing that such language would likely cause Ms Carlyle to wince.

# SETTING THE STAGE

Annabel was seated at her desk, one side of her face illuminated by a banker's lamp. He could tell it was her Constitution Press office; Addison was peering over her shoulder, either at the screen or down her generously unbuttoned blouse. Images of that evening remained fresh, had buoyed him up on many a cold night in Ballyhannah. Could he have been her first, her only workplace playmate? Probably not. Might there be residual microscopic traces of his DNA on the green leather surface? He was imagining the desktop as a palimpsest, gossamer films of seed overwritten by later additions. 'Sebastian!' He pulled himself together. Time to get down to business.

The hotelier had never attended a book award ceremony, the publisher had. Should the Parnell aspire to be something along the lines of the Oscars or BAFTA—albeit on a less extravagant scale? That's what he'd been asking himself. Only a fool would settle for a fifteen-minute presentation with a glass of plonk and a cold sausage roll. Given that people would, in theory, come from far and wide, the budget approach would not pass muster. The Parnell had to transcend the Rathboffin norm, ideally in the process establishing a new benchmark for event planning in the area. Meticulous preparation would be of the essence. Staged events have a way of unravelling, the causes ranging from a screeching microphone to a malfunctioning fire alarm, from an inebriated speaker to a catering mishap. The overall organization of the evening, the choreography of the ceremony itself and the quality of cuisine would all play a part in shaping both stakeholders' and the public's perceptions of the tyro prize. Annabel underscored Brendan Byrne's point: get it wrong first time out, and there'll not be a second chance. Still, Sebastian reckoned, if a smallish town like Wexford can host an internationally acclaimed opera festival, then, surely, Rathboffin can stage a three-hour, cock-up-free party.

Annabel had anticipated most of his thoughts and concerns. 'Sit-down supper, but not black-tie, is my suggestion. You're dealing with literary types and they're typically more comfortable with shabby chic or the mildly eccentric. Thought about music? If yes, then I recommend against canned. Live works best. Nothing raucous, of course. Traditional is a possibility, though not hundred-miles-an-hour reels or that dreadful wailing stuff.' 'Sean-nós,' he spurted out, happy to display his erudition. 'Something like the gentle tunes we heard in the pub after the memorial service. Remember?' She rattled on. 'Complimentary wine with the food, sit-down food. Any other kind of booze they pay for themselves. All four short-listed authors absolutely must be present on the night, along with their publishers and hangers-on. Try, if possible, to get some network TV coverage of "the reveal." Even a twenty-seconds slot on national media will be an enormous boon. You know, it really doesn't matter whether it's 'The Great British Baking Show' or 'Strictly Come Dancing,' deep down everyone, obsessive fan or unremitting critic, wants to know who the winner is. You could, of course, just tear open a sealed envelope, cut to the chase: "And the prize goes to…" Instead, I would suggest tasking each of your judges in turn to say a few words about one of the finalists. It doesn't have to be their personal favourite; they're not making a pitch, after all. Ensure they keep their remarks brief and engaging, like a trailer for a movie. Speaking of which, you've got to create a video record of the event for uploading to your website, even if the TV networks are present. The key to success is structure and seamlessness. Draw out the proceedings, build a sense of excitement among the audience until the spotlight lands, literally, on the winner. Think of it as foreplay leading up to the money shot.' Her smile filled the screen; his penis inflated his underpants. 'Now, when I said you could announce the winner, I didn't necessarily mean that it should be you personally who does the announcing.' She paused before continuing. 'Do you have someone in mind; or maybe you really would like to do it yourself?' Since their first meeting she'd had the impression that he wasn't entirely averse to the limelight. Wasn't there a bit of the performer in every academic? His 'I won't say I am not considering it,' she took as a periphrastic affirmation.

'A really important aspect of the whole thing is the live audience. I assume you're working closely with your PR people on the invitation list. At the risk of being a bore, you've quite a few bases to cover. In addition to the four finalists and their entourages you'll want to have a representative sample of publishers, large and small, plus a selection of literary types, everything from agents, critics and academics to talking heads from the culture industries.' Sebastian could still not bring himself to use culture and industry in the same sentence, even though the Parnell Prize was an instantiation of the concept. 'Naturally, you'll want the up-market papers in attendance, literary magazines and, no less important in some respects, the regional press. And we mustn't forget town councillors and local luminaries. You'll want these people on your side in the years ahead. If you can get a critical mass of key players to attend, then you'll have created a powerful networking venue. That'll persuade people to return in future years. Schmoozing makes the world go around. Of course, it helps if the venue and local hotels are up to snuff.' Much of what Annabel said chimed with Brendan's advice, but redundancy provides reassurance: just ask the captain of a Boeing 747.

Sebastian had been looking as well as listening. The bottom half of his computer screen was given over to cleavage. As she spoke his eyes would drift down, then remember where they were supposed to be. But she knew what she was doing. And he knew she knew. Even so, he didn't want to give the impression that he was in thrall to his libido, utterly incapable of self-control. Off screen and below desk, plesiosaur-like, his erection. If she'd tried desk sex with others, it was a safe bet that she'd given phone sex a go, maybe even Skype sex. What was the worst thing that could happen? Session terminated with a single click. 'Do you remember,' he began, 'the last time, the winter light, the rather too warm gin? We've certainly refined our technique since The Conyers debacle.' She was smiling, all crow's feet; it was clear where they were headed. 'Have you ever masturbated to images of that night?' she enquired with a brazenness that caused his penis to stiffen further. 'Since you ask, not more than once a day.' Only a slight exaggeration. She undid the remaining buttons of her silk cream blouse, revealing two familiar beauties. 'Pretend these are your hands,' she teased him, as she fondled breasts and nipples with the sensitivity of a master potter. Sebastian was unzipping, struggling to extract the beast. With practiced lasciviousness she inserted two fingers into her mouth, all the while locking his gaze. Next thing the digits disappeared off screen. She was rubbing a nub smarter but smaller than a penis, emitting gentle moans. 'Let me see it,' she demanded with the authority of a dominatrix. He stood up, moved back, forward, left, right, as instructed. Now her screen was almost completed occupied by a pinkish, fleshy rod. It looked like a museum specimen of some kind. 'Rub it, rub it,' she exhorted him. 'I want to see you come. I want to see what I didn't see last time.' He did as bid, his hand sliding up and down his shaft. Low grunting sounds merged with moans. 'Oh my God! Fuck!' The hyper-ventilating language of loss: loss of control, loss of liquid self. He jerked several times in spastic fashion. A jet of warm semen splattered against his computer screen and slithered slowly downwards like a deliquescing candle. He slumped onto the swivel chair; his trousers concertinaed around his ankles. 'Holy Christ!' was all he could manage, his head turning back towards his virtual fuck buddy. Moans, louder and more drawn out than before, could be heard coming from Bloomsbury Square. Later, as he relished the memory, Yeats came to mind: 'Time drops in decay, / Like a candle burnt out.' It had been battered into him at grammar school.

# TECHNO-SEX

After hanging up, Sebastian, drained but exhilarated from his teleworking experience, poured a large glass of Sauternes—an unusual early evening choice for the Bordeaux boy—and perched himself on one of the weathered-oak barstools he had ordered from an interior design store in Bray. It had now reached the point where the mere sight of either a kitchen island or an office desk triggered a potent mix of memories and fantasies. He was no better than one of Pavlov's poor dogs. Their Skype session, with its fusing of novelty and transgression, had hit the sweet spot: peer-to-peer perfection, he'd go so far as to say. Even so, he'd be upgrading his workstation for a larger model. Annabel's anatomical assets deserved no less than one-to-one scale on screen. Why, he wondered, didn't the company market itself as the planet's leading provider of safe sex software—no unwanted pregnancies, no STDs, no regrets? 'Skype to my Lou' would make the ideal soundtrack to accompany the TV advertising slots, he smiled to himself. Consumers, of course, would demand absolute reliability, even though the service was free: something for nothing was never enough for some. Loss of signal at a critical moment would be just as bad as coitus interruptus, and in the west of Ireland connectivity was often patchy. He had been lucky first time out; it might not always be the case. Next time it might be Annabel's frozen boobs. Of course, that was hardly the worst thing that could happen.

Was there any modern communications technology that could not be co-opted to serve man's sexual needs? For decades the porn industry had at been the cutting edge of IT, developing ever more sophisticated products to feed a voracious global market, a market that was as ethnically and racially diverse as a politically correct HR manager's wet dream. The much-maligned, much-loved business had a history of continuous experimentation and innovation, all the way from 3D photography in the nineteenth century to, later, stag films, video, and online bulletin boards through to twenty-first century interactive digital tools and technologies. Sebastian understood the nature and underlying dynamics of the smut sector— hadn't he been a professor of information systems with a particular interest in socio-technical issues? Still, an intellectual understanding was one thing, erotic reality another. Good old fashioned phone sex on a landline relied a lot on imagination and synchronized dirty talk. With Skype the visual cues and clues enriched the dynamic in important respects, allowing for easier coordination and at the same time greater spontaneity. The interaction felt less artificial, less scripted. Even so, dirty talk still played a major role in the proceedings, not least as a way of easing into the session. Against that, the video element meant there was no place to hide; everything, from the droopy to the wrinkled, was on show. Now, the participant at the other end couldn't pretend to be doing something he or she wasn't. There was less scope for fakery, which didn't necessarily mean that the moans he heard weren't as artificial as a porn star's boobs. It did mean that she could, for instance, tell whether he ejaculated or not, and confirm just how much juice he had delivered. One small additional take-away from his inaugural session was the importance of having screen-cleaning wipes at hand along with a multi-purpose tissue or two.

Just imagine if he could remotely operate a vibrator inserted inside Annabel's vagina by twiddling a joystick attached to his computer in Rathboffin, while she, for her part, was digitally manipulating an electronic glove wrapped around his stiff penis from her London office. Remote-controlled sex toys would revolutionize long-distance relationships, no two ways about it, was his thinking. The age of teledildonics—a term he had first heard used by computer science guru Ted Nelson—was dawning. Merely thinking about some of the possibilities gave him an almighty hard-on, not something to be taken for granted at his age, the age at which many of his coevals started to pepper their conversations with the p-word. Prostate problems had a nasty way of derailing a rake's career. Virtual reality and immersive sex must surely be imminent. Somewhere in the not-too-distant future, customized sex robots, designed to satisfy punters' every predilection, would be available for home delivery, as faithful and pliant as a pet Labrador. Any perv, incel or closet gay with the necessary means would be spared the spectre of rejection or public humiliation. All being well, a perma-smiling bint-in-a-box would come to his rescue by the time he was toothless and incontinent. Plastic dolls and artificial insemination, such might well be his long-term future. For now, though, the prospect of messy, fleshy sex was only a few months away.

Annabel, to his delight, had informed him of her intention to attend the award ceremony. Naturally, he offered to put her up at Ballyhannah in either the barn or cottage, but she was concerned about appearances. What if one of the two authors submitted by Constitution press were to be shortlisted or won? There might be mutterings about conflict of interest or favouritism. It made more sense for her to stay at The Conyers. On her advice, he would be reserving rooms for the four jurors. The finalists should stay under a different roof to avoid any suggestion of impropriety. It would not look good were a paparazzo to snap the eventual winner huddled with a juror or two in a corner of the hotel bar the night before the announcement. Sebastian put down his glass, grabbed a tissue and headed for the bathroom.

# TASTE BUDS

July broke records. It was if the rain gods couldn't turn the faucet off. A case of cats and dogs, day in, day out. Despairing tourists, shrouded in Gore-Tex, trudged from shop to shop in search of respite, like colourful figures in a North African souk. For many it was their first visit to the Emerald Isle; for some it would be their last. If greyness was what they wanted, then this was on a par with Lapland in November. The Conyers, however, remained impervious to climatic extremes, a carefully curated oasis of comfort, style, and affability; the Iberian dream team made sure of that. As a rule, its guests had either anticipated or knew how to cope with the elements, waxed Barbours and green wellies almost always getting the nod over garish cagoules. For those caught short, monogrammed umbrellas stood ready to serve.

On a couple of occasions, Sebastian wondered if he had bitten off more than a dilettante could chew. Even with Brendan Byrne masterminding the promotional campaign and Declan—now employed full-time—developing and maintaining the Parnell website, there were myriad tasks that required his attention, ranging from meetings with the facilities manager at the town hall to fielding questions from journalists, literary agents and publishers, quite a few of whom seemed either unable or unwilling to read, never mind follow, the submission instructions provided on the website. He had also wasted no time creating a spreadsheet to track all expenditures associated with the prize. Fay & Florin required transparent record-keeping of the highest order: to every item its invoice. Any unverifiable purchases would come out of his own pocket, a great motivator of meticulousness. Sebastian's day-to-day involvement in the life of The Conyers was dwindling.

By mid-August, they had received almost fifty submissions from publishers. At this stage no decisions needed to be made. The quartet, he assumed, would be giving each book the once-over the moment it landed on their doormat. He would defer substantive discussion until late autumn, while making a point of popping up regularly in their inboxes with updates on the roll-out. To their credit, all four had been quoted in the press on multiple occasions since the initial public announcement and Nic Langdale had twice made sober mention of the prize on TV, as indeed had Sebastian, albeit on an RTÉ arts round-up that went out at an hour guaranteed to net an audience in, at best, the very low thousands. Worse, he found himself fielding queries about George Kingsley and their friendship when what he really wanted to do was focus on the national, indeed international, significance of the prize and the distinguished nature of the selection committee. Once the September closing date arrived, he would instruct the panel to carry out a swift triage to identify any books that failed to meet the stated criteria. It was conceivable that a wily publisher might try to sneak in a work of young adult fiction, escapist romance or popular fiction under the guise of literary fiction. One major publishing house would, in fact, have the temerity to submit a previously unreleased piece of juvenilia by a celebrated septuagenarian, arguing that since it had been penned by the author when he was in his late twenties and published within the designated timeframe, it thereby met the submission criteria.

The distinction between literary and popular fiction may not have been a subject that heretofore occupied Sebastian's mind. He remembered Annabel saying at one point that Sir Thomas Bodley dismissed *all* fiction as 'idle books and riffe raffes.' For the director of the Parnell Prize, it was another case of knowing something when you saw it, like pornography. Given his new role, he had begun to reflect on his own reading behaviour over the years, on the determinants of his literary preferences. JK Rowling and Dan Brown might be two of the world's top-selling authors, but he knew instinctively their work would not appeal to him. It was a defensible prejudice: all you needed to do was read a page or two. Not many people would equate the likes of Julian Barnes or Philip Roth with Danielle Steele or James Patterson. Of course, that didn't prevent some readers from switching between genres, depending on their mood—writers included. He recalled his exchange with Annabel about cross-over authors who wrote for both markets using different names.

Writers like Roth and Patterson belonged to incommensurable worlds as, by and large, did their respective readerships. Weren't there multiple aesthetics as sociologists argued, ranging from high-brow to low-brow? Few of those who switched on weekly to watch *Coronation Street* would sit through a Tom Stoppard play and vice versa. He could imagine himself in McTigue's saying to George: 'If you like milk chocolate you probably also like Impressionism; if dark chocolate is your thing, then you'll be a fan of Constructivism.' The former professor was beginning to wonder if perhaps markets for cultural goods operated on something akin to the principle of self-organization. That didn't mean you couldn't enjoy Mozart in the morning and Metallica at a nightclub. But the two could not be compared. Simply put, some things were intrinsically better than others, and the best of the best constituted the canon. Although notions of canonicity and cultural hegemony were as welcome as herpes in certain parts of academe, the owner of Rathboffin's finest hotel knew that freewheeling relativism was an invitation to anarchy.

The stratification of taste was observable in every walk of life, every minute of every day. And yet, the more he thought about it, the less sense it made to think in terms of a simple binary since some books managed to combine genuine literary merit with a gripping storyline. Surely, if the writing met the tacitly understood threshold of literary quality, then it should be deserving of consideration, no matter how it might be classified by publishers, booksellers, or librarians. Thinking in terms of a spectrum seemed to make more sense, though the problem of drawing the dividing line remained. One of the reasons he had been giving some thought to the matter was to be prepared lest a question such as 'How exactly do you decide if a book is a work of literary as opposed to popular fiction?' or 'Who actually gets to decide what is and isn't literary fiction?' was raised by an interviewer. How should he respond? That serious fiction demands more of the reader because the author doesn't spell everything out; that the author expects the intelligent reader to grapple with the big issues raised in the text. Continuing in that vein he'd likely add that popular fiction is typically plot rather than character-driven, thus requiring less effort from the reader. It's for the complex characters and grand themes—*la condition humaine*—that we read heavy-duty fiction, not plot, not excitement, not easy laughs. For serious writers, the storyline is not an end-in-itself and characters are much more than ciphers. That would be his two cents worth. It would soon be time to hear what the experts had to say.

# GLOVES OFF

To avoid interminable rounds of email when it came to scheduling meetings, Sebastian had asked Declan to tutor the four jurors in the use of Doodle. In Amelia's case, patience was required. The young man's west of Ireland accent and his tendency to mumble when experiencing social anxiety had complicated communication. In the end, though, it was time well spent. As a thank-you, Amelia had sent him a copy of her latest book. It would be re-gifted at Christmas. The first proper work session took place ten days after the closing date, the aim being to eliminate any submissions that failed to satisfy the formal criteria and to collate the quartet's first impressions. Sitting at his desk, facing the bay with an unmarked, freestanding flip chart behind him, Sebastian contacted each member of the team in turn.

Two ziggurat-like stacks—review copies, presumably—bookended Nic's unshaven face. Papers, magazines and books blanketed every square inch of his desk. A butt-filled ashtray perched on top of the *SOED*, evidence of an unbreakable habit. Behind him, wall-mounted shelves, lined with paperbacks and CDs, sagged in the middle. Not a single artwork or potted plant, dead or alive, relieved the scene. In Rye, Ms Carlyle, mindful that her abode would be on show, had spent time that morning determining the optimal placement for her computer. In-built brown shelves were brimming with neatly arranged books, old and new. Tooled leather bindings gleamed in the foreground, strategically placed to attract the viewer's eye. A tall Mason vase on her clutter-free desk contained a selection of cut-flowers, brought for the occasion. Wrapped in a mauve pashmina and coiffed to perfection, she epitomized literary gentility.

It was obvious to all that what Goffman called the presentation of self in everyday life mattered to Amelia. If it did to Hyala, you would never have guessed. She was seated in her third-floor apartment in Galway's Salthill Promenade, a sea view just about discernible over her left shoulder. To her right, a functional sideboard; in the foreground, on the Ikea desk, a draft manuscript, and some papers. She was wearing a loose-fitting black top over black yoga pants, not that Sebastian could see anything below her abdomen. Nothing would have been arranged differently had there been no Skype call. She didn't need to work on making an impression the way Sebastian had done throughout his life: her poise and writing did that for her. Had there'd been a prize for the most impressive room, Con's college digs would have won. With its stone mullioned windows, floor-to-ceiling dark wood panelling and period fireplace his workspace looked like a set from *Brideshead Revisited.* Both the professor's desk and a nearby table were heaving under the weight of scholarly tomes. Off to one side, a scarlet gown, and a black tasselled bonnet. All the traditional signifiers of donnish erudition were on show, but in unforced fashion. He was wrapped in a chunky blue cardigan, knitted by his wife. It had yet to acquire elbow patches.

Sebastian had received copies of all the books but opened none. In fairness, though, he did make a point of reading the publishers' blurbs. If the submitted works were as brilliant, as original as promised, then the selection panel faced a monumental task. Most of the authors were new to him but since he was not part of the literary establishment, that came as no surprise. The pile included quite a few first-timers, so presumably almost no one, including the judges, would have heard of them. With minimal discussion and no contentiousness, three titles were eliminated from consideration for failing to meet the criteria. 'I know we're not announcing a long list, but if I were to ask you to name up to, say, ten that you felt deserving of serious consideration, could you?' Sebastian figured they each had a longish shortlist of sorts, possibly even an early favourite or two. He wanted to eliminate as many titles as possible in the shortest possible time and then home in on the most deserving candidates. He could easily have asked one of them to set the ball rolling but didn't want to imply that he had already identified one of them as either socially or sapientially *primus inter pares*. On the other hand, with such a heterogenous mix, direct comparisons were difficult not to say invidious: Con was an academic, Nic a media maven, Amelia a traditionalist and Nyala a voice of the diaspora. They operated in discrete if overlapping spheres, addressing different audiences in different ways—just another instance of product differentiation and market segmentation as the Sebastian of yore would have put it. That is not to say, for example, that those who read Con's *magnum opus* might not also read one of Nic's comedic novels. One thing united the four disparate spirits: their passion for language and storytelling. They were all baubles on the tree of literature.

A catarrh cough heralded the alpha male's opening salvo. Sebastian imagined he heard a soft sigh coming from Rye. 'Bloody hell! I mean, do all Paddies think prose is an excuse to write long-winded poetry with a few punctuation marks thrown in? Just how many ways are there to describe the still surface of a fresh-water lake, an alder in the winter sunshine, an ancient stone circle in Kerry? Only a couple of these newbies are writing about the New Ireland, the dismal bankrupt mess left behind by the Celtic Tiger. Does their gaze never rise above their damn navels? And snowflake after snowflake writing yet another coming-of-age novella set in drug-raddled north Dublin or west Belfast during the Troubles that could have been produced by a computer. Some of these kids probably can't even spell *Bildungsroman*.' Before Nic could cause further offence Sebastian cut in. 'I take it, Nic, you have been less than impressed. But right now, what we need to know is which books, if any, you feel merit our collective attention. Serious discussion we can keep until later. Of course, if you, if all of you feel none deserves shortlisting, in theory, we could decide not to award the prize. That would be quite a turn-up for the books. Imagine the headline. "Major new prize fails to make an award in its inaugural year." We'd certainly save money and generate a ton of publicity.'

With that Sebastian picked up a red marker and positioned himself beside the flipchart. Nic, inured to scolding and sarcasm, added something to the effect that the insufferable Irish seemed to think they were God's gift to world literature, but, with further chiding from the ringmaster, begrudgingly offered up four titles, one of which, was written by Farha Musharraf, not a name any of them knew. 'I thought this must have been included by mistake until I read that she was born in Sligo,' Nic chuckled. 'Still, it's a daring and creative piece of work, uncomfortable but necessary. Maybe Farha Musharraf is a pseudonym for Mary Murphy,' he added with a self-congratulatory snigger. Hyala was so surprised to hear Nic praise a young female writer, one moreover from an ethic minority background, that she overlooked her slight reservations about the book, which, though unquestionably a fearless and exquisitely crafted examination of diaspora and dislocation, could, she felt, be seen by some as incendiary for its unsparingly honest portrayal of Islam's less than appealing aspects.

The sighs from Rye were neither imagined nor inhibited. The doyenne of English stylists had heard enough. 'Perhaps if you had actually read the books you were sent with an open mind and clear head you might have realized that amid the so-called dross lay a handful of beautifully wrought novels, some of which deserve and will, I don't doubt, receive wide acclaim for their poise, their deeply-felt humanity.' A snort of sorts was the sum of Nic's rejoinder. Seven titles were added to the first four, some being greeted with murmurs of approval, others with a polite 'Oh, really?' Sebastian invited Hyala to go next. 'I find myself in part agreement with both Nic and Amelia and I am pleased to say that of the seven titles I'd like us to consider in depth, three were in fact proposed by Amelia and one by Nic. The only other thing I want to say is that more than half of the books were authored by females. Can any of you imagine that being the case even twenty years ago. I hope, Sebastian, that this statistic will be given the publicity it warrants. It can only be good for the award.' At least she hadn't launched into a vapid speech about the silencing of women's voices or male hegemony. A gracious delivery could make the unpalatable almost tolerable. Hyala possessed the skills of a diplomat while the Langdale fellow routinely confused aggression with suasion. A grateful Sebastian added her recommendations to the board, most of which were accepted without contention. He wondered just how selective their reading had been, how deep their engagement with the texts.

Con was happy to bring up the rear. When it came to speaking at conferences, he liked to come on last. That way, he knew what his colleagues/rivals thought and could adjust his material or style of presentation accordingly: forewarned meant forearmed. He was also mindful of the recency effect: that people in the audience were more likely to recall what they'd heard last. There was, of course, an attendant risk: that people would skip the last session for the serious business of booze and networking. Academics believe that they know best, better than their peers, better than the public. Narcissism of the intellect is an occupational hazard. Fortunately, a few enlightened members of the professoriate are mindful of the tribe's failings and while still adhering to the conviction that they know best also know well enough to mask the fact, at least some of the time. Con Digman was one such. Deep down he was as arrogant as the next chair holder, but his apparent willingness to listen to his interlocutor, combined with a general agreeableness of demeanour, made it almost impossible for people to dislike him, apart, that is, from those at Cavendish College who resented success as a matter of principle.

'I wouldn't be as harsh as Nic. Overall I think the call has netted a very respectable catch. I've skimmed or read every one.' Without effort he was making it clear that not only did he take his responsibility seriously but that he was a man capable of managing a heavy workload. 'Some of the first-time authors show definite promise but too often can't sustain the narrative arc or are simply trying too hard to create narratological novelty. I agree with Nic, up to a point. As an Ulsterman, the novels about the Troubles seem to plough the same furrow, even though, as Amelia notes, there is plentiful evidence of a powerful humanity in much of the writing. I wonder if that might not have something to do with the number of female authors addressing the subject of late? In any case, I concur with Hyala about the heartening gender mix.' By this point, Con had managed to say something positive about each of his fellow jurors. Just the sort of chap one wants chairing a meeting, thought Sebastian, even if he does seem to like the sound of his own rather grating voice. Con's names were duly added to the list, duplicates scored out, and a first cut of eleven established. They could have stopped at this point, congratulated themselves on a job well enough done. The odd expletive apart, it had been no worse than a typical faculty meeting, in Sebastian's estimation. Since the iron was hot, he decided to strike. 'Let's see if we can't whittle down this number. Is there any one of the eleven that someone thinks has no right to be on this list?' When the iron is struck, sparks usually fly. Sebastian was bracing himself.

Almost at once an Exocet missile was launched from an antique desk in Rye, one of Nic's nominees locked in its sights. 'I recommend eliminating *Lost in a Remembered Garden*. The staccato, self-consciously pared-back writing style feels both forced and derivative. I read one of Baldwin Staunton's earlier novels and he struck me as a would-be Hemingway.' Amelia was enjoying herself but did not let it show too much. 'Moreover, there's an off-putting machismo about the central character. It all seems so terribly dated.' 'Like yourself,' Nic muttered. We're off to the races, Sebastian thought to himself. He let Nic reply briefly but reined him in before he could say something that even he might regret. Support from both Con and Hyala saw Baldwin Staunton bite the dust. Nic, in the spirit of St Augustine's doctrine of the just war, fired back proportionally. 'There's one book on the list that wouldn't survive a class critique at a creative writing course for beginners. How it ever found a publisher I'll never know. Oh, wait. I do. It was brought out by Feminx Press. Let me tell you, *Amid the Marram Grass* reads like a pastiche of *Catcher in the Rye*, full of artless humour and saccharine prose. I've never heard of Breda Hanley, but if she writes like this all the time, I hope I never do again. You'd find better in *Ireland's Own*.' He went on to castigate the author for her lack of imaginative agency and much else, not that Sebastian understood what he meant by imaginative agency. There was a feisty back and forth before Ms Hanley was sent packing. And so, it continued until they were down to eight. Time to call it a day. A month hence they'd reconvene to debate the merits of those still in the mix, with vigour and, he hoped, civility. By December they'd be down to the final four, at which point detailed discussion of each contender's pros and cons would be expected. Before ending the call, he informed them that all their travel and accommodation expenses would be covered in connection with the February award ceremony. Their hotel rooms had already been reserved at The Conyers. 'Ah,' exclaimed Nic, with characteristic facetiousness, 'so our esteemed leader is also the Conrad Hilton of Connaught.' Sebastian continued to find it difficult to warm to Mr Langdale.

# KITCHEN CABINET

Once again, the annual slugfest involving Bing, Noddy and the Pogues was in full swing. Christmas was still weeks away but already almost every retail outlet and hostelry in Rathboffin had succumbed to seasonal song. Not The Conyers, where good taste prevailed: minimalist yet elegant decorations with a perfectly symmetrical, eight-foot fir gracing the foyer. Sebastian had been helping out at the hotel more than usual of late, in an effort to ensure that Carla did not feel abandoned or exploited. She'd not be returning to Galicia for the holidays. At some point, though, she would have to take time off; then they'd need a backup plan. But such worries were for another day. Sebastian's immediate concern was making the necessary catering arrangements for the ceremony. Hundreds of invitations had been sent out to publishers, authors, journalists and others. Detailed planning was complicated because he had no way of knowing the level of interest; replies were still coming in. The final number would be somewhere between zero and five hundred.

At a pinch, the auditorium, with its reconfigurable seating, could accommodate three hundred for a sit-down meal. The challenge was finding someone capable of catering a three-course affair for such a large number. The town hall lacked on-site facilities. There wasn't a single stove, oven, warming tray, microwave or fridge. In a perfect world he'd have called upon the services of Claude, but such a large event would exceed the restaurant's capabilities. Plan B would have been to phone Daisy and ask her to wave her magic spatula. But she had fled. George, ironically, had complicated the organizing of his own event. Of course, if he hadn't done what he had to Daisy, there'd have been no event in the first place. Can't have your cake and eat it as his late friend might have said. Carla reminded him of Calum

Corcoran. It was his former colleague who had put him in touch with Daisy in the first place. The pair agreed to meet that very evening in the bar of the Slievemore where Bing's 'White Christmas' album reigned supreme.

They hadn't seen one another since the memorial service, but Calum was his usual genial self, though when he laughed, which was frequent, there was discernibly more jigging of the jowls than before. The outward signs of incipient decrepitude were becoming harder to ignore. And it wasn't just Calum. Sebastian was confronted daily with evidence of facial flaccidity when he looked in the mirror; slight, to be sure, but incontrovertible. For some people it might take no more than a paunch or pouch to trigger a mid-life crisis. With time, all things drift downwards, while the southerly bits—prostate, bowels, bladder and what have you—inevitably start to malfunction the way an old banger does; first it's the spark plugs, then the big end and before you know it the engine's kiboshed. The prospect did not thrill him, having in recent months become conscious of his own stuttering motor: once or twice he'd nearly been caught short on a long car journey. In the words of Galway's populist bard, Kevin Higgins, 'Our bladders will be busy writing their declarations of independence.' But at least his northwards-pointing penis continued to buck the trend, proving that the spark had still not gone out of that particular plug.

Calum gave Sebastian an update on life at MCAT and the strategic vision of the newly appointed president. 'You can't go anywhere in the FE world these days without a vision. Good luck to him, I say. And before you ask, yes, I did throw my hat into the ring and, to be fair, they did interview me, but I always had the feeling they wanted an outsider for the job. Anyway, I'm happy enough where I am, content to leave the vision thing to others.' Calum had always been a glass-half-full kind of fellow, hale and hearty to the tips of his pudgy fingers. And that was no small part of his charm.

Daisy was greatly missed by both her colleagues and students. Everyone at MCAT had been taken aback by the abruptness of her departure. She had subsequently emailed Calum to offer an apology, indicating that unavoidable and complicated family issues lay behind her decision. 'But people don't just leave their job, basically disappear from the face of the earth overnight, Sebastian, do they? There's more to it than meets the eye if you ask me. I've heard it said that there was something going on between her and, you know, your late friend.' He was angling for some titbits, but Sebastian would go no further than say that he'd heard similar sorts of things. He knew that gossipers as a rule were disliked in society, even though most people loved hearing tittle tattle. Telling tales out of school might buy you short-term popularity but in the longer-term you ran the risk of becoming a social pariah; dish the dirt, get dumped. As for the notion that the pair had been in a serious relationship, such, he assured Calum, was preposterous. With that, they moved on to other things.

Over a second pint, Sebastian outlined his predicament. 'No bother at all,' was Calum's casual-as-can-be response. This was just the kind of real-world challenge he wanted the Department of Hospitality Management to take on, a stretch goal in his words. 'It's all very well catering for a dozen or so dignitaries at the campus, but the true test is whether they can scale up and maintain quality levels in an unfamiliar context, under pressure. Admittedly, it'll be a bit of a logistical challenge, getting several hundred three-course dinners from the MCAT kitchens to the town hall and keeping the lot warm before serving, but what an opportunity for the students, what a way to get them out of their comfort zone. Daisy's replacement is a woman by the name of Ivy O'Malley. She's no Daisy, but she's rock solid. Served for a time in the Defence Forces. Here's her number. I'll let her know we've spoken. You can take it from there.' 'Splendid! Knew I could rely on you. And, naturally, I'll send you a couple of tickets for the award ceremony. Fingers crossed, it should be a night to remember,' said a grateful Sebastian. 'Wasn't that the title of a film about the Titanic?' quipped Calum, flush of cheek.

Ivy was one of those people who grew on you over time, as evidence of competence and obligingness became daily more evident. A dumpling was how Sebastian had first described her to Carla, whose scolding frown would prove justified. Two weeks later she was presented with a revised assessment. 'Not so much a regimental sergeant major as an adjutant. That one could organize a royal banquet never mind a dinner in Rathboffin,' was Sebastian's take on the heavily built former catering manager from Monaghan. Carla didn't know what he was talking about. Within a matter of days, Ivy had come up with three menu options and suggestions for wine, all fully costed out. She was direct without being brusque, respectful without being a pushover. Sebastian had one less thing to fret about.

# TURFED OUT

The Skype backdrops looked the same, with one exception. Con was marooned in Boston where he'd been attending a conference on trends in neo formalism. A nor'easter had shut down the airport. From his hotel room window, many of the city's tall buildings could be seen, a forest of snow-dusted stalagmites in the frigid morning light. Old Bing would have felt right at home. The exotic setting helped break the ice and afforded Nic an opportunity to talk about the time he had been snow-bound in Toronto for two days and how his ex-wife had refused to believe his story. Sebastian wondered if he was detecting the first intimations of a developing rivalry between the two male members of the jury. He had still not read any of the eight books. Having no skin in the game, he could hardly be accused of taking sides if the discussion became, as it surely would at some point, testy. Truth be told, he was not much interested in what any of them thought and had no desire to grant them free rein. People like these were congenitally incapable of not speaking whenever an opportunity presented itself. He imagined they viewed themselves as the Lipizzaner stallions of literature, surrounded by dray horses and pit ponies. Maybe not Hyala. She seemed grounded, disinclined to showboat.

Standing by the flip chart he proposed what he believed would be the most expeditious approach. 'Let's start at the end and work back to where we are now. Presumably, we all agree that what we want is to be able to garland a book that when read by literary critics and intelligent readers alike will make a lasting impression. The work we are going to choose should be able to stand the test of time. People ought to be reading it twenty, fifty years from now. That, surely, is the litmus test.' No pushback. 'But first we need a shortlist to feed into the PR machine. It's essential that we build buzz between December and January before what our PR mastermind, Brendan Byrne, calls the big reveal.' He then proposed they each divide the eight books into the four they'd keep at all costs and those that could be eliminated. He'd give them a few minutes to gather their thoughts, not expecting consensus. Time-pressured they'd have scant opportunity to debate the merits of their favourites. To his great surprise, there was near instant consensus on three that should make the cut: Diarmud O'Carroll's *The Playboy of Belclare*; Sharon McGilligan's *Heartbreak at Cobh*; Gerald Fitz Allen's *The Last Harrumph*. To his and no doubt Annabel's delight, Constitution Press had published Fitz Allen's tome. That must be worth a blowjob at the very least, he reckoned. 'Well, wasn't that painless?' Amelia ventured, equally surprised. There were two contenders for the remaining slot. Both had secured two votes apiece. The thought crossed his mind that there must have been some horse-trading going on behind his back in the preceding days, but he couldn't decide who might have been the instigator. In any case, block voting of the kind he associated with ice skating competitions didn't make much sense when there were only four jurors and no clear ideological clusters. Yet, statistically, the odds on four very different individuals exhibiting near unanimity in the highly subjective matter of literary taste were exceedingly slim. But all was moot. This felicitous outcome made his life that much easier. Part of him, though, relished the idea of an online ding-dong between his four eminences.

*The Last Harrumph* was a short, experimental novel about the place of turf in the Irish psyche. The narrator was a long-eared donkey, a creature attuned if not inured to the rhythms of bog life. Con conceded that while the idea of an animal voice was hardly a novel device, this deconstruction of rural culture through the eyes of a not so dumb animal operated successfully on multiple levels—he did not actually specify what those levels were. 'And the sequel will feature an old Irish goat, I suppose,' came Nic's predictably sarcastic response, before adding, 'To be fair, the writing is assured but I just don't think he pulls off the conceit. Still, a good first try. Probably not something I'd want to hang a prize around.' Although Amelia had never visited either a peat bog or a donkey sanctuary, she had been greatly impressed by the acuity of the fictive animal's observations; felt she was amid the heather of time—that was how she phrased it. 'The narrator may have been a dumb animal, but throughout I almost felt as if I was seated at a Donegal fireside listening to a cottier or indentured servant chronicling the hardships of times bygone but with quite original and penetrating insights. The parallels between peasant and beast of burden I found persuasive, the freshness of perspective laudable.' She would be siding with Con. 'Sadly, I simply could not get Eeyore out of my mind while reading this,' was all Hyala had to say. Her terse though not intentionally cruel dismissal elicited a couple of 'Uhs.' The voting went as follows: Amelia and Con for, Hyala and Nic against.

Farha Musharraf's debut novel, *The Callous Crescent*, produced another split vote, Nic and Hyala advocates this time. According to the blurb, the author was born in Ireland shortly after her parents immigrated from Bangladesh, grew up in Dublin in a closely-knit ethnic minority community and started writing short stories when a scholarship student at Trinity. She was the first member of her extended family to attend university. In the dust-jacket photo Farha could be seen wearing a loose-fitting hijab. 'This is not a coming-of-age diaspora story dressed up as a novel,' Hyala began. 'The central character, after all, is a twenty something male working in a halal factory. I read this book with care and if I hadn't known in advance that the author was female I would never have guessed. Ali, the central character, is as credible a portrayal of a male by a female writer that I have read. More than that, the writing reminded me at times of Orwell's *Down and Out in Paris and London*.' Nic butted in. 'Hyala is absolutely right. Farha whatshername has done a brilliant job. Young Ali is torn between the attractions of the flesh, and I don't mean the dangling carcasses in the abattoir, and the strictures of his culture, the demands of his faith. The juxta-positioning of his revulsion at the practice of female genital mutilation in his own community and the nature of his day job creates a powerful duality.'

It was clear to the other two that Nic and Hyala were unlikely to yield. Con, however, had not altered his view that certain passages in the book were likely to cause upset in the Muslim community. 'Better to get hurt by the truth than comforted by a lie,' interjected Nic, who would have continued but for an assertive 'Let Con finish' from Sebastian. The Slutsky Professor, diligent to a fault, provided chapter and verse to support his assertions before Hyala stepped up to bat again for Ms Musharraf. The controlled passion of her delivery and the evidence of her meticulous engagement with the text were making a strong impression on Amelia, who had read the book less closely than the others. After a further ten or so minutes of arguing pro and con, she announced that she had been persuaded to change sides having listened to Hyala's arguments. 'Imagine if the first Parnell Prize were to go the child of migrants,' she mused out loud. 'I think we may be jumping the gun,' said an authoritative voice from Boston. 'Do we want to run the risk of alienating a small but growing segment of the Irish population. I have no doubt in my mind that some of the statements in this book will cause offense to Muslims.' And so, it continued in similar vein for another ten minutes until Sebastian brought proceedings to a close. 'Time to wrap up, I'm afraid. We need to choose between Ali and the donkey.' Nic sniggered; Amelia stiffened in her spindle chair. Two minutes later, the donkey was headed for the knacker's yard. They had their final four. An announcement would be made imminently, publishers informed, the website updated, and the media encouraged to contact the short-listed authors. Sebastian concluded the meeting by reminding them once again that the winner would be selected on the eve of the award ceremony. Their first and last face-to-face meeting would be held in The Conyers. Between then and now he'd have to read the four books himself, prepare for the inevitable jockeying and jousting. What would the interactions between the four be like when they were seated cheek by jowl in the bijou surroundings of Rathboffin's finest hotel? How George would have wanted to be a fly on the wall that day.

# DUCKS IN A ROW

From mid-December until Christmas, when everything ground to a complete standstill, Brendan Byrne and his team in Dublin orchestrated a media blitz. Profiles of the shortlisted authors and synopses of their books appeared in the trade press, in national and local newspapers, on both radio and TV, and across social media. Feedback was positive and the level of buzz around the prize commensurate with Brendan's best expectations. Apart from some understandable and mostly unexpressed jealously among less wealthy prizes, the only sour note was an almost Swiftean piece, 'Parnell as Prophylactic?' It appeared in a second-tier literary magazine and asked why the world needed yet more Irish writers, given the country's already staggering literary output. Maybe, the provocateuse suggested, the prize should be used to pay authors to *not* seek publication. As an attention-seeking stratagem, it worked, even bringing a smile to Sebastian's face.

The four jurors continued to do their bit without much prodding from either Brendan or Sebastian. They may have been talking about the new award and its significance to upcoming writers, but each interview represented a not-to-be-wasted opportunity to showcase themselves and, by extension, their latest book. The composition of the jury had met with general approval, as much for its gender mix— in particular, the inclusion of a female person of colour—as for the literary credentials of its members. As far as he knew, there had been no public speculation surrounding the jurors' sexual identities, not that he knew or cared whether they were hetero-normal, bisexual, gay, transgendered or some other classification that he might not have heard of. For the liberal intelligentsia virtue signalling seemed to count even more than substance. Of just as much importance to

Sebastian as pigmentation was the fact of Hyala's haunting beauty. If skin colour could provide you with a leg up in life, why not looks? Given a choice between two individuals of otherwise comparable intelligence and sensibility, he knew which he'd choose. And if the looker happened to be yellow, brown, black or whatever, so much the better. After his experiences in the US, he was all for affirmative inaction. And one other thing he'd have added had George been within earshot, if looks didn't matter, how come so many writers—Amis, Bukowski, Mailer, Roth and Rushdie to name just five at random— end up with gorgeous looking women on their arm or in their bed. Wordsmiths—poets maybe more than most—were blessed with an extraordinary talent for pulling babes that not even halitosis or monomania impaired. George, the most unlikely of Lotharios, seemed to have been sprinkled with some of the same stardust. Sebastian had learned about Daisy and Jenny late in the day, and there may conceivably have been others.

Pundits wasted no time in expressing opinions. A few Irish bookmakers were offering odds, but unlike with horses there was no form to go on since all the authors were first timers. Still, it added to the growing excitement. Barstool bores in Dublin's literary pubs were having a field day. As so often, the more dogmatic an opinion, the less likely the speaker was to have read or even seen the book in question. But didn't hot air keep a balloon rising? Coverage across rural Ireland was particularly heartening and the *Rathboffin Chronicle*, not wanting to be outdone, devoted an entire section to the upcoming award ceremony. It even included an extended interview with Sebastian, who by now had come to realize that he was rather enjoying the limelight. There was a certain predictability to the questions directed his way. How did he come to be in the role of director? How long had he known George Kingsley? Why was the prize named after Parnell? Instead of having a panel of four judges why not make it a people's prize with the winner chosen by popular vote? What happens if there is a split decision? The constant attention reminded him of his conference flitting days, of keynote addresses, boozy receptions and casual sex, though now the sex was mostly mediated. As might be expected, the local bookstores got in on the act. Window displays, amateurish in the most charming of ways, featured the four shortlisted titles and, in one case, photos of the jurors along with some of their recent publications. Hotels, large and small, were reporting heavy bookings for the award weekend. Come January, municipal workers would be erecting a giant banner across the facade of the town hall and just before the big day the *cathaoirleach's* impressive chain of office would be burnished to within a glint of perfection. Since returning to Ireland Sebastian had been struck by how there seemed to be an inverse relationship between the size of a local authority and the length of civic chains sported by elected officials. In the west, council chairmen liked their bling.

On the logistical front, Ivy and her team had sourced enough extra-large chafing dishes to ensure that the food would be kept piping hot while being transported the few miles from MCAT's kitchens to the facilities-deprived town hall. Her students had made several dry runs, cooking all three main courses and the two dessert options. There would be no hiccups on the night, at least not when it came to serving. When ordering the food supplies, Ivy built in redundancy to avoid disappointing guests on the day: carnivores would not take kindly to a vegetarian dish and vice versa. She had devised a comprehensive plan of action and walked the students through the various steps on multiple occasions. It requires military precision, she pointed out, to ensure that tables are served in the correct sequence, that food arrives swiftly, that they don't collide with one another as they weave between tables, that they don't spill food in designer laps or muddle up diners' requests. She explained when and how the wine should be served. They should act like Victorian children, seen but not heard. If there were well-known faces in attendance, they should be treated no differently from other guests. Anyone caught asking for selfies or autographs would be court-martialled on the spot. Naturally, given her military background, she had instituted contingency plans in the unlikely event of something going awry on the night. An additional incentive for a top-notch performance would be the presence of MCAT's president in the audience. Ivy would inspect their uniforms before they left campus: no stains, creases and absolutely no costume jewellery. 'I'm sure you know the drill by now' was all that needed to be said. Her platoon would rise to the occasion.

So, too, would the four musicians Carla had rounded up in town to perform on the evening—referring to them as a quartet might be something of a stretch since they had never previously played together. By February, however, the classically trained Spanish guitarist—who developed an immediate if unrequited crush on his compatriot Carla—the German bodhrán player along with the local fiddler and a gifted flautist would have fused into a creditable ensemble, such that they'd be invited to submit a demo by one of the guests. Foot-stomping reels and jigs would not, however, be part of the playlist, so the challenge was to ensure that their more delicate melodies remained audible over the general chatter and clatter. An up-market literary convention was hardly the place for a hooley fuelled by rebel songs. Cries of 'Up the 'RA!' accompanying the chocolate fondant might guarantee press coverage but would almost certainly prove to be the kiss of death for the infant award. Ralac—as they baptized themselves for the occasion—selected their tunes with care and rehearsed with the kind of thoroughness that would have earned Ivy's approval. All the auguries looked favourable.

# CHRISTMAS CHEER

Annabel was heading to Chamonix with a group of university friends for their biannual skiing jolly. 'Mornings on the slopes, but deffo no off-piste bravado, to be followed by Gluhwein, then more Gluhwein,' was how she put it with an exuberant laugh. 'Beware bronzed, blue-eyed instructors. And no ski poles going where they shouldn't,' was Sebastian's advice. It was their last session before she'd fly out for a guaranteed white Christmas. By now they'd become quite adept at talking dirty on Skype, having broken through the shyness barrier; not that a snifter or two didn't help move the show along. High comedy resulted if there was a lag in transmission, or the screen froze when one or other of them was in a state of visible arousal. She'd giggle on seeing his erect penis, motionless like a heraldic sword, beguiled by the bulging blood vessels and the smooth tip with its thin slit that seemed ever so vulnerable. He'd pump even harder when her stationary boobs filled the screen. Up close he could make out every detail on her auburn areolas. Once or twice in the heat of passion he had rubbed his knob against the screen. Was there a neologism for digital frottage? Over the weeks they refined their respective techniques, synchronizing their moves, becoming more emboldened with each interaction. Completely naked, she'd sit back in her office chair, legs splayed, expensively shod feet on the desk either side of the computer, its camera directed at her vagina. He could see close-up her fingers manipulating a receptive clitoris. Her moans were the real deal, not like those of the girls panting monotonically on sex chat sites. He'd masturbate at her command: 'Fast! Faster! Slow! Hold it! Pump! Shoot!' When uncontrollably fired up he might come twice, chuffed to bits with his oh so caricaturable self. In a month or two, real pussy would replace the pixelated kind.

During the holiday period he intended to read the four shortlisted books. Even if there wasn't a split vote, he would at some point be called upon to comment. As the public face of the prize, the media would expect him to have an opinion. Parroting from the judges' citation would not suffice. He had also determined to be more of a presence around the hotel, which was fully booked: occupancy remained constant, whatever the season, whatever the festivity. Not once had they offered discount rates. Naturally, the Iberian dream team could not be expected to work every day and in the run-up to Christmas Carla had brought on board some temporary help, both of whom—mature ladies—had previously worked in the Slievemore. They quickly learned that boutique was shorthand for near obsessive attention to detail. Sebastian wanted to be available to help Carla in any way she might want. Together they hosted the evening tapas sessions, neither an especially onerous nor disagreeable task. With the decorations and crackling log fire, guests lingered as long as possible, reluctant to swap in-the-moment seasonal good cheer for the chilly walk to *Chez Claude* or whenever their evening plans might take them.

It was almost eleven before Carla and Sebastian could sit down alone by the fire. Tongues of light flickered up over the bloodied torso of the saint, still as much a conversation piece as he had been on the day the hotel first opened its doors. He removed the empty Prosecco glasses from the recently introduced Damascene table—one of a pair secured at auction in Athlone—and walked over to the fridge where he had secreted a Dom Perignon. With a soft and sibilant pop, the cork was released, and liquid merriment spilled into two flutes. Gestures, large and small, meant a lot to Carla. It didn't have to be a pay-rise or an Audi; a whisper of thoughtfulness was all it took. Their free-wheeling conversation first covered workplace issues such as staffing, the website and how Declan was performing, then moved on to the general economic climate, local gossip, arrangements for the award ceremony, her family and George. From time to time, she wondered whether and to what extent her boss missed his old friend. Sebastian was almost always busy, but she could tell that he didn't have anyone else in his life remotely like George. If there was a social scene or an in-crowd in Rathboffin, he was not part of it. She did, however, know him well enough to know that he probably had a female on the go somewhere, but there was nothing whatsoever to suggest that he might be in a permanent relationship. Annabel and she had met briefly at the time of the cremation, but at that stage Sebastian and Ms Hyde were not an item, had exchanged neither saliva nor any other kind of bodily fluid. It was inconceivable that Carla might share the publisher's passion for Skype, while the mere thought of Sebastian waving his willie around in front of a computer screen would have revolted her. Fortunately, she tended not to have thoughts like that, let alone thoughts like that about the owner of The Conyers. She'd seen his inner clown more than once, but there was a huge difference between mischief and degeneracy.

Shortly before one, Carla retired for the night, without the hug she knew she shouldn't have been hoping for. The building was church quiet. Sebastian fetched a bottle of tawny port from the bar and settled back into his armchair. One swig led to another. A late returning guest would probably not have noticed the slumped figure with his feet on the brass andiron staring into the exhausted embers. Edging towards the middle of his seventh decade he could discern no underling pattern, no obvious plan to his life. Purpose should not be retrofitted; post-hoc rationalization was an easy way out, unworthy of him. It had never been his ambition to own a boutique hotel, let alone manage a literary prize. Those were not options suggested by his career guidance master back in nineteen sixties Castletownmorris. It was, with hindsight, a quixotic trajectory, one that some individuals might envy. But what, ultimately, did or would it all amount to? More than a sow's ear perhaps, but no silk purse.

# PROZAC PLEASE!

Sebastian's every day was driven by external demands which kept him productively active. Rarely if ever did he experience loneliness; idleness, too, was an alien construct. Busyness left no time for introspection. Rather, it created a sense of purpose, albeit one that atrophied the moment one was no longer busy. Life could be like musical chairs. You suddenly found yourself standing, side-lined; no longer part of the game. So much for self-importance. Retirement meant oblivion for most people. Nobel laureates and a sprinkling of sporting greats might milk their living legend status, but once cut adrift from the madding swirl the vast majority was soon forgotten, the luckiest ones memorialized in clay or oil or buried in a footnote. That's when the nagging doubts start to creep back in; the vexing, rite-of-passage questions that he and generations of undergraduates had wrestled with when drunk, when sober. Decades on and those same questions would be lying in wait the moment the flimflam was stripped away. 'What's the point of it all?' seemed no easier to answer in Rathboffin than it had more than four decades earlier in Dublin.

    He saw George—not in an ectoplasmic sense—sitting opposite him. With no effort at all he could imagine how the exchange might go, how his friend would push him to clarify his thinking. 'Why look for transcendent meaning, for meaning of any kind? Life is what it is, a congeries of experiences, agreeable and disagreeable that add up to naught. Remember Beckett's "nothing to be done"? Pointlessness is the point. Accept it, get over it. Every moment, be it joyful or painful, edifying or banal, carries within itself the seeds of its own extinction. Nothing lasts, not even the universe for all I know. Maybe only nothingness is everlasting. The very instant excitement or joy is experienced, we are assailed with a debilitating sense of its imminent loss, if we are being honest with ourselves. Such is the nature of life. It can't be overlooked, can't be changed, so no sense in complaining. The best we can do is conjure up ostensibly meaningful activities that get us from dawn to dusk with the minimum of effort and discomfiture. Wasn't it Monsieur Camus who said, we fornicate and read the papers? There is no afterlife, no higher purpose, no Allah. For many the *Sun* and a shag is as good as it gets. We're here and we've simply got to suck it up, to paraphrase Zeno.' Sebastian would have struggled to disagree.

'Take sex,' George might have continued, 'at the very apogee of arousal, there is an excruciating tension between the need for release and the desire for prolongation. The pleasure that should dominate the moment, excite us to our very core is vitiated by the knowledge that it can't be captured the way sound can be captured on tape, or images on film. If pain is pain, and pleasure, reductively speaking, is nothing but sugar-coated pain, why on earth do we slog through seventy or eighty years of mundanity and misery? What is the point of exhorting people to "*Carpe diem*!" when nothing can be grasped, when absolutely everything slips through our fingers, dissolves into metaphorical dust before our eyes? That's the great existential paradox. The more we love life, the more we can't hope to enjoy it because it is only a matter of time before it will be taken from us. Just imagine how much worse it must be if you're a narcissist. Life's a cruel tease, a drawn-out dance of the seven veils that, ultimately, reveals a skeleton. All happiness, my friend, is illusory.' By this point a thirsty George would have been reaching for his glass, providing Sebastian with an opportunity to interject.

'I hate to say it, George, but we are of one mind on this. Do you ever ask yourself how victims of the Holocaust survived, hour by hour, day by day, week by week, month by month under conditions of almost unspeakable barbarity? What sense of purpose, beyond a hardwired animalistic urge to live and maybe a humanitarian desire to bear witness, kept them going? Many were devout believers but their experiences in the deathcamps convinced them that God was dead, that Nietzsche *was* right. It's the Nazis we must thank for providing the modern world with the perfect instantiation of the argument from evil. Although it is almost impossible to countenance, something kept these Jewish prisoners going; from somewhere they found the willpower necessary to survive. And yet, even those who escaped the ovens, were destined to die a couple of generations later. The best any of us can do is postpone the hour and hope to experience a few fleeting moments of ecstasy along the way, whether watching porn, listening to Mozart or snorting coke. Life is a struggle to prevent the inevitable, and that's why, over the centuries, we have crafted heart-warming tales of love, resilience, redemption and compassion in a fundamentally pathetic if understandable effort to make the unbearable bearable. We consume these narratives the way we do antidepressants. If we didn't, we'd top ourselves. And as for those who chunter on about having had a good innings what can you say other than that they're bloody delusional?' At that point, Sebastian took yet another mouthful, forgetting that pleasure is inherently unsustainable. Next morning young Isabel was more than a little surprised to find her dishevelled boss comatose in front of the fireplace, a drained bottle of Warre resting on his ruby-stained lap.

# PART IV

# A GOOD READ

Over Christmas, Sebastian read the four shortlisted books, annotating and underlining as he went along, just as he used to when reviewing scholarly papers. Each one's strengths and weaknesses in terms of structure, characterization and language were noted. He would be able to hold his own in any roundtable discussion, if needed. Sharon McGilligan's *Heartbreak at Cobh* could only have been about one thing, and so it proved to be, except this time the effects of the Famine were seen through the eyes of jobbers and stevedores, quayside eyewitnesses to the misery of mass emigration. It was in both form and tone a conventional historical novel and the author had taken great care to replicate the vernacular of the day. The proliferation of characters made the story difficult to follow at times and McGilligan's tendency to freight the text with ponderous descriptive passages only exacerbated matters. Sebastian made it to the end but not without refilling his glass multiple times. Ms McGilligan was not quite ready for primetime. That she had reached the final four surprised him.

The same was true, though to a lesser extent, of Gerald Fitz Allen's *The Last Harrumph*, as far from an historical novel as one could get. The futuristic satire was set in Northern Ireland in the year 2038 when the province finally ceded from the United Kingdom and joined with the Republic to create a unified nation. All the action occurred within the space of a politically vexed and emotionally fraught week. Although the author possessed a mordant wit, the humour at times seemed forced. The cast of characters, as with McGilligan's book, was enough to fill an epic, the result being that the reader soon started to lose track of who was who. Yet, for all its shortcomings, *The Last Harrumph*, published by Constitution Press, was a meritorious if over-ambitious debut.

*The Callous Crescent* was not set in the Georgian splendour of late eighteenth-century Bath, but in a rather dismal Dublin suburb where immigrants from sub-Saharan Africa, post-Communist Europe, the Maghreb and the Indian sub-continent were dipping their toes into the melting pot. Ali, the book's anti-hero had elements of Meursault, the central character in Camus' *The Outsider*: seeming indifference coupled with honesty. His starkly matter-of-fact descriptions of life in a meat factory might not have been original in themselves, but the counterpointing of what went on in his workplace with what happened in less enlightened parts of the world in terms of female genital mutilation proved effective and deeply affecting. In the book, Ali struggles to find satisfactory answers in either the Quran or the hadiths, the sayings of the Prophet Muhammad. The more he reflects, the more he is puzzled by attitudes within his extended kinship and community networks. The reader, to quote the blurb, 'follows Ali on his remarkable journey of self-discovery, a journey that results in his splitting from his beloved family and rejecting the Muslim faith.' The blurb was less well written than the book. Squeamish by nature, Sebastian found the subject of cutting off-putting. Nonetheless, he was highly impressed by the author's daring, though he couldn't imagine the book making the bestseller lists in Egypt or Pakistan.

According to the dustjacket, Diarmud O'Carroll was rendered paraplegic following a motorcycle accident in his early twenties. Perhaps that should have been a clue. But Sebastian was part-way through *The Playboy of Belclare* before it dawned on him that the potbellied charmer at the novel's centre was himself wheelchair bound. That, of course, gave him automatic license to say things that an able-bodied author would not have been able to get away with, just like black dudes in the States calling one another nigger with impunity. It was something that had struck Sebastian as comically absurd, but, as he had come to appreciate, identity politics had little truck with logic. The *Playboy* was anything but a misery memoire and brought a smile or two to his face. A decent picaresque novel, felicitously written but hardly prizeworthy was his assessment.

His mind was made up, not that his opinion would necessarily be sought. If that was all it took to pick a literary award winner, then it was money for old rope. Presumably the judges had by now come to a decision and were busy compiling evidence to both support their and neutralize the opposition's choice. If it was obvious to him which title should get the nod, how could it not be to people who wrote (and read) for a living? But that would be to miss the point. If you're an anointed expert then you feel duty bound to demonstrate your domain knowledge, the subtlety of your taste, your aesthetic sensibility. It had been no different in academe. The moment you put more than two professors in a room, the flatulence ramped up geometrically. Maybe if you're a Pasternak or Proust, you've earned the right to ego, but lesser mortals, educated ones especially, should know better. And, indeed it was the case; all four were at that very moment rehearsing their dual roles, as defenders and prosecutors. If, by magic, they were all in agreement from the outset, then the formal business could be wrapped up in no time allowing the group to spend a leisurely day seeing the sights in and around Rathboffin before heading to *Chez Claude* for dinner with Sebastian on the eve of the award ceremony. But given the number of possible permutations with four books and four jurors, he didn't get his hopes up. Still, even if it took an hour or two of back and forth to reach consensus, he'd be content. In the end, what did it matter to him personally if the paraplegic playboy pipped Ali the apostate at the post?

# PHATIC COMMUNICATION

Both Nic and Amelia flew into Dublin from Gatwick, but at different times of the day, traveling on to Rathboffin separately by train and then taxi. Con, who had been attending a conference in Edinburgh, landed at blustery Knock airport where he picked up a rental car. Hyala drove up from Galway, arriving shortly after six, the last of the group to check in. Carla was on hand to receive each one and attend to their needs. Very nice people, that was how she described them to her boss. And she meant it, with one possible exception, Nic Langdale, whose over-familiarity had strained but not defeated her ability to sustain a smile. He had reeked of nicotine and alcohol. Dr Conyers would be joining them in the bar for pre-prandial drinks before heading to the town hall to oversee final preparations. Dinner could be ordered from *Chez Claude*, an excellent French restaurant, and eaten in either their room or the lounge area, or perhaps they would prefer to explore Rathboffin's gastronomic hot spots, individually or together. In any case, tonight was theirs; next day Dr Conyers would be hosting a dinner in their honour. Amelia was immediately impressed by Carla's poise and by the hotel décor. She had been expecting something less stylish. Admittedly, it had been a few years since her last visit to the west of Ireland, but this was not how she remembered it.

Sebastian strolled into the foyer wearing a navy goose-down gilet over a bold striped shirt and colour-coordinated cords. He looked a little tired but dispensed the heartiest of greetings to his literary lions who had been shepherded to one side of the large space by Carla. An hour earlier Annabel had texted to say that she'd not be able to make it to the event; her aged mother had just been rushed to hospital in Kent, a seizure of some kind. Probabilistically, there was a fifty percent chance that that statement was true. Now he'd not be getting laid. As the other guests sipped Prosecco, oblivious to the literati in their midst, Sebastian uncorked a magnum of Tattinger without fuss or spillage. Six glistening glasses converged, clinked chaotically. Nearby stood an array of freshly made tapas dishes to line their tummies. He had asked Carla to stay, primarily to ensure that the conversation didn't careen off into discussion of serious business. This was the group's first face-to-face meeting, and as such should be no more than opportunity to establish multilateral cordiality. Yet, behaviours he had observed in their virtual meetings were already beginning to exhibit themselves, which is to say Nic spouted a lot, Amelia appeared to bristle, while Con started to look like a long-suffering parent who knew he'd have to intervene at some point. Hyala again spoke least, her stunning eyes missing nothing. He'd have given a lot more than a penny for her thoughts. She wouldn't have needed to spend even a single penny as she could tell what kind of thoughts typically occupied his mind. Sebastian had been nothing but courteous to her when they'd met in Galway, but she had a sixth sense: one of those naughty-but-nice types had been her first impression, the naughtiness cloaked in suavity. Messrs Langdale and Conyers were in their different ways exemplars of the heterosexual male, Nic, the pettish oaf, defining one end of the spectrum, and Sebastian, the charming rake, the other. They both, first and foremost, viewed women as sexual objects. They couldn't help it. Nor did they see it as something to be problematized. For now, she was unsure whether Sebastian's self-restraint and all-round good manners were sufficient to grant him temporary reprieve from reprobate classification. She'd make her mind over the course of the next forty-eight hours. As regards voluble Nic, she shared Carla's assessment. He was beyond forgivingness or redemption.

    Sebastian could sense the general watchfulness among the quartet. Although belonging to the same world, they occupied different vectors and while they may not have lacked self-esteem, being as they were writers of some note in the public imagination, they felt that esteem was their due. It was a form of entitlement that didn't fade. Of course, they knew they mustn't allow themselves to be seen as needy or insecure in any way. That was an absolute no-no. Name dropping, however, when done with contextual appropriateness, was an effective way of establishing one's credentials. So, too, an *en passant* reference to an invited talk one had just given or a gong that had unexpectedly come one's way. Con, as was his wont, played a measured game, reacting more than instigating, though once or twice he edged close to pomposity. Having spent the previous three days discussing life narratives, a particularly hot topic in his field, he could be forgiven for slipping back into professional mode. But the moment any one of them alluded to the four finalists or mentioned one of the books in contention, Sebastian issued a schoolmasterly rebuke.

Amelia, as impeccably dressed as she had been the first time Sebastian met her in London, regaled the group with a slightly risqué story from her time at the Yeats Summer School in Sligo. It was pitch perfect for the occasion and had the added benefit of locating her in a status-enhancing milieu. That prompted Nic to say that he'd always felt Yeats was an overrated fogey. Even before the real target of his dismissive assessment could respond, a quiet voice intoned. 'Tread softly, Nic, because you tread on my dreams.' The oaf's trap stayed shut. Hyala followed up with a smile that was both placatory and triumphant, revealing teeth that matched the blistering white of her eyes. It was as if she was illuminated from within. Ms Getachew-O'Hare would have been beautiful even if she had been a male. But—and this was for Sebastian the interesting thing—he found her somewhat lacking in terms of sex appeal. Beauty and sexual attractiveness were not two sides of the same coin; they were distinct categories, which was not to say that one did not possess elements of the other. Sebastian could have spent all day just looking at Hyala, the way he might have, say, the Cliffs of Moher or Caravaggio's 'Cardsharps.' But any arousal he experienced would be more aesthetic than sexual in nature. A thing of beauty, such as Hyala, was a joy forever but probably not a fuck buddy. That was—had been—Annabel's role.

'We'll convene tomorrow morning at ten, over there in the far corner,' he said pointing beyond the bar. The area will be screened off and I'll make sure we have copies of the four books on hand and anything else you may need. Let's see if we can't conclude our business by lunchtime. Once we've picked a winner, I would like one of you to take a stab at drafting a citation that can be read to the audience on the night and released to the media, something, naturally, that the four of you are happy to sign off on. After all, it will be the statement of record, an indicator of what the prize aspires to be.' Shortly after, Sebastian took his leave and Nic headed off in search of a pub accompanied by a somewhat reluctant Con while the ladies brought their drinks and *patatas bravas* closer to the inviting fire. 'Now, that's not the kind of art one expects to find in a small-town hotel in the west of Ireland, is it?' asked Amelia. 'But then neither is the corporeal Sebastian the kind of person you expect to find running a book prize,' came Hyala's response. And with that their conversation turned to the subject of literary merit. A similar if spikier conversation was underway in Keenan's bar and would last for three pints and the same number of chasers. The Slutsky Professor of English Literature, not by nature a boozer, would later reprimand himself.

# STALEMATEYNESS

Five chairs were grouped around a rectangular table covered with a crisp, white linen cloth, five stacks of books, writings pads and pens. Water, juices, coffee, tea, scones and fresh croissants sat off to one side. The decision makers were greeted by a familiar flip chart, the first sheet of which was filled by a large grid. Across the top, four names: Amelia, Con, Hyala, Nic; along the side, the words Cobh, Crescent, Harrumph, Playboy. The sixteen cells of the matrix were blank. He would begin proceedings not by asking each of them in turn to give their views on each of the books, but by having them nominate their first and second choices with supporting arguments. The idea was to determine the level of starting agreement, eliminate any book that had no support and focus discussion on the serious contenders. In Sebastian's dream world the number one would appear in all four cells of one row. Having found a winner, they could then discuss in harmonious fashion what had set the work apart from the rest before turning their attention to the also-rans, highlighting their meritorious aspects. A feature of the award ceremony would be having each juror make a brief presentation about a different book. They would also be expected to read a few passages from each one for the benefit of the audience, the way Oscar ceremonies showed clips from the contenting movies. Only after that would the winner be announced. This may not have been the approach the quartet expected or would have proposed but Sebastian was in the driving seat. Amelia thought it had considerable merit, being both efficient and democratic, and said as much. Nic, fiddling with his cuticles, said nothing, nor did the other two. They sensed, correctly, that the chairman had made up his mind. Unfortunately, *they* were not all of one mind.

Amelia gave her top vote to *Cobh*, her second to *Crescent*; Con gave first place to *Harrumph*, second to *Playboy*; Hyala ranked *Crescent* top and *Cobh* second while Nic placed *Playboy* first and *Harrumph* second. Each of the four books had been voted top once and each had secured one second spot. Sebastian's manoeuvre had stalled. The stalemate would only be broken if at least one of them could be persuaded to convert one of their second choices to a first. It was clear to Sebastian that discussion could not be avoided. Who could be persuaded to reconsider? Or would doing so be interpreted as a sign of weakness? Which of them was motivated enough to want to fight for their favourite? Who, if anyone, owed another a favour or wanted to curry favour? As far as Sebastian could tell, there was nothing in their behaviour to suggest that alliances had formed or were even perceived as necessary. They each seemed to be strong willed, sure of their opinions. The fairest way to proceed was to have each of them make a case for their number one choice. He'd give them five minutes apiece to champion their product then invite discussion. Perhaps by highlighting elements of the book that had either been overlooked or underappreciated they might be able to swing a vote their way.

They went from left to right. Con made his pitch for *The Last Harrumph*, focusing more on the underlying political history and satirical intent than the formal or stylistic strengths of the novel. Once or twice, he took a swipe at the competition, notably *The Callous Crescent* which he felt to be disrespectful if not downright offensive to Muslims. That didn't endear him to either Hyala or Amelia who had picked Farha Musharraf's book as their first and second choice, respectively. Amelia, who had as much knowledge of Northern Irish politics as she did interest in satirical writing would do whatever it took to prevent the award going to such a contrived piece of work. 'Since this is a literary award, I take it we are in agreement that demonstrable mastery of prose writing isa given.' Hyala paused, almost forcing the rest to mumble their agreement. 'That being the case, there *is* no competition. Even if the subject matter of *The Callous Crescent* is not to your liking, the writing must surely be, given the ease with which it shifts from interiority to exterior action. But when exemplary craft skills are coupled with a story that is both deeply affecting and morally significant, I don't see why we need to spend too much time debating the merits of *The Playboy of Belclare* or *The Last Harrumph*. A master's in English literature or a doctorate in literary theory is hardly a prerequisite for appreciating fine writing.' As always, she spoke with a lilting softness, forcing the others at times to lean in. It was a technique she had refined over the years.

By now Nic's cuticles looked like a war zone. If he'd had a bit, he'd have chomped through it. In the wake of a phlegm-clearing cough he delivered his apologia for the maligned *Playboy* with as much enthusiasm as he could muster. He began by invoking literary precedents, from JP Donleavy to Tom Sharpe, then proceeded to show why he thought O'Carroll was a master of comedic writing by reading aloud excerpts from his well-thumbed copy. 'Drollery. Is the Parnell Prize to be awarded for sophomoric drollery?' The Slutsky Professor, his forehead as furrowed as his beige cords, had heard enough. This intervention did not sit well with the *Playboy's* rubicund sponsor. Hadn't Nic introduced Con to a twenty-one-year-old Bushmills single malt only the previous evening? And now here he was mounting his high horse in the hope of impressing the ladies. The gloves were off, and the ladies, as surprised as they were secretly thrilled by the eruption, sat up in their seats for a ringside view of the slugfest. But after a feisty thirty seconds or so the referee intervened to stop the fight. 'Gentlemen, enough. Why don't we see what Amelia and Hyala have to say about Mr O'Carroll's literary talents? Perhaps agreement can be reached without noses being put out of joint.' Ms Clayton, who had been impressed by Sebastian's deft handling of their Skype meetings, was no less impressed by this display of cultured assertiveness.

The morning vanished in a non-stop series of thrusts and counter-trusts; quotes and counter-quotes. At times it resembled a fractious game of cards, as each sought to trump the other. To a neutral observer their determination to stand by their top choices seemed unshakable, a stalemate inevitable. Sebastian proposed a thirty-minute lunch break, as much to escape the morass as catch up on his backlog of emails. In a little more than twenty-four hours the show would begin. He needed a decision soon so that he could head back to the town hall to liaise with Ivy and the janitorial staff before meeting up with Brendan and his team who were due to get in from Dublin late that afternoon. Lunch, a tray of delicately sliced sandwiches, appeared, prepared by Isabel, whose chatty presence provided brief respite. They all walked around the room to stretch their legs, nibbling or fiddling with their phones. At one point Sebastian noticed Hyala and Amelia huddling in a corner. The meeting resumed, with Hyala, politely to be sure, explaining why her second choice, *Heartbreak at Cobh*, lacked that certain *je ne sais quoi* one would expect of a clear winner. The great thing about *je ne sais quoi* was that nobody else really knew what you meant. If you had to ask what it was, then you obviously weren't made of the right stuff. As a result of Hyala's intervention, Amelia broke ranks, announcing that she now felt *The Callous Crescent* to be more deserving of the prize than *Heartbreak at Cobh* and proceeded to offer detailed reasons why. 'That was a quick change of heart. I'd have thought someone like you would have known *je ne sais quoi* when you saw it.' Nic was just warming up, partly because he felt she was not being honest and partly because he liked pissing her off. He'd always thought that she was a tad too full of herself, one of those people who wrote about but hadn't lived life. Not for the first or last time, Sebastian had to restore civility. Half an hour later Nic had reversed his initial rankings. Now both he and Con were supporting *The Last Harrumph*. Had the menfolk been conniving or was Nic changing his preferences simply to spite Amelia? Sebastian couldn't decide. Meanwhile Con was launching a powerful defence of Fitz

Allen's futuristic satire, eloquent if ultimately ineffectual. By mid-afternoon, civility levels had declined precipitously. Acerbity combined with repetitiousness could only be tolerated for so long. The chairman intervened and did so with the kind of decisiveness he had exhibited during his spells as department chair in Edinburgh and Groverdale. 'With some regret, it appears that I am going to have to exercise my prerogative.' All four registered surprise not to say shock. He didn't wait for them to comment or question his right to do so. They had had their chance.

# CROSSED SWORDS

Sebastian's decision to grant the prize to *The Callous Crescent* was received warmly by the female members of the jury. Nic contented himself with a sarcastic guffaw; Con delivered a brief statement with donnish gravitas. 'I respect your right, Sebastian, to cast the deciding vote but not when the vote goes to a novel that can only be described, whatever its putative literary qualities, as an insult to the vast majority of the world's Muslims who are respectful, peace-loving individuals. Ireland, as I am sure you all quite aware, has in recent years become home to one of the fastest growing Muslim populations in Western Europe. This book, if given the oxygen of publicity, will unquestionably damage community relations in the country by fostering suspicion and enmity. The last thing the New Ireland needs is the New Right crowing at the success of Musharraf's incendiary book. As arbiters of public taste, we have a moral responsibility to consider the wider consequences of our actions, to look beyond stylistics, character devices, plot and so on. Free speech does not mean you can shout "Fire!" in a crowded theatre just because you happen to have a refined accent.'

Sebastian could see that Hyala was itching to respond but he was not going to reopen discussion. 'Con, I think I can understand your position but, while the book does contain passages that some may deem, incorrectly in my opinion, Islamophobic, there is nothing in Ali's tale of socio-cultural emancipation that allows the reader to infer that either the character or indeed the author herself is in any way racist. Moreover, as Hyala has explained, neither female genital mutilation nor misogyny is an exclusively Muslim practice. The book takes issue with certain tenets of Islamic ideology and challenges their legitimacy in civilized society. But don't forget, one can be critical of

Islam, especially its most extreme varieties, without being critical of, or demonizing Muslims. Let me domesticate the argument for a moment. Most if not all IRA activists in this country were drawn from nominally Catholic communities but that's hardly grounds for tarring all Catholics with the same brush. It's easy to confuse categories, but harder to undo the consequences of lazy thinking. Quite apart from which, *The Callous Crescent* is, in my humble opinion, a masterful piece of writing, the very thing the prize was set up to celebrate. Nowhere in the submission criteria is there anything to the effect that a book should be excluded from consideration if it makes the reader feel uncomfortable. We could do worse than heed Wilde: "There is no such thing as a moral or immoral book. Books are well written, or badly written. That is all."'

Con, holder of a named professorship in a venerable university, did not take kindly to the chairman's *de haut en bas* tone and determined to ratchet things up a notch. 'If Musharraf is to be awarded the prize, then I am not sure I can continue to be a member of this jury.' The ladies exchanged glances. Nic looked up from his cuticles. Sebastian called the puffed-up professor's bluff, if bluff it was, without missing a beat. 'Well, you signed a legally binding document and received half of your honorarium in advance. It was made clear from the outset that in the event of a split vote I would cast the deciding one. There is no reason why tomorrow the distribution of votes needs to be made public. All that needs to be said is that the jury has chosen *The Callous Crescent*. I am not sure what is good is achieved, beyond ego satisfaction, by publicizing a dissenting opinion, unless, that is, you want to draw even more publicity to a book that, from what I hear you say, you'd presumably rather not see garnering attention in the first place.' Con, exasperated but worldly-wise, said nothing further and would do nothing, bar sulk for a few hours. Nic, who might have been expected to launch a tirade, remained silent, to general relief. As soon as the meeting was over, however, he'd leak news of the split decision to a mate in the mainstream media, sit back and wait for the fun to begin. Although they were bound to secrecy, he was convinced that the breach could not be traced back verifiably to him.

As planned, the group reassembled at seven for an aperitif, dinner to follow. Tinged with frostiness, that's how a novelist might have described the atmosphere. Unlike the previous evening, conversation was stilted, everyone self-monitoring, glancing downwards or sideways. Carla, unaware of the underlying tensions, chatted away about the long-established restaurant and the not-so-healthy appetites of the *patron*. Sebastian's arrival did little to elevate the mood. But after top-ups all around, the frostiness began to fade. Con, perhaps feeling that he had over-reacted, made a special effort to engage with Hyala. At one point during the afternoon meeting, she had revealed that her mother came from Ethiopia, a mixed religion country where, she explained, cutting was not just a matter of faith but also custom and culture. She didn't go on to say whether she belonged to or had been raised in any particular faith but Con figured that if someone of Ethiopian descent—and possibly also Muslim—was not affronted by *The Callous Crescent*, then, perhaps, he needed to take a step back. Nic, having just taken the steps necessary to ensure that the shit would hit the fan, decided that he might as well enjoy the complimentary booze and food while waiting for the ordure to splatter into the public domain. Amelia, relieved that bloodshed had been avoided, was wondering if per chance she might find herself seated next to Sebastian at dinner.

# TABLE D'HÔTE

Wrapped in winter coats and armed with hotel umbrellas, the quintet headed off down Church Street. The rain had abated, the south-westerly wind strengthened. It was a night for upturned collars, fur-trimmed in Amelia's case. Nic, enveloped in an RAF blue-grey greatcoat, sucked warmth from his cupped Benson & Hedges. As expected, the restaurant was jam-packed, many of the faces unfamiliar to Sebastian. The Parnell was clearly doing its bit for the local economy. What happened next could have been predicted by both Carla and Sebastian. Claude ziplined from the back of the restaurant straight to where Hyala was standing. At first, she was unsure whose hands were spidering across her shoulders, touching her hair, or indeed why. Claude had used one of his favourite tricks, the surprise flank attack. Under the pretence of removing madam's coat, he had penetrated her first line of defence, positioned himself closer to her than would have been deemed acceptable. Silver-tongued compliments were tumbling out of his garlic-infused mouth. Had it been an amateur dramatic performance the director would have chided him for over-egging the French custard. But shamelessness was one of the *patron's* distinguishing traits and exaggeration came to him as naturally as curtseying to a lady-in-waiting. A sternly quizzical 'Do you mind?' from the affronted beauty effected no change in his behaviour. Not for the first time, Sebastian would intervene, defusing a potentially ugly situation. And not for the first time Claude wondered how on earth Sebastian managed to find himself in the company of so many attractive women. It was a badge of honour, in his eyes, the sort of thing that merited a special classification of the *Légion d'honneur*.

As the preposterous *patron* escorted his guests to their corner table, quite a few heads turned, not just because both Hyala and Amelia, in their different ways, were head-turners but because at least someone at every second table seemed to know at least one of the latest arrivals. If a bomb had hit *Chez Claude* that February night, literary Britain might never have recovered. Despite the earlier contretemps, Claude behaved as if nothing had happened, *comme l'eau sur le dos d'un canard*, Sebastian mouthed inwardly. The ladies were ushered to their places, chairs pulled back and starched napkins dropped into laps. There being no seating plan, Claude took it upon himself to arrange matters and thus it was that Amelia found herself at the host's left. For that, she would overlook the Frog's hyperbolic tendencies, which resumed with a florid recitation of the evening specials. That, in turn, was followed, and without any apparent drawing of breath, by a panegyric on the merits of a recently acquired 2009 Côtes de Nuit-Villages. Hyala's question pertaining to vegetarian options he had either not heard or chosen to ignore, but when re-submitted by Sebastian on her behalf, Claude said he would see what could be done, as if vegetarianism was worse than the clap. Con was bemused by it all, Nic visibly amused. Had this been London, Claude would by now have been placed on an endangered species list. But, without too much further ado, orders were taken and off he swanned. Minutes later a trainee sommelier sidled up and the usual pantomime ensued.

Thanks to the wine, conversation skirted contentious issues. Mere mention of Burgundy was all it took to send Nic off down memory lane. His attention-demanding story involved a boozy weekend with fellow undergrads in Dijon. Minus the layers of laddish embellishment, it hinged on his threatening a gendarme with a furled copy of *Le Monde*, the incident resulting from a late-night drinking-session in a back-street bar that had turned sour over a game of table football with some locals. It was a story he enjoyed listening to as much as telling, that was clear. Con wondered if this could really be the same Nic Langdale who was sometimes bracketed with Kingsley

Amis and David Lodge. Amelia, as much to impress her host as raise the tone, proceeded to describe a week-long literary festival she had attended in Aix-en-Provence the previous spring, at moments matching Nic in terms of superfluity of detail if not vulgarity. Sebastian decided to spare them the one about the time he had endeavoured to get the leg over a svelte *documentaliste* at a conference in Grenoble. The arrival of their starters provided further opportunity for pontification and one-upmanship, Con garnering very few brownie points for his disquisition on *pâté en croute*. For the life of him, Sebastian was unable to comprehend why dinner table conversation couldn't just be light and easy, bouncing around like a beach ball between people instead of degenerating into a series of unsparing monologues. Didn't the likes of Con live and die by the sharpness of their wit at high table? Droning on about making the crust for a loaf of what Rathboffin's wags called *Paddy en crôute* would hardly have enhanced his stock at Cavendish, yet here he was hogging the conversation. Hyala avoided the trap, but maybe went too far in the other direction. Sebastian was continually wondering what went on behind those mesmerizing eyes, as did many other males. By the end of the main course, Nic had upped and left and was now chatting to a literary agent at a nearby table, an attractive Jewish-looking woman in her mid-forties. Their body language suggested something more than professional acquaintanceship. Meanwhile Con continued his charm offensive with Hyala. Their disagreement of earlier in the day, if not entirely a thing of the past, was in no way impeding an exchange of views on Edward Said's contribution to post-colonial theory and in the place of activism in academic life. At one point, Sebastian overheard Hyala asking Con whether he felt the professoriate should be assailing the barricades. Her exact words were, 'Do you think we should be deconstructing barriers, or should we stick to deconstructing texts?'

For the remainder of the evening, Sebastian and Amelia would have the pleasure of one another's company, and not a minute would be wasted discussing subalternity. They had turned their chairs and were now seated at forty-five-degree angles to one another, across the table from the other pair. In fact, they were so close she'd be able to tell if he had blackheads on his nose. Sebastian's scrutiny of his companion failed to detect a single blemish, while also confirming what he suspected, namely, that she made minimal use of either perfume or make-up. In fact, if she weren't so busy writing novels, Amelia could without doubt have carved out a career as a model for one of those mail order catalogues targeted at the over-fifties. On a couple of occasions her knee had brushed against his thigh but she neither apologized nor blushed and he certainly didn't mind. She seemed relaxed yet showed no overt sign of inebriation. Once or twice, in order to be heard over the crescendo of chatter, she had leaned in such that he could feel her warm, Burgundy-scented breath across his face. She was wearing a soft grey woollen crewneck sweater that complemented her silver hair and invited stroking the way a Red Setter does. The conversation switched almost at once to personal lives, or, more accurately, Amelia directed questions at Sebastian in the way that a narcissist could only dream of. Her probes, of course, granted him reciprocal rights. Both were willing to open up about themselves, interested, too, to learn about the other.

# FUCK FICTION

If you are single, in your sixties and a writer of literary fiction domiciled in Rye, then it may well be that you don't fantasize about having casual sex with a west of Ireland hotelier. Or if you do, you justify it to yourself by saying that it'd be grist to the mill: a case of fucking for the sake of fiction. On the other hand, maybe there is no need whatsoever for justification, if mood and moment are aligned. Amelia's public persona was as carefully maintained as her appearance, but if a book should not be judged by its cover, why should an author be judged by her demeanour? People like Nic and Con were professional acquaintances and the Amelia they interacted with was the official version. Like many others in their circles, they either failed to see or chose not to look beyond the cover. They could not have known that she had long ago lost the love of her life, a photojournalist. Jeffrey, to whom she had been engaged in her mid-thirties, died unexpectedly of Dengue fever on assignment in west Africa. The statistical improbability of such an event had made the loss even harder to endure. One of the few people who knew the story was Annabel and she had not mentioned it to Sebastian, or anyone else. Since her fiancé's death, Amelia had foresworn neither relationships nor sex, but she had exhibited a degree of selectivity in affairs of the heart alien to the likes of Sebastian or Nic Langdale.

Amelia had warmed to Sebastian during their first meeting in London, the blend of intelligence and savoir faire. Hadn't he shown those traits only a short while earlier in the evening with his handling of the frightful restaurateur? Other commendable attributes that had revealed themselves over the course of their Skype meetings were organizational competence and self-assurance. He could be authoritative without resorting to bullying, decisive without being dismissive of alternative viewpoints. She knew that he had been an academic at one stage, but nothing about his field or where he had worked, except that it wasn't connected to the publishing world. Not least she had been impressed by his ability to discuss the relative merits of the four shortlisted novels with the so-called experts. The menfolk may have resented his casting the deciding vote the way he did, but they could not really fault the manner in which he marshalled his arguments in favour of *The Callous Crescent*. It could not be said of Sebastian that he had arrived at his decision as the result of either whimsey or petulance. Throughout the process he had exercised his role as chairman in exemplary fashion.

Those qualities aside, some aspects of Sebastian's appearance and physique reminded her of Jeffrey, notably the longish hair, even if several shades darker, and his still slim, six-foot build; the nose, though, was less refined. By now Sebastian and Amelia were seeing off the remnants of the third bottle. It was a good thing that the wine had ended up in well-lined bellies. Both were mindful of the important day that lay ahead and were showing some restraint: agreeably tipsy rather than intoxicated would have been a fair description. Hyala and Con were now deep in conversation about the political situation in Ethiopia, while Nic, destined for drunkenness by night's end, was doing his level best to bag the Jewish agent. Sitting slightly forward on their seats, Amelia and Sebastian were scanning one another intently, like a pair of metal detectorists looking for anything that might signify attraction. Micro clues were embedded in their every twitch, movement, sound, expression, gesture and gaze, but capturing and decoding them was an art form; there was no bodily equivalent of the metal detector's high-pitched beep. Sebastian did wonder if she could conceivably sense what was happening in his underpants at just that moment. Did a swelling penis emit micro signals that could be picked up by an aroused female?

By the time Claude returned with the bill, the issue, it seemed fair to assume, was no longer whether but when. First, Sebastian had to secure safe passage for the ladies, from their table at the rear of the restaurant to the cloakroom, thence into the street. He did so with aplomb. Claude's attempt to help Amelia into her overcoat was repelled with a stare of such controlled ferocity that for once the Frenchman had to back off. Hyala and Con, heads bent into the wind, pressed back to the hotel on their own, Amelia having discovered that she'd left her wrap at the table. Forgetfulness was not the explanation. The ruse created the temporal and physical space the pair needed. Sebastian was impressed. He had underestimated the lady from Rye. He held the umbrella mid-shaft, she linked with his left arm, leaning in almost nuzzling up against him.

There were 'What if...?' questions to answer. What if the other jurors saw them? What if Carla was up and about? What if one or other of them had a faulty metal detector and the attraction proved to be lopsided? Sebastian favoured the hide in plain sight approach: behave as if nothing were out of the ordinary. To his relief, Carla was not about when they walked into the lounge area. Two guests, neither of whom he had seen before, were at the bar, finishing off their drinks, oblivious to their presence. Amelia stood by the lifeless fire while Sebastian fetched a nightcap. She probably wasn't the type to get down on her knees and give a five-minute blowjob beneath a full-length portrait of St Sebastian. Much though he fancied submitting a request for such, he knew better than to risk rejection. What, though, if *he* were to drop to his knees, run his hand up underneath her dress, draw down her panties and let his tongue loose? Again, fear of rejection held him back. Pushiness wasn't what every button wanted.

'I'm sorry, Sebastian. I fear I may have drunk a little too much. A glass or two is my usual limit.' And with that his fantasy house of cards came tumbling down. Amelia's withdrawal had not been premediated. She, too, had been all a-tingle with anticipation. It was as if an override switch had been thrown. But how, why? As she lay between the Egyptian cotton sheets retracing the course of the evening there had seemed an inevitability about the outcome, one that she had desired as much as he. She imagined him lying at her side, his fingers gently exploring the moist cavity between her thighs. Sebastian, no less puzzled, looked at his watch, remembered what awaited him the next day and stuffed a couple of mints into his mouth before heading home. If the Gardaí were mounting road checks between town and Ballyhannah, the Parnell Prize would be awarding itself next day. Fortunately, they weren't, convinced that no one in their right mind would be out and about at such an hour in such conditions.

# FATWA CHANCE

A persistent ringing ended a night of fitful sleep. Groggy, Sebastian bumbled barefoot into the kitchen, picked up his phone. 'I've been calling for the last hour. Have you seen the news?' asked Brendan. '"Literary Prize to go to writer of Islamophobic novel." It's all over the morning papers, on the news. Even the red-tops have picked up on it.' 'Huh?' grunted Sebastian, distracted by the throbbing in his left temple. 'We've got to kill the story. Failing that, we need to get out front, shape the narrative.' Brendan paused, realizing that he had omitted to ask a rather basic question. 'Of course, it's untrue,' came Sebastian's peevish response, 'It's no more Islamophobic than *Winnie-the Poo* and you can quote me on that. I can quote myself on that, come to think of it.' Within minutes they had a drafted a concise statement for widespread distribution to all the major media outlets to the effect that none of the four works shortlisted for the prize was Islamophobic in nature and that the name of the winner would be revealed that evening. For the rest of the morning Brendan and his team fielded queries from journalists and publishers, deviating not at all from the message, entertaining no speculation, providing no amplification. The Parnell Prize was now well and truly in the public eye, but for all the wrong reasons. Neither Sebastian nor Brendan wanted anything remotely like a repeat of the Rushdie affair, nor—it can be safely assumed—did Ms Musharraf, who would have been appalled to learn that her work had been characterized as anti-Muslim in sentiment. She'd probably forego the €75,000 prize rather than have a fatwa placed on her by some crackpot mufti.

There were only four people on the planet who could have been behind the leak. On the assumption—reasonable if not incontestable—that neither of those who voted for *The Callous*

*Crescent* would have been the source, the finger pointed at either Nic or Con. Sebastian's gut told him that Nic was their Judas. His general obnoxiousness did him no favours and, of course, he had connections in Grubb Street, knew many people in the wider media world. But what about motive? Sour grapes because his choice had not won? Personal animus toward one or more of his fellow jurors, or Sebastian himself? Childlike mischief? Thirty pieces of tabloid silver? Speculation was otiose as nothing could be proved. In any case, the clock was ticking down and myriad small and not so small details still had to be dealt with by Sebastian, Ivy and sundry others if the ceremony was to proceed on schedule and according to plan. While Brendan and Sebastian were firefighting, the judges, including a crapulous Judas, were finessing the wording of the citation that was to accompany the announcement of the winner. They had a couple of hours to come up with something on which they could all agree.

But what would Nic do? If he truly believed the book was anti-Muslim in tone and intent, then he'd be morally bound to refrain from signing off on the joint statement—all the more so since he had leaked the accusatory story, unless, as Sebastian suspected, his action had less to do with morality than devilment. Furthermore, if he refused to sign off, it would be suggestive of guilt. Thus, the question facing Nic was: to what extent, if at all, would his professional reputation and friendships suffer if it were to become known that he had been the whistle-blower? The question for Sebastian was whether, in his dealings with the committee, the best tactic would be to take the sting out of the leak story by brushing it aside as just one of those things, utterly without foundation in fact. Such an approach might be sufficient to disarm Nic, enough to keep him onside until the proceedings had wrapped up. Now sober, the backstabber might just feel that the path of least resistance—refrain from saying anything self-incriminating, behave like a good citizen—had a lot to recommend it. And so, a statement was duly agreed upon, one that was neither equivocal nor sensationalist but fittingly laudatory. Nyala took responsibility for crafting the final version, which would be embargoed until Sebastian had formally announced the prize-winner in the town hall. Throughout the quartet's deliberations Nic seemed if not chastened at least more subdued than usual. He must have sensed that his colleagues suspected him even though not a word had been said. The state of his cuticles offered evidentiary support for such speculation.

The committee members spent the remainder of the afternoon selecting the passages they'd read from their chosen book and preparing encomia. Sebastian raced back to Ballyhannah, showered and dressed for the event: navy-blue lounge suit, white shirt with cut-away collar and a dark knitted tie. The tip of a white handkerchief peeked out of his breast pocket. At six-thirty, he pulled up outside The Conyers. Nic, wearing a black blazer and creased grey slacks, sat up front in the passenger seat, the other three in the back. Hyala was the quintessence of stylish understatement, Con almost presentable in an off-the peg suit that had sat through many a conference dinner and Amelia radiant in a mid-length tuxedo dress beneath winter coat. A cocktail of colognes and after-shaves filled the interior of the BMW. It was a chilly evening, but dry. A light breeze ruffled the banner over the illuminated façade of the town hall. A few people were gathered outside, including two uniformed members of An Garda Síochána. 'No sign of protesters,' joked Con. The officers recognized Sebastian and pulled the no-parking cones aside.

Inside, the stage had been set up: in front of a maroon curtain a semi-circle of seats for Sebastian and his colleagues; at both sides, floral arrangements, near the footlights a lectern. Technicians were busy finalizing the lighting and sound systems. Off to one side, Ralac were tuning their instruments and testing the mics. Two TV cameras were set up in the wings. Darting in and out between the fifty or sixty decorated tables he spotted Ivy chivvying her students, making final checks. Minutes later a large white van pulled up outside the building and offloaded a platoon of food warmers. The first guests started to file into the foyer where two bars had been set up. In a meeting room at the back of the building, Sebastian and his team convened for the first time with the four shortlisted authors to go over the format of the evening. They would be seated, along with their publisher, friends or whomever, at front row tables. Each would be asked to stand up in turn after extracts were read from their book, then the literal spotlight would move to the next. When Sebastian announced the winner, he or she would be invited onto the stage where the presentation would be made after the citation had been read out. The formal proceedings were set to follow the desert course. So far everything was going as planned. The town hall had a festive feel, and the mood was vibrant. Many of those attending knew one another. It was certainly the glitziest evening Rathboffin had seen in a long time, possibly ever. Sebastian, having recovered from the effects of the night before, now felt upbeat. George, looking down from his celestial seat, would have been impressed by the results of his friend's endeavours. The Parnell Prize was in safe hands. So much for the capering clown.

# BULLISH

In fifteen minutes, Sebastian would step onto the stage, welcome the assembled guests and announce dinner. At that point MCAT's uniformed trainees would swarm into orchestrated action. As soon as they had left the meeting room, Nic beetled off to the bar for a quick one, Con spotted an old friend and Hyala headed to the loo. It was the first time Amelia and Sebastian had been together since the damp-squib ending of the night before. She, too, had slept fitfully, wondering if she hadn't made a mistake. Her hair was pulled tightly back and held together with a bejewelled clasp. She looked seigneurial sheathed in her tuxedo dress. Her figure was that of a woman twenty years younger. In her left hand she held a suede leather clutch bag. In her right she now held Sebastian's arm. She steered him to a room marked 'Maintenance' adjacent to the one they had just come out of, turned the handle and bullied him inside. It was almost pitch black. Not one word would be spoken. This quickie would be a candidate for the record books.

Dress up, flies undone. Knickers around ankles, penis rampant. He was maximally aroused, she was wet. Their colliding tongues dashed around teeth and tonsils, like a pair of pups let off their leashes. She grabbed his cock, put it where it should have been twenty-four hours earlier. He shoved it as far up as it would go, like an over-zealous chimney sweep. This was no time for foreplay or technical refinement. It was a bull meets cow moment. Pump, pump, pump. Up down, in, out. She rubbed thigh against thigh, grabbed his butt with her left hand, dug her fingernails in. He was pumping, ever faster. She issued muted moans. The bull came, with a muffled snort of sorts. There was something to be said for rapid ejaculation. Its elemental animalism appealed to him. Her upper body sagged, as tension and passion found much needed, near instant release. Hurriedly, they rearranged their clothes in the gloom, exited one at a time and headed straight to the toilets. Con was coming out of the gents as Sebastian entered. 'Your flies are undone, old chap.' 'Desperate,' came the face-saving reply. The professor said nothing about the smudge of lavender lipstick. As the Director of the Parnell Prize stepped onto the stage, tracked by a spotlight and polite applause, he was tingling, walking on air, invincible. He may not have set eyes on Amelia's breasts or vagina, but, by God, he had experienced them in a way that few others would. If only George could see him now. He spoke with brevity and returned to his seat.

Conversation at the top table proceeded without incident. Whether or not they would have admitted to feeling nervous, it was pretty clear that they were each thinking about the remarks they were about to make: Nic on *The Playboy of Belclare*, Hyala *The Callous Crescent*, Con *The Last Harrumph* and Amelia *Heartbreak at Cobh*. They might be singing the praises of fellow writers, but the quality of their own singing would be judged by their peers in the audience. Under the table, Amelia's shoeless foot was caressing his ankle. Above table, she seemed no more interested in his than anyone else's contribution. Occasionally, between courses, visitors would stop by their table, exchange air kisses and 'Darling!' one another in a fashion that made him want to puke. It could be seen as a form of paying homage, but to pay it you had to be one of those who mattered. The very fact that you could walk up to the top table underscored your status. All the while, the far from deafening sounds of Ralac could be heard. Just as the main course was being served, the intended occupant of the empty chair arrived. Once the tapas tables had been cleared, Carla had gone into Cinderella mode. The deep-red knitted dress worked a treat with her green eyes. She slipped between tables, attracting more than a few admiring glances as she worked her way to the front of the crowded room. The smitten guitarist fluffed a cord or two when he spotted her. Sebastian could tell that she was thrilled to have been invited. So could

Amelia, who the very first day had sensed that Sebastian's right hand might have had a crush on her boss.

Ivy's troops were performing with distinction. The food arrived at table hot, people were served what they requested, and wine glasses were rarely allowed to reach empty. Admittedly, one tray-load of empty plates had gone for a burton. The crash momentarily silenced a corner of the room, but apart from that everything went as Ivy had hoped it would. She and her team had done Rathboffin proud. Those cosmopolites expecting a plate of boiled ham, cabbage and mash would have been surprised. 'Much better fare than high table at Cavendish,' declared the Slutsky Professor after devouring his almond torte and licking his lips in a manner that surprised Amelia. Even the vegetarian option favoured by Hyala garnered praise. Royally fucked and fed, Sebastian walked up the few steps to the stage, took a small card with keywords on it out of his inside jacket pocket and assumed his position behind the lectern, adjusted the mic, standing back enough to avoid deafening the masses, and began his formal remarks in a clear and confident voice. Most of the people in the room had never seen nor heard of him before, so instead of continuing to chat, as so often happens at events of this kind, they sat back, curious to learn more. After a preamble about George, he went on to describe the nature and aim of the Parnell Prize. Next, he introduced the jurors, before turning to the four hopefuls sitting at nearby tables, all doing their best to mask nervousness. Amelia's eyes never once left him. Nor did Carla's.

# STAGE PRESENCE

Sebastian had assigned Nic the opening slot in the hope that he'd still be sober. The bounder mounted the stage with no notes and a glass of wine. Rising above the weight of his own self-regard, he managed to focus exclusively on the book. 'This is the *real* playboy of the western world. A paraplegic who'd rather make fun of himself than be labelled alternatively abled. Someone for whom a wheelie is just as much a thing of life-affirming fun as it is for a nine-year old. And this is a book that does not confuse sentiment with sap. Laugh with me it says, not at me, but not in po-faced fashion. Of course, the wheelchair is a metaphor for the constraints that bind all of use, be it prejudice or shyness, religion or sexual confusion. In fact, Diarmud O'Carroll has challenged common prejudices about prejudice itself and done so with a mélange of wit and sensitivity that deserve our admiration.' By the time he had finished his remarks, the glass was empty, but Mr Langdale had inflicted no damage on his public image.

Next up the dark beauty. For three or four or maybe forty seconds she said nothing, just looked out into the glittering room. No one spoke. Sebastian was riveted. Was it her skin colour or her indisputable beauty that guaranteed submissiveness? Hyala took the elephant in the room by the tusks. Farha Musharraf had written a novel of searing power, unflinching and humane. To call it Islamophobic was a gross insult to both the author and those who rightly exposed the evils done in the name of Allah. You could have heard a pinafore drop in the room. This was no Marine Le Pen but an award-winning novelist, someone who, for all they knew, could have been a practicing or cultural Muslim. Labelling the book pro- or anti-Muslim was meaningless. The point was that the author had captured the emotional and ideological struggle faced by her hero with unflinching honesty and empathy. The compassionate reader came away enraged at the treatment of young women in the name of the Prophet. The Hampstead and Highgate elites in the audience, along with their Dublin counterparts, at first didn't know whether to applaud or boo, so did neither. In the end, after Hyala's reading of a passage describing the cutting of Ali's youngest sister, she left the stage to spontaneous applause.

Con immediately realized he'd got the short straw. The well-meaning professor with the provincial accent did his level best to re-enthuse the audience. But it was like sex. If you've just come, it's hard to do it all over again without a period of recuperation. From his remarks, one could tell that he had read the novel with great attention to detail. The donkey-as-narrator device, he argued with seemingly genuine conviction, worked quite brilliantly at times. His selected passages, wisely, avoided some of the imaginary dialogue and centred on the mores and material culture of Ireland's rural west, and how these had been captured in photographic prose by the author. Apart from the fact that one or two hoots of laughter could be heard from the rear of the room when he first mentioned that the narrator was a big-eared donkey, Con was a dutiful ambassador for Fitz Allen's book, published by absent Annabel's company.

Last up was Amelia. She extolled the literary merits of *Heartbreak at Cobh* and the novelty of perspective brought to the Famine tale by first-timer Sharon McGilligan. In the kind of voice that accompanies a serious documentary she read two heart-rending paragraphs describing the agonizing death of a seven-year-old on a coffin ship headed for New Brunswick. That got the room's attention. By the end she had them in the palm of her elegant hand. As Amelia walked off the stage, she was aware of Sebastian's cum trickling ever so slowly down her inner thigh. Part of him had been up there with her, and no one among the hundreds of guests had the faintest idea. As she settled back into her seat, she allowed her hand to brush against his hair. He had had a partial erection much of time she was talking.

Now the four judges and Sebastian returned to the stage, sat in a semi-circle. The photographers in the room, pushed forward with their phallic lenses, settling in near the tables with the four finalists ready to capture expressions of joy, fake joy, and quite possibly disbelief for the morning editions. This time Sebastian took a sheet of paper from his inside pocket. He would read the exact words agreed by the committee. The statement outlined why *The Callous Crescent* had been chosen as the winner but did not reveal the fact that the final decision had been contingent on Sebastian's casting vote. Some in the audience found it strange that having heard Hyala's presentation of the book they were now listening to the views of a committee on the very same book, a committee of which Hyala was a member. It was an unconventional approach but one with which Sebastian felt comfortable. The committee praised the winning submission for its creativity, stylistic assurance and high moral tone. Once again, the elephant in the room was acknowledged, but perhaps not as forthrightly as it had been by Ms Getachew-O'Hare. Nonetheless, the audience was assured that it would require wilful misreading to interpret any part of the book as Islamophobic in nature. 'And without further ado,' Sebastian concluded in time-honoured fashion, 'I would like to ask Farha Musharraf to come up on stage and receive the inaugural Parnell Prize.'

The semicircle beamed, the audience applauded, and Sebastian drew an envelope containing a large check from his jacket pocket. 'Perhaps you'd like to say a few words.' Ms Musharraf, wearing a floral waisted dress and nothing suggestive of ethnic parentage, seemed genuinely surprised to find herself standing in front of several hundred smiling faces, seventy-five thousand Euro richer than she had been just thirty seconds earlier. Her remarks were unscripted, devoid of pretence. Yes, she was thrilled to have the literary merit of her work acknowledged by writers whom she admired, but she also hoped that her book would open people's eyes to the barbarism that was female genital mutilation. Those who practiced, as well as those who sanctioned or passively condoned cutting should be exposed and prosecuted where appropriate. Equivocation was obviously not her style. Neither culture nor religion could be used to justify what was unjustifiable. Unscripted or not, diminutive Farha was taking full advantage of the platform presented her, concluding with a quote from Rosa Luxemburg: 'Women's freedom is a sign of social freedom.' The well-oiled literati were lapping it up, the loud applause now enlivened with a bravo or two. As Sebastian escorted the winner and judges off stage, flashbulbs popped, and a melee of press photographers scrambled for close-ups. Carla gazed up at her all-conquering boss, with pride and more.

# FIRED-UP

Just as Sebastian returned to his seat, a commotion announced itself at the rear of the hall. The sound of breaking glass and crockery could be heard. Amid the din, shouts of 'Allahu Akbar!' and 'Kafir scum!' were audible. The band did not play on. Sebastian could see a group of six or seven youngish men, some with long beards, a couple with Islamic religious garb and skull caps. Three were holding aloft signs that read 'No hate speech,' 'We love Muhammad,' and 'No to Islamophobia.' Another was pointedly knocking over wine bottles and glasses. Some of the guests, emboldened by an evening of free alcohol, took exception to the intruders' lack of basic good manners and a scuffle broke out. Soon the interlopers were trading punches with the well-groomed diners, swinging their placards in manic fashion. In true Keystone Cops fashion, the two Gardaí officers who had been on duty out front came panting onto the scene, only to be pepper-sprayed by the tallest protester. Sebastian, with Con's ready assistance, bustled Hyala and Amelia up onto the stage and behind the heavy velvet curtain. Nic, like a man possessed, headed straight for the melee, and hurled himself at the nearest skull cap. Several male guests were equally up for it but within a matter of minutes baton-wielding reinforcements had arrived from the garda station. By then, several of the protesters had fled the scene while the rest, bruised and bloodied, were being treated like park benches by indignant diners ably assisted by Ivy, who had relished the opportunity to put her underutilized military training into use. The photographers and camera crews simply could not believe their good fortune. Off to one side sat Brendan Byrne, slumped across the table, head in hands. The Parnell prize was off to one hell of a start. Ms Musharraf's book was guaranteed overnight success, for reasons good and not so good. After a suitable lull, Sebastian, Con and the ladies emerged from backstage. By now the room was mostly empty, the protesters having been hauled away with Ivy busily marshalling her troops, trying to calm them and ensure that everything was packed away and tidied up.

A visibly unsettled Farha Musharraf was driven to her hotel by a female officer, while Sebastian, Carla and the four jurors, all to varying degrees distressed by the unsavoury events, eventually set off for The Conyers. No one was quite sure what to say. Nic was high as a kite, not having been involved in a proper brawl for quite some time. It was if he had completely forgotten that the unholy episode had been set in train by his leak of the previous day. Someone might have been killed because of his selfish, cavalier action. The mood was sombre. Realizing that he was now a pariah, he slinked off in search of a late-night bar. As the group reached the hotel, Sebastian could see that something had been spray-painted onto the wall beneath the illuminated sign. The message in red was simple: 'There is no God but Allah.' They looked at one another, in disbelief, said nothing. Once inside, Sebastian offered everyone a nerve-steadying drink. Hyala declined and went straight to her room. Although upset, she realized that her support of *The Callous Clown* was not only justified by the actions of the protesters but essential. In the space of twenty-four hours fiction had become fact.

As much as by the events themselves, Amelia was horrified by the fact that zealots would take violent action based on mere hearsay. Probably not one of the goons had read a single word of the putatively offensive book. Such tripwire sensitivity defied comprehension. It was irrational and irresponsible, symptomatic of underlying insecurities. 'Hate speech is whatever they want it to be, so very Humpty Dumpty,' she mused out loud. 'So odd, so odd.' Con recalled his trip to Paris in 2011 when the offices of *Charlie Hebdo* were firebombed; publishing a caricature of the Prophet constituted a death sentence in post-Enlightenment France. 'Even little Ireland, at Europe's westerly rim isn't safe any longer. I wonder what the morning papers will make of the night's events.' With that Con took his leave, followed closely by Amelia. It appeared that post-prandial pandemonium did not constitute an aphrodisiac as far as she was concerned. Carla would contact the Gardaí first thing in the morning, have the graffito removed. Sebastian took her in his arms, the hug providing the reassurance she so desperately wanted at that moment. It was almost midnight and he had to drive home, once again over the legal limit. 'Please be careful,' was all she said.

Sebastian had just entered REM sleep when the phone rang. He didn't hear it the first time; nor the second. On the third attempt Carla got through. In his confusion he knocked over the bedside lamp and lurched against the wardrobe. 'On fire?' He put on the clothes he had taken off only a few hours earlier, climbed back into the car and drove like a boy racer along the deserted coast road. The sky was clear and star-studded. Church Lane was closed off. At the far end he could see several fire engines and emergency vehicles, lurid lights flashing. Gold-red flames were shooting into the sky and an acrid stench filled the night air. He explained who he was and dashed towards The Conyers. Guests, some in dressing gowns, others wrapped in blankets and overcoats, were huddled at a distance from the hotel, which was engulfed in flames beneath a pall of black smoke. Part of the roof had already collapsed. Multiple jets of waters poured down from aerial ladders onto the stricken building and the arrow-riddled saint. Sebastian sprinted towards a tearful Carla. Everyone was safe, as far as she could tell, though Nic remained unaccounted for. Amelia was shaking unstoppably despite the best attempts of a paramedic to calm her. If only she hadn't switched her vote to Farha Musharraf to support Hyala and spite the odious Nic, then none of this might have happened, she repeated over and over, not that the paramedic had the foggiest idea what she was on about. Daybreak saw The Conyers, the region's finest boutique hotel, reduced to a smouldering mass of rubble encircled by Garda crime scene tape. *The Callous Crescent* had lived up to its name.

# PART V

# WHY ME?

*A Trifecta of Tribulations.* It came to Sebastian as dawn slinked in over Rathboffin, streak by salmony streak. Would make a cracking title for an autobiography, especially one with transatlantic aspirations. Less pretentious than *Peripeteia*—a word choice that would have come as no surprise to George—and less demotic than *Fucked!* Think of it: first, he is hounded out of academe on trumped up charges of sexual harassment and racial bias; second, his wine and art business is scuppered by a global recession and then, in his moment of glory as a small-town hotelier, The Conyers is burned to the ground. And he could easily have added another for a non-alliterative quadfecta: the fantastical kidnapping attempt by Abdullah al-Hashim during his spell with the Midwest College of Applied Technology. Bad luck be damned; this was the rolling wrath of one decidedly implacable Allah. Sebastian was being singled out, branded for life. But why? For teenage wanking? For unyielding narcissism? For haughty irreligiousness?

Viewed from almost any angle, the punishment seemed disproportionate, given the mundanity of his misdemeanours—mere stumbles on the foothills of heinousness, as George might have put it. He was no Stalin, no Pol Pot, not even in the Jimmy Savile or Harold Shipman leagues. Granted, he may have broken a heart or two careening along life's byways but others he had just as likely gladdened: a bit of a rake but hardly a career Casanova. More to the point, did he not provide employment for grateful locals, pleasure for his discerning guests and much needed stimulation for the regional economy? A case of wronged decency, he preferred to think. It didn't add up. In any case, he had no intention of writing an autobiography. Never quite understood what motivated certain people to put pen to paper. What did it say about their sense of self? A severe case of inflammation of the ego seemed the most obvious explanation. My deepest thoughts, my private life, my accomplishments, my peccadillos; you will, of course, want to read all about these, so here they are, filleted and diced, chronology and contextualization to my (or my ghost-writer's) liking. Surely, there should be some tacitly understood threshold, some minima, whether in terms of one's historical significance, moral exemplariness or enduring cultural legacy. Mark Twain, Nelson Mandela, justifiable self-indulgence on their parts you'd have to say; superannuated crooners and snooker legends...gimme a break. Although aware of his cosmic insignificance, Sebastian could, nonetheless, see how the last twenty or so years of his life might, in the right—that is to say sympathetic—hands make for an amusingly ribald book, albeit one of qualified originality, the sort of thing you'd stuff into a week-end travel bag if the *Decameron* seemed like a slog. Hardly hubris, though; hadn't he been the inspiration for George's *The Capering Clown*?

Disconnected thoughts jostled with one another like paparazzi around a Hollywood celebrity as he stared into the smouldering rubble, his red-edged eyes aggravated by the lingering smoke. Overhead, territorial rooks circled and cawed, displeased by all the commotion. He found them Hitchcockian, with their surgical beaks and corvine arrogance, an arrogance that on a whim could morph into directed, all-too-personal aggression. Helmeted firemen, faces basted with soot-peppered sweat, were still dousing the scarred shell of the building, its former purpose divinable only from the warped metal sign on which the letters h, t, and l could just about be discerned. He thought he spotted a piece of the martyr's gilt frame, but nothing could have survived the inferno. Saintly Sebastian, from day one an incongruous yet unfailingly benign presence above the fireplace, had finally given up the ghost. How many conversations had he sparked into life during his tenure? How often had he helped melt the social ice at cocktail hour? How many indiscretions had he observed from his all-seeing perch? Sebastian was going to miss his arrowed namesake.

At some point a forensics team would ride into town to confirm—with politically correct caveats and clodhopping periphrasis—what the nation's press had already concluded beyond any reasonable doubt. Several years of toil and ingenuity had been wiped out overnight by a handful of Islamist zealots, fuelled by a combustible mixture of ignorance and hatred of western values. In reality, of course, they enjoyed many aspects of occidental culture just as much as their kafir neighbours, from grooming underage girls to scoffing bacon butties. Hadn't Mohamed Atta and his fellow 9/11 hijackers hung out at Shuckums Oyster Pub & Grill before launching their dastardly assault on the Great Satan? And hadn't one of the Saudi perpetrators paid for the services of a hooker prior to the fateful day? Perhaps it was an earthly insurance policy in case the promise of seventy-two *houris* in the afterlife didn't pan out. Funny, he imagined himself saying to George, how sex on-tap with a flock of doe-eyed virgins gets a green light in the afterlife but is deemed a big no-no in this one. Religions had a way of trying themselves up in knots. There ought to be a sub-field of topology devoted to the subject.

Muslims weren't alone in their delusionality, of course. Until his dying day, Sebastian would remain perplexed that educated Catholics could accept such inherently preposterous notions as the virgin birth or transubstantiation. It made believing in UFOs and the Loch Ness monster seem positively enlightened. You didn't have to read the latest treatise on the cognitive bases of religion to realize that people needed to believe in something transcendent; seemed to flounder in the absence of external, preferably anthropomorphized, agency. Fancy thinking that you could have your way with several dozen virgins as a reward for blowing up a handful of non-believers or chucking a blindfolded sodomite from a tall building. Allah knew what made the men's minds tick—probably modelled the male urge on his own almighty appetites. Hadn't it been drummed into him at primary school that God made man in his own image and for his own glory? Lust remains the great equalizer, oblivious to creed, race or status. 'Don't blame me, mate; it's evolutionary biology. Just boys being boys. Seed shooters, that's all we are.' Sebastian had heard (and indeed deployed) that justification more than once. It didn't fly these days, dismissed in *bien pensant* circles as risible self-exculpation, not merely pathetic but downright misogynistic, as *passé* as Sebastian's coral cords. Still, he might have countered, what about the stash of video porn found by SEAL Team Six when they burst into Bin Laden's compound in Abbottabad? Just another Allah-invoking old goat. Wasn't that further proof—as if further proof were needed—that biology has a way of trumping ideology? He'd be sticking to his position, neither abashed nor defensive in argument. The evidence spoke for itself, unless, that is, you turned a deaf ear. For every sex scandal that made the headlines, a dozen hovered below the waterline. Nooky was the norm, not the exception. Lust made the world go around. The designer-in-chief was no fool; he knew exactly what he was doing. Our urges stem from the Almighty himself. There's no escaping the fact: we exist to fuck, and fuck to exist. Fucking great!

Intriguing, isn't it, how so many slut-shamers, be they mega church pastors, fulminating imams or preacherly priests, are not averse to a little slap and tickle themselves? Horniness is the universal disruptor, routinely sending careers and marriages into a tailspin, dragging governments and institutions into the unforgiving mire. It's life's great wrecking ball, swinging away like Foucault's pendulum, skittling the indiscreet, the haughty, the hypocritical. Where there's testosterone, there's trouble, as Sebastian knew only too well. Cue images of his acrobatic bar-top shag with Annabel in The Conyers and the broom cupboard quickie with Amelia in the town-hall just before the award ceremony. He allowed himself a partial smile. Standing in front of the gutted hotel, how could he not acknowledge the tragicomic nature of life, even if in his own case the ratio of tragedy to comedy warranted recalibration? Late, lamented George would have empathized. In short order, the capering clown's life had lurched from mild farce to cruel absurdity. All his (and Carla's) hard work had just gone up in a very large and noxious puff of smoke.

It would have been devastating enough to learn that the hotel had been put out of business because of an electrical short or a kitchen fire—after all, accidents do happen—but Sebastian was struggling to accept that his livelihood had been destroyed in the name of Allah by skull-capped loons who took exception to a book they had not read, one that he had neither written nor published. Worse still, it was possible that some celebrity-hungry mufti in Dublin or Dhaka had by this time issued a full-on fatwa to have poor Farha Musharraf neutralized in the name of all that is good and holy even before she could deposit her winner's check. There was much to process, and he had yet to read the morning papers, speak to the PR people or deal with the authorities. Apart from twice emptying his bladder behind a thick-trunked cypress in the nearby park he had spent the entire night in Church Lane, senses dulled, thoughts muddled, anger simmering. It wasn't that long since George had been reduced to ashes, now it was The Conyers' turn. His departed friend wouldn't be coming back, but might the hotel rise Phoenix-like from its still glowing embers? It was too soon to address such a question with anything approaching analytic incisiveness.

Carla, a night-long fixture by his side, continued to emit intermittent, hiccup-like sobs. Finding alternative accommodation for the distraught, blanket-swaddled guests had been her priority, such that it hadn't dawned on her that she, too, was now homeless and bereft of possessions. A sadness pressed down on her like a goose down duvet on a warm night, but it had nothing to do with the particulars of her situation. The magnitude of what had happened, from the fracas at the award ceremony to the firebombing—if that's what it was—of the hotel had numbed her. Every now and then, Sebastian would drape a comforting arm around her slack shoulders. Her thereness also provided him with reassurance, not that he realized it at the time. More random thoughts entered his head, sensemaking having gone out the window. Odd how she hadn't needed to relieve herself even once all night. Another case of Mars and Venus?

He was approaching his mid-sixties, an age at which men experienced prostate problems. He remembered his father referring to issues with the waterworks, a coy euphemism that had perplexed him on first hearing. The issue, however, was not one to which he had given much thought, though of late he did seem to pee more than usual. Nights, he'd get up once if not twice. Sometimes during the day he'd have to contend with dribbling. Neither shaking nor milking provided a complete solution. That pesky last drop seemed to have a mind of its own. Minor inconveniences in the arc of a picaresque life to be sure, but such weaknesses—for that was how he perceived them—didn't jibe with his self-image. The embarrassing episode on Achill Island with Helga from Düsseldorf had not been forgotten. Being caught short half-way up tree-less Slievemore was no laughing matter. Still, he neither looked nor felt his age. Damned, though, if he'd allow his style to be cramped by a piddling matter like peeing. He lined up with Gertrude Stein: 'We are always the same age inside.' A tap on the shoulder from a portly garda brought the urological reverie to an end.

# AFTERSHOCKS

Two thousand and thirteen had come out of the blocks like Usain Bolt. It had promised to be an *annus mirabilis*. His bank account bulged, The Conyers was thriving, and the inaugural Parnell Prize seemed set fair for a spectacular launch. Almost everything had proceeded according to plan, from the integrated PR campaign to the finely tuned organisation of the gala ceremony itself. Even the shortlisting process had proved less acrimonious than might have been expected; no one had resigned from the jury and fisticuffs had just about been avoided. It remained a moot question whether Nic Langdale's last-minute attempted sabotaging of the process had been premeditated or simply the kind of behaviour one associates with attention-seeking boors. Had he leaked the story to the tabloids in exchange for moolah, out of spite for not having had his way when it came to the final vote or for the sake of mischief pure and simple? In the end, it really didn't matter; the outcome would have been the same. Whether the dyspeptic juror had hoped for quite such an incendiary response—or any kind of response for that matter—from members of the Muslim community would, presumably, be an issue for law enforcement to consider, though it'd be well-nigh impossible to demonstrate a direct causal connection between his leaking of the story and ensuing events in either the town hall or Church Street. Six males, all with addresses in Dublin or Waterford, had since been arrested and charged with violent disorder, but nothing more. In due course, they would appear in court, unlikely to serve time unless they had previous or in the interim attempted to flee the jurisdiction. Still, on the basis that there is no such thing as bad publicity, the Parnell had brought home the bacon, so to speak.

The town was reeling. Nothing quite like this had happened before. Admittedly, there had been some dastardly deeds during the War of Independence when the detested Black and Tans had looted businesses and torched buildings, but the televised highlights of the town hall brawl, combined with live footage of the burning hotel, served to magnify the sense of indignation. 'Miracle no lives lost' was the banner headline in the *Rathboffin Chronicle*, one echoed by the red-tops on both sides of the Irish Sea. The local guards, with help from the Big Smoke, were busy trying to establish means and motive, and determine whether any kind of warning had been phoned in, an approach sometimes used by the IRA. Pudgy, pug-faced Sergeant McGarry had the unenviable task of addressing the world's press. A standard-issue clip-on tie is not a compelling look at the best of times, much less so when wedged beneath a protuberant and hyper mobile Adam's apple. It was clear to the assembled hacks that McGarry's training hadn't prepared him for such intense scrutiny. They smelled blood. Nerves as much as fear of saying something that would land him in hot water with his superiors explained the slightly tremulous, dry-throated delivery. The force couldn't run the risk of being labelled Islamophobic. It had been drummed into him and his peers that the rights and feelings of minorities must be respected at all times. That was a defining feature of liberal democracies and thus essential to creating a more diverse and inclusive Ireland. A platitudinous 'all lines of enquiry are being pursued' proved to be his stock response to most questions. But what, the more persistent reporters asked, about those who had lost not just their belongings, but could so easily have lost their lives in the conflagration? Did the feelings of the dozen or so guests who were asleep in the hotel at the time of the attack somehow count for less? Homicide not arson could have been the focus of the ongoing investigation. The mistreatment of her husband by the snotty journos incensed Mrs McGarry to such an extent that she directed a bowl of semolina along with a hearty obscenity at the TV screen mid-way through a live press conference. Her friends in the

Family Rosary Group would have raised a collective eyebrow; the only time her voice went up an octave was when she intoned a well-earned 'Amen!' Within a matter of days, the hapless officer found himself back on desk duties, the face of the force now a seasoned superintendent from Sligo. In time, the story faded, updates dropping further down the inside pages of the dailies. Empathy, like fresh produce, had a limited shelf life. On the other hand, *The Callous Crescent* seemed destined for a lengthy run in the public eye. In next to no time, it had shot to the top of the best-seller lists, not though in either the Middle East or Indian subcontinent. There, the usual rent-a-mob protests saw pirated (and one imagines unopened) copies being committed to the flames along with life-size effigies of the offending author. Back in Ireland, a spooked Ms Musharraf was already in hiding.

Sebastian would not forget the spring of 2013 in a hurry. Assisting and placating traumatized guests, helping the police with their investigations and dealing with municipal bodies, when not filing or fielding insurance claims, filled almost every waking hour. He declined interview requests from the popular press, deferred those from representatives of the book trade and literary magazine editors. A week after the fateful night he Skyped Brendan to fashion a boiler-plate response to the blizzard of media queries coming their way. The draft press release opened with a rhetorical question, turning defence into attack: 'How can a book that is as compassionate as it is literate, as engaging as it is empathic, trigger such senseless, such murderous hostility in the twenty-first century?' The notion that *The Callous Crescent* was in any way offensive, even under Ireland's medieval blasphemy laws, was batted aside. Brendan, remembering when Salman Rushdie had been on the receiving end of a fatwa, co-opted a term vogue at that time, 'armed censorship.' It had resonated then and would again. The final version concluded by quoting the Universal Declaration of Human Rights and promising that those associated with the award would not be cowed. In fact, Sebastian had yet to give any thought to his (or indeed the prize's) future; he was up to his oxters in the present.

Being by disposition neither uncommonly brave nor given to pusillanimity, he—as would have any right-minded person—hesitated before assenting to Brendan's wording. Sebastian rather liked the seamless connection between his head and neck and had no desire to see an altering of the status quo. In the end, the PR professional prevailed, assuring his apprehensive client that since he was neither the author nor publisher of the offending book, there really wasn't any need to fret about imminent assassination. With the arson attack, they—whoever *they* were—had made their point, would be lying low. Looking ahead, the likelihood of the next award going to another 'Islamophobic' work were effectively zero. The brouhaha would subside in due course. 'Think of it this way. All the money in Connaught couldn't have bought the publicity Farha Musharraf has secured for you,' said Brendan, almost purring. 'Yes, but at what cost to Farha? And, at the risk of sounding crassly self-interested, what about my hotel? Seems to me that I've paid a rather hefty price. Maybe, as you imply, they don't shoot the messenger these days, just reduce his livelihood to ashes. Can't say I'm not grateful for the guards' presence around my house right now, though.' Sebastian seemed to smile to himself, before adding, 'It's just the sort of thing that would have appealed to George's diabolic sense of humour, his love of Grand Guignol.' He recalled their earnest teenage discussions about Descartes' idea of a malevolent demon overseeing the universe and yanking man's earthly chains just for the hell of it. 'Daft though it sounds, it's no dafter than believing in the existence of a benign deity, at once omnipotent and omniscient, who tolerates untold human misery and suffering without so much as a shrug of the divine shoulders. The yearning for a celestial comforter is as persistent as it is misguided. Funny, isn't it, how even the brightest of people can be so dim? It was Yeats, I think, who said that the world is the excrement of God.' Brendan twiddled his Staedtler pencil like a drum major in a marching band, nodding noncommittally as an animated Sebastian launched into an impromptu disquisition on the opiate of the masses. No skin off his nose: billable time was billable time.

# NEAR NEIGHBOURS

The fire brought Carla and Sebastian closer together. Her new home was the same converted barn where, more than a decade earlier, he had assumed grace and favour tenancy on arriving from the US, unemployed, if not exactly unemployable. On her first night in Ballyhannah they visited McTigue's where Pádraig's stout refusal to accept payment partnered a promise that if he spotted any dubious-looking Muslim types within an ass's roar of the property, he'd pepper the ne'er-do-wells with buckshot. Now of a morning, she could, if so minded, pop out in her PJs, knock on Sebastian's door, cadge a pint of milk and be back in her kitchen in under ninety seconds. Not that she would: unlike many Gen Xers, she knew where life's invisible lines were drawn, understood punctilio. He swatted her protestations aside. It would be rent-free, as it had been for him, on top of which he would continue to pay her salary. For the hotel staff, a generous severance package and guaranteed reemployment when—Sebastian intentionally used when rather than if—the business was back up and running. By that time, the Iberian Dream Team would likely have moved on, but it was a thoughtful gesture and appreciated as such. Simple acts of kindness provide welcome reassurance at moments of uncertainty, like scaffolding around a dangerously derelict dwelling. In due course, the old order would be restored, and life resume pretty much as before; such was the intended message. On hearing all of this, Carla's heartbeat had accelerated, though not for the same reasons or in quite the same way it had that siren-filled night.

On her way back from Galway she stopped off in Oughterard, on the western edge of ruffled Lough Corrib. At Sebastian's insistence and with €500 in crisp notes pressed into her reluctant hand, she'd spent a blustery morning clothes-shopping in the city. Her innate sense of style attracted laudatory comments from glammed-up sales assistants with seasonally impossible tans. Often it took but a single accessory, and not necessarily an expensive one, to render the ordinary eye-catching, or a little bit of daring to combine garments that at first glance might seem as un-pairable as catfish and claret. It was a skill Spanish women possessed in spades: the French didn't have a monopoly on style. She sat down in front of the inviting fireplace. The stook of bone-dry turf glowed, burning with the laziness of a well-packed pipe. Her chilled core began to warm. On the dark wooden mantel an array of west of Ireland knick-knacks. One caught her eye, a plaster figurine of a red-skirted shawlie woman, the kind you'd see in a Paul Henry or Sean Keating painting, clichéd but just the right side of kitsch. It catapulted her back to *Rhopos*, to her encounter with Sebastian in front of the McSweeney canvas that had drawn her in on her very first visit to the shop *cum* gallery. Like a puppy he had been, keen for attention, desperate to impress. Those traits remained, engendering almost as many suppressed sighs as involuntary smiles. She treated herself to tea and a fruit scone. The butter and home-made strawberry jam, pip-filled and tangy, came in cute little pots, the kind you might slip into your handbag for re-use at home. An affable, acned lass—a transition year student in all probability—brought the fare on a quivering tray. Apart from two elderly porter-supping men at one end of the curved bar, Carla had the establishment to herself. The pair sat hunched and mute, leathered hands cupped around near drained glasses. Three pints and as many sentences later, they'd trudge out the door, as they had done every weekday since retirement. Walking past them, the unmistakable aroma of stale urine and tobacco drifted up her nostrils. She didn't warrant so much as a turn of the head or grunt. But for the smell they might have been Tussaud dummies. Little would be happening in the small town that chill afternoon. The season had yet to kick off; several gift shops and restaurants continued to hibernate.

Recent events, for want of a better term, had knocked her equilibrium for six. Although not herself a direct target of the

Islamicists' ire, she had been appalled by what she had witnessed up close, horrified by the thought of what might have been. Because you find the subject matter of a work of fiction not to your liking, you are entitled to threaten the lives of others? What kind of world must such people inhabit, she wondered? And more to the point, what kind of God would thank them for their actions on his behalf? After centuries of pogroms and persecutions, men—for it was almost always men— still sought to erase from the face of the earth those with whom they disagreed on matters metaphysical. What if innocent people had been trapped in the hotel? What if she had been in her ground floor quarters only to find her escape route blocked by burning debris? Her thoughts turned to Farha Musharraf, a gentle, literary-minded soul, now living in constant fear, freedom of movement in addition to freedom of expression denied her by some. What if Sebastian had perished in the conflagration? Imagining his absence from her lifeworld made it clear just how much he meant to her. He functioned like a long-chained anchor that secured but didn't constrain her, allowing her to drift and bob to her heart's content. The analogy might have surprised him.

Carla had spoken to her father almost every day since that awful night and for the first time thought about contacting her estranged mother. The moment Matteo had come out, home life at the Delgados had changed forever. His wife remained uncomprehending, adamantine in her refusal to acknowledge her husband's true sexual orientation. She had been married to a *marica* all these years, to a man leading a double life? Fernanda's sense of betrayal seemed boundless. She considered her husband's behaviour both sinful and perverted; *contra naturam,* as she had said on more than one occasion. Her reaction to Matteo's homosexuality was as inexplicable to Carla as her mother's subsequent committal to Opus Dei, a quasi-cult with fetishist leanings. Almost at once, Fernanda had left the family home and sought an annulment, one to which the Church hierarchy had little trouble in assenting: Leviticus 18 came in handy at such moments. And so it was that Matteo Delgado, noted Galician photographer, became the single parent of a teenage daughter and a ten-year old son, Pablo. Carla could not understand how a mother would simply walk away from her offspring as if they were lepers, somehow tainted by association. What about charity beginning at home, the Christian notion of forgivingness? Later, Fernanda moved to Salamanca and remarried; Matteo's replacement was an antique dealer who introduced his new bride to the Opus Dei. Fernanda joined him in the business and on the spiritual path outlined by the secretive Order's founder. Together they would honour God in daily life, in the buying and selling of *objets d'art*, period furniture and antique paintings. Since marrying and joining Opus Dei, Fernanda's views on the subject of homosexuality had calcified. Same sex relationships constituted an abomination in the eyes of God. Growing tolerance of, and support for, gays in civil society had not caused her to modify her mindset. She would stick to her super-glued guns, in that regard little different from millions of fundamentalist Christians and Muslims around the world. Carla's mother espoused views that were currently unfashionable in liberal democracies, but she did so with an almost commendable steadfastness; intransigence, after all, was not a synonym for inauthenticity. Nazis hated both Jews and homosexuals but that hatred neither derived from nor depended on religious conviction. Fernanda did not hate homosexuals, for that would be unchristian, nor did she advocate any form of coercive intervention; she disapproved of their chosen lifestyle for the simple reason that it flouted God's law. As in all other spheres of her daily existence, she was following holy scripture not indulging a baseless loathing for a vulnerable minority. Whatever her failings, she could hardly be accused of moral lassitude or deemed guilty of having committed a hate crime, though intransigent human rights activists might beg to differ. Certain tenets of her faith were non-negotiable: the practice of homosexuality, a perversion only marginally less degenerate than bestiality, was one; abortion and capital punishment—legally sanctioned murder—were others. Even if the rest of the world considered her views outmoded and odious, she was entitled to them. Carla could just imagine Sebastian, ever the contrarian, acting as her mother's defence counsel and saying something to the effect: 'I disapprove of what you say, but I will defend to the death your right to say it.' Over the years neither mother nor child had ever essayed reconciliation. Carla remembered Sebastian once saying something to the effect that an eye for an eye mentality took all parties down a blind alley. To no avail: she remained unbending. Now, however, by the comforting fire, the outlines of an imaginary dialogue with her estranged parent were taking shape. Her ruminations ended when a sleek people carrier pulled up outside the hotel and disgorged its contents. A flock of tricolour lanyards lumbered through the double doors. A loud 'Hey, hon, just look at that fire,' heralded a chorus of strangulated 'Wows!' With a reflexive smile, Carla ceded her cosy roost to a middle-aged woman wearing a Green Bay Packers beanie and headed straight to her parked Audi. The heated seats were a godsend. Yet one more reason to be grateful to Sebastian.

# A SMILE IS JUST A SMILE

For meetings, they used his spacious kitchen, except, that is, when McTigue's lounge bar assumed the role. Sebastian gave Carla a key to the house and was insistent that she should feel free to come and go—it was their ersatz office, after all. Before long, an end-of-day walk to the pub had become routine—just as had been the case with George—blurring the lines between work and leisure, collegiality and companionship. The regulars said nothing, but the unspoken assumption was they were an item. A few of the younger crowd would steal envious glances at the green-eyed newcomer from Spain.

Declan, eager to assist his former (and possibly future) boss, had acquired and set up all the necessary home-based technology for the pair—from workstations and laptops, copiers, printers and shredders to the latest iPhone—needed to handle the myriad issues spawned by the clusterfuck. The hotel's hardware, including backup systems, had been destroyed. A direct hit from a Tomahawk missile would have been no less devastating. Having no flight recorder or back box to fall back on, they were flying in the dark. The young man, however, rose to the challenge with geekish focus.

An inventory of the hotel's contents, a requirement for insurance purposes, would have to be recreated from memory and by using information scraped from the hotel website. Having invested so much effort in setting up the business, from initial design and construction through launch and stabilisation, Sebastian's lack of motivation—to call it inanition would be going too far—came as no surprise to Carla. Tasks that needed doing were addressed with diligence but without the palpable enthusiasm and energy of yore. She suspected that he might be drawing a line under the hotel business: a case of, been there, seen it, done it. Time was when the former life coach would have parroted something like 'Pick yourself up, dust yourself down and start all over again' to a client in a similar pickle, but anyone who knew him realized he couldn't stomach such fatuousness. The free spirit was likely hankering after a fresh start and the option existed of selling off the property to either an independent operator or large chain once the insurance claim had been settled. That would remove one shackle. The complicated matter of the Parnell Prize, however, remained.

The Monday following the St Patrick's Day weekend saw a dramatic spike in sales of Aspirin and Alka-Seltzer. From Ballina to Ballsbridge the falsely reassuring fizz of slow-dissolving tablets could be heard; the entire nation was hungover, or so it would have seemed to an anthropologist from Mars. Not, though, Carla and Sebastian. He despised the manic Paddywhackery, could not comprehend why the occasion had been hijacked the world over. The saint's feast day had metamorphosed into a mindless aping of Mardi Gras. It was, he informed Carla, an egregious instance of cultural appropriation. Most of those with green-painted faces, sipping green-coloured beer probably couldn't locate Ireland on a map let alone say in which century the holy man lived. Not that they gave a flying fig: poor old Patrick was merely a pretext for a jamboree. The country's revered patron saint could have been an alcoholic horse thief with a brood of illegitimate children for all they knew or cared. Odd, Sebastian continued, how blackfacing is taboo but green facing is quite acceptable. Carla looked perplexed. Her boss had a way of going off at a tangent.

As she entered the pub, a likely lad lounging against the bar said something that triggered a smile. It didn't, contrary to expectation, cause her to break stride or respond. His smart-aleck follow-up was stillborn, to the amusement of his sniggering mates. This member of McTigue's darts team would be eating humble pie for supper. Sebastian observed the cameo, one he had witnessed before. Some people are blessed with a smile that simultaneously disarms and charms. The very best function like a powerful passport, opening doors and securing admission denied others. Carla's was a thing of beauty, natural and effortless, bestowed in equal measure on young and old, male and female, firm and infirm. He had once described it to George as the poster child of equal opportunity smiles. That Duchenne smile had worked wonders for The Conyers (and indeed *Rhopos*). It really did constitute a valuable intangible asset and should have appeared on the company's balance sheet. The occasional chancer might read more into it than was warranted, but Carla had only very rarely been discommoded. Wolf whistles and lascivious asides bounced off her like bullets off a Panzer's armour plates. She used but never abused her charm, a charm for which Sebastian's appreciation had only sharpened since her relocation to tiny Ballyhannah.

'Do you miss your parents?' Both the question itself and its directness caught him off guard. With Carla, he had come to expect diffidence coupled with graceful circumlocution. If even the slightest possibility existed of a question being construed as intrusive or overly personal, she would lard it with qualifiers and deliver it with winning politeness. Whether that was due to inherent cultural differences or indicative of her exceptional good manners, Sebastian couldn't decide; both possibly. In any case, it produced results. Not once had he seen her lose her composure with a customer. He, on the other hand, could be snarky or combustible, words she might not have known. 'I suppose so,' came the unconvincing response. 'We were not particularly close and after I moved to the UK, we just drifted further apart, locked in our respective orbits. Now, having said that, once they were both gone something did feel different. It was as if I had been orphaned very late in life, left to drift, oh I don't know, like a canoe on the currents of Lough Corrib.' She smiled. 'To some extent,' he continued, 'one's parents act like a security blanket. Even if you don't return that often to the nest, the sense persists that they will always be there even if everything else in your world should vanish around you.

You could say that parents are, to use an Americanism, the original safe space for some. We grow up, we push out into the world, build a career, marry and have children of our own, but in our parents' eyes we remain forever kids, never wholly emerging from the chrysalis of childhood.' With that and an 'excuse me' he headed to the loo for a second time.

She took a longer than usual swallow of her drink, a 'super zesty Sauvignon Blanc infused with the flavours of the Tropics' and grimaced; it tasted like liquid zinc. The label was playing loose with the truth. She blinked the thought of it away, looked straight at him. A steadying inhalation of breath, then a two or three-second pause. He felt like a patient expecting to hear bad news from his GP. Out came the full story of her parents' separation, her mother's deserting of the family and subsequent marriage to an Opus Dei member. She told it without tearing up but with unconcealed emotion. The nuclear family had imploded, destroying the sense of security that both she and Pablo had felt growing up. Although Matteo proved to be an even more caring and dutiful father than he had been up to that point, the abruptness and finality of the break-up unsettled the children. Sebastian observed every facial tic, every hand movement. The expressive power of the Spanish astonished him, so much nuance. It was the difference between a bicycle with three gears and one with fifteen. Carla was making full use of all fifteen. Were the English emotionally stunted, he wondered, because they were born with stiff upper lips or were the stiff lips a product of their native expressive reserve? Or had it something do with the weather? And why were the Finns so saturnine, the German so blunt and humourless? National stereotypes existed even if the PC brigade begged to differ. Carla may have hailed from cool Galicia but right now she was exhibiting the paralinguistic range of a fiery Carmen from Granada. Abandonment had affected her, maybe more deeply than she had realized. '*Madre mia!*' she exclaimed. 'Oh, I am sorry, Sebastian.' She clamped his arm just above the wrist. 'I didn't mean to be so, erm, so demonstrable. Is that the word?' 'Demonstrative,' he chuckled, throwing an incautious arm around her shoulder, and drawing her in. The dart player felt a pang of jealousy. The old fella with the hair had hit the bullseye.

# ON REFLECTION

Concerned that she might have committed the sin of garrulousness, Carla spoke hardly at all on the way back to the cottage. By coincidence, both were thinking of the awkward fumbling that had taken place shortly after George's demise, on that strange night almost a year earlier in her flat near the harbour. The image of the gas fire, spluttering and hissing with geriatric disapproval, had stuck with Sebastian. Tonight, as then, nothing could be said, which explained why he neither hugged nor embraced her. Not that the urge didn't exist. She cut quite a figure, striking in her naturalness; possessed a *culo* would have been labelled pert by jaded tabloid sub-editors. But pert it indubitably was, thanks in no small measure to the slim-fitting cord jeans that had attracted the dart player's (and Sebastian's) gaze earlier in the evening. If she weren't who she was, he'd have the hots for her. In fact, the Geiger counter in his trousers told him he already had. Vigilance would be required in the weeks and months ahead to ensure that liking and admiration continued to define the upper bounds of his attraction. The only permissible intimacy could be that of mind. One drink too many by the pub fire or a well-intentioned hug that morphed from companionable to romantic under a seductive moon would be enough to upturn the applecart.

Stretched out on the sofa with *Recuerdos de la Alhambra* all a-tremble in the background he loosened the reins on his imagination. Just imagine if he'd been a classical guitarist, any kind of musician for that matter. Who wouldn't want to be a Segovia or a Bream not to mention a Furtwängler or Bernstein, a potentate of the podium, with a thousand eyes fixed on your every gesture, an entire orchestra in thrall to the subtlest uptick of your baton, the merest arching of your eyebrow? Mastery in any art form translated into pulling power, compensating for runtiness, halitosis, narcissism, insensitivity, pomposity, penury even: Jagger and Hendrix, Picasso and Freud, masters of their craft, lady killers to a man. And as for bloody poets! Enjambement was all it took to get the leg over. He was powerless, lacking the kind of magnetism that derives from God-given talent and compels adulation on its own terms. The tiny platform provided by his run-of-the-mill professorship in Middle America had been taken from him; The Conyers, a congenial stage for an ageing roué, had been swept away. There was nowhere for him to strut what little stuff he had left.

The belligerent Atlantic rain battered against the triple-glazed windows. March could be a mean month in the west, a time when the lucky few headed to Knock Airport, dinky gateway to the sun. A vintage Port geed him up. Hotel or no hotel, he was cash rich and far from asset poor: the converted cottage and renovated barn between them must be worth a million, even after the property market collapse. He raised a ruby-red glass to George. Did he really want to live through a rebuilding of The Conyers, greeting guests, supervising staff, managing inventory, filling out VAT forms? He had proved to George, and moreover to himself, that he could incubate a successful venture. It had taken a once-in-a-lifetime recession to wipe out *Rhopos*; a wholly unpredictable terrorist attack to destroy The Conyers. In good conscience, he could not be faulted; it was a case of fortuity at its cruellest.

Refill in hand, he directed his thoughts to the other elephant in the room. This one loomed larger and would be harder to handle. The Parnell Prize had become, depending on one's viewpoint, a *succès de scandale* or a life-menacing liability. Police enquiries continued with plodding diligence; Islamophiles and Islamophobes exchanged bile on social media; the chattering classes debated the inherent desirability of literary prizes; rabid imams demanded that Ireland's exemplary blasphemy laws be used to prosecute Farha Musharraf and, for good measure, the organizers of the prize. Since the outrage, all four members of the jury had been asked repeatedly for their reaction to events and, with the predictable exception of Nic Langdale, had eventually obliged, each offering a choice blend of bromide and cliché. They probably wished they had never been contacted by Sebastian in the first place. Rarely had writerly solitude seemed so appealing, celebrity less attractive. For weeks, Brendan Byrne had been pestering him to speak to the press, to undertake a couple of TV interviews, to let the world know whether and on what basis the prize might continue in the years ahead. The Dubliner persisted in his view that the worst would soon be over, leaving the prize positioned for a spectacular relaunch.

Casting his mind back to his first meeting with Arthur 'Lurch' Dooley, Sebastian tried to remember the exact wording in the will pertaining to the prize, specifically the *quid pro quo* (inheritance in exchange for directing the literary prize). It had struck him at the time that it was an essentially unenforceable condition. Certainly, the lugubrious solicitor had not dwelt on it. And even in the unlikely event that there was a legally binding requirement of some kind, surely death threats would be sufficient grounds for him to break the terms without triggering disinheritance. Not even George would have expected him to risk life and limb for thirty pieces of silver. In principle, there was no reason why someone else, a recognized literary figure or experienced event organiser, shouldn't step into the role, appoint a fresh set of jurors and reboot the prize. Brendan's (or another) PR firm could be hired to pre-empt any potential blowback. That way, he'd hold onto his inheritance and the Parnell Prize would continue on its way. Thoroughly geed up, he poured himself an ill-advised third glass. Tomorrow he'd get in touch with Lurch. Liberation beckoned.

# IN THE LURCH NO MORE

'Terrible! Simply terrible! Heaven alone knows how no one perished. A miracle, nothing less. We are all absolutely outraged at what happened. So relieved you weren't hurt, Sebastian.' Her bosom swelled with nativist indignation. 'After the effort you put into getting that lovely hotel up and running. A crime, an absolute crime. And as for the antics at the town hall. I hope that lot end up jail, get what they deserve.' Patricia Dooley, sporting a nubby, ochre cardigan that would have been perfect for a harvest festival, was visibly upset but not so upset that Sebastian could get a word in. 'I don't understand it, just don't. We open our doors to these people and in next to no time they're telling us what we can and cannot do in our own country, a Catholic country at that. What in God's name has Allah got to do with the likes of us? Just imagine if we went to their country and insisted that they follow our rules, adopt our beliefs. Imagine, too, the reaction if we burned down their buildings, threatened the lives of innocent people in their towns and villages. I tell you, it's simply not good enough.' The guards may not have completed their investigations, but in light of the circumstantial evidence Mrs Dooley had already made up her mind as to who the culprits were, as, in fact, had most people in Rathboffin. 'Frankly, I hold the government responsible, letting every Tom, Dick and Harry, or should I say every Muhammed, into the country willy-nilly.' She had always voted Fine Gael but might have to break a lifetime's habit come the next election. Just then, a stringy figure in a tired grey suit with a face to match appeared in the doorway directly behind her, hovered briefly. 'Dr Conyers, do come in.'

Dooley was his habitual self, a settled blend of exactitude and dullness. His countenance resembled an oil painting with early onset of craquelure. He, too, expressed his sympathy, while studiously avoiding his wife's judgementalism. If he had emotions, he didn't wear them on his shiny, slightly too long sleeve. Sebastian's eyes took in every corner of the artificially lit room: even more of a firetrap than before. Poor old Lurch stuck all day in an office that had the personality of a hoarder's spare bedroom or out defending miscreants in drab county courthouses; such was the man's life. Litigants' names might change but the diet of case work varied little. Four decades of this and he could devote himself to philately or performing good works with the local branch of St Vincent de Paul Society. Sebastian understood the appeal of high-profile criminal lawyering. Who wouldn't want to be a Perry Mason or Rumpole of the Bailey, centre-stage in the cut and thrust of the courtroom? But the bread-and-butter stuff, the numbingly archaic language, the reams of paperwork? Could it be that the finer points of conveyancing and probate law provided rectitudinous Lurch with all the job satisfaction he needed to keep on getting out of bed in the morning? Sebastian tried to see it through eyes other than his own. The profession had status and attracted some of the finest minds. There must be good reason. Well, for one thing, the law is codified, based on due process and precedence; it advances in rational and forensic fashion. Such a career would appeal to a certain kind of person. He could see how you might think of law as a scaled-up version of chess, requiring mastery of rules, deep concentration and the ability to strategize in real time. Of course, not everyone could be a Kasparov or Fisher. For every grand master there were thousands of Lurches in the lawyerly trenches. By way of contrast, neither obsessive attention to detail nor love of conformance had been a distinguishing characteristic of Sebastian at any stage in his adult life. Flourish and flare seemed to count for more. He liked to think of himself as a big picture guy not a miniaturist. The devil, they say, lies in the details, but the devil-may-care professor-turned-hotelier in mustard corduroy would likely beg to differ.

He stared at the expressionless, whey face across from him. Some couples so defied explanation that you yearned to be a voyeuristic fly on the wall. Who knew what went on in the Dooley's marital bed, whether either party ever ventured across the saggy median in search of comfort? It would be like a stick insect trying to hump a toad, a grotesque case of interspecies mating; that was how he envisaged it, having seen the pair close-up for a second time. But perhaps their marriage, a childless one, had devolved over time into a sexless arrangement—always assuming it hadn't started out that way—a union cemented in convenience. Or maybe buxom Patricia fulfilled the role of small-town solicitor's beard, a titivating prospect. Throughout their conversation, Lurch kept his personal opinions relating to the recent violence to himself, focusing instead on the legal matter in hand. His flat, near monotonic delivery conveyed a sense of professionalism and impartiality. Or so he imagined. Sebastian could not tell what the inscrutable figure sitting across the paper-strewn desk thought of him, if anything. Throughout their meeting, Lurch blinked with metronomic consistency. What made people like him tick? Did they ever experience a Dionysian urge, crack a dirty joke or fart in polite company? If men are from Mars and women from Venus, it seemed reasonable to assume that Lurch and his ilk hailed from Uranus.

'We do find ourselves in a somewhat unusual situation, I must admit, but then I would not have described Mr Kingsley's will as altogether usual. Although Fay and Florin are responsible for managing the funds associated with the prize, they have no formal oversight role regarding the directorship, whether in terms of appointing or appraising. Their role is entirely fiduciary in nature.' The words came out of his dry mouth with the consistency of widgets rolling off a Detroit assembly line. 'One can only assume that Mr Kingsley would have intended the prize to carry on after your time at the helm. In my judgement, and please be aware that I am merely expressing an opinion, your inheritance would not be rendered null and void should you be indisposed for reasons of, say, ill-health or a threat to your person and thereby felt a need to demit office. Moreover, were you to take the steps necessary to ensure the continuing viability of the prize, you would, I venture, be adhering to the spirit of Mr Kingsley's request. As such, I can't think how anyone might reasonably object to your stepping aside once a good faith effort has been made to find a suitable replacement.' After a pause, he added: 'Well, perhaps there is one person: Ms Kynaston, you late friend's distant cousin, whom you may remember.' Not even a flicker of a smile crossed his face. Sebastian's stomach clenched; mere mention of that name functioned as a noxious stimulus. 'But even if she were to mount a legal challenge of some kind, which would, I assure you, be a potentially costly move, I can't see her making much if any headway. Since both your life and livelihood have been threatened in the performance of your duties, I find it difficult to imagine that any judge would rule in her favour and strip you of the inheritance, whether in part or whole. So, as for next steps, Dr Conyers, might I suggest a courtesy meeting with Florin and Fay in Dublin to inform them both of recent events and of your plans, if you have not already done so?'

Less than five minutes later, the reluctant hero of free speech took his leave of the Dooleys, Patricia's heartfelt good wishes ringing in his ears. He strolled along Church Lane beneath a blue sky garnished with a single cauliflower cloud. Chain-link fencing corralled the charred remains. He imagined a piper silhouetted against the rubble, one foot resting atop the fallen lintel of the entrance, issuing a lament. The incubus would soon be off his back, but even so he felt a twinge of sadness corkscrew through his innards. He had put a great deal of sweat equity into The Conyers, given the short-lived venture his all. Sometimes the Fates could be fickle beyond belief.

# STOP, START

Sebastian detested call answering services. As a sometime professor of information systems, he understood that they were designed with the express purposes of crushing customer resolve and bamboozling all but the most persevering: the antithesis of user-centred design. If only the rest of the world followed the example of Israel, making it a legal obligation for large companies to get back to their customers. Since the fire, his limited reserves of patience had been depleted. George had never allowed his emotions to be held hostage. Sebastian might know what he needed to do but lacked the capacity to modify his behaviour accordingly: anger would too often take control. There was hardly a day when he was not attempting to get through to someone at HEX Insurance or busy re-reading the countless exemptions, exclusions and contingencies buried in the heretofore ignored small print of his prolix policy. Maybe the Lurches of this world got their rocks off navigating the hair-splitting minutiae of such documents, not Sebastian. Taking out the policy had been straightforward, trying to lodge a successful claim anything but. HEX's modus operandi soon became clear: prevaricate whenever possible; change the contact person within the company; request gobs of additional information; challenge every expensive item on the loss inventory; fail to follow up; repeat the process. In any case, nothing would be settled until the company's loss adjustor had determined the reason for the fire, a matter still under investigation. If the cause were shown to be arson, the policy, he gathered, should cover the damage, but if the fire-bombing proved to be an act of international terrorism—a term HEX had not yet seen fit to define with anything approaching legal exactitude—then coverage might be vitiated. After a couple of weeks Sebastian had had his fill of corporate gamesmanship and decided to hire an independent loss assessor from Galway to fight his corner. It might not be cheap, but in the long run he'd save money and possibly his sanity. The visit to HEX's offices in the capital had been the final straw.

In late April, Sebastian and Carla had travelled to the city for an overnight stay, the plan being to hand-deliver documents to the company, documents that a pettifogging jobsworth twice claimed not to have received via email. They'd also use the opportunity to meet with Gavin Fay and discuss next steps. To his credit, Gavin had phoned Sebastian after hearing the shocking news from Rathboffin, but the pair had not had an opportunity to talk at any length since then. Sebastian and Carla also planned to meet with Brendan to craft a transition plan and determine how best to handle the fallout. It would be her first visit to Dublin in several years; anticipation filled her veins. She hadn't asked but gleaned that they'd be staying in a small hotel, The Plurabelle, not far from Stephens Green. The rooms and public spaces, Sebastian informed her, were *hygge*, judging by the images on its website. It sounded a little like hug but made no sense to her. Rooms like hugs? Anyway, there would be no returning to the exorbitant Shelbourne, no reliving of those heady days with Aoife O'Malley, about which he imagined she knew next to nothing. Decorousness was now in the ascendant.

They departed shortly after nine, heading towards Athlone via Cong and Tuam. With April came showers, but then they did with every month. Why privilege April? He watched tiny tadpoles of rain slip down the windshield only to be swept aside by the imperious wipers. The greasy surface called for caution. Sebastian's valued cargo hummed a soft refrain that he thought he recognized: something by Albéniz? He told her a little about the monastic history of Cong but nothing about the afternoon he had spent there with Helga sitting by the jet-black river beneath a willow tree. If he weren't careful, he'd experience an erection. Interesting how the verb choice makes it seem as if one has no agency, that erections happen *to* you. The old term 'morning wood' came to mind—a phenomenon once referred to memorably by his RE teacher in Castletownmorris as nocturnal penile tumescence. Something to do with the autonomic nervous system. Language like that reduced sex to mechanics and pimply teens to convulsions. He had blushed that day, deeply. Still did on rare and unpredictable occasions; an unfixable Achilles heel it continued to be.

Sexual encounters constituted major sites in the topography of Sebastian Conyers' memory. For him, they could assume the importance of the death of a parent, birth of a child or purchase of a house. These signature moments, as he liked to call them, functioned as pornographic punctuation marks, taking him from one chapter of his life to the next. His self-esteem remained tightly coupled with his ability to appeal to the opposite sex. He needed affirmation like a diabetic needed insulin; in his sixties and increasingly bladder-aware, the craving remained as elemental as ever. Not that he was either priapic or desirous of sex multiple times a day, the way historic studs like Mussolini or Kennedy had been. In many respects he was Mr Average with normal appetites, but one for whom validation mattered to an above average extent. If that constituted a failing, it ranked low on the turpitude scale, in his eyes at any rate.

'Overhanging the abbey's yews, a medieval mist, cotton wool dense and damp with dreaminess...' Was he talking to her or to himself? Poetry perhaps? 'Oh, that's nice. What is it?' she asked. 'Just a couple of lines from a short poem I found flicking through a book last night.' He carried on. 'Mutes matinal sounds, shutters solstice sun... Can't remember much more of it. Nothing of great consequence.' She admired his cultural intelligence no less than his business acumen. He knew the kinds of things you'd expect an educated individual to know, but you also sensed that he held considerably more in reserve. It was a stratagem he had developed by observing George's way of luring strangers into discussion, letting them believe he was a lightweight or barstool bore; intellectual entrapment, he called it. His friend, he had come to appreciate, tended to approach life from an oblique angle rather than straight on. To describe him as contrarian or nonconforming, however, would be not quite right. Inscrutable got close, though offered no insight into the underlying personality dynamics. In terms of appearance and manners, George regressed to the mean and that surface normalcy caused people to underestimate him. To be taken for a bogtrotter by some pipsqueak could almost give him as much pleasure as draining a pint of expertly poured Guinness. What might be construed as self-abnegation was to his way of thinking the epitome of self-control. Of course, once the interlocutor had exhausted his knowledge stock or run out of *bons mots*, a sly smiling George would counter like a professional poker player cleaning out a novice. While most people, not least Sebastian, sought explicit acknowledgement of their talents and charm, George seemed to derive a perverse pleasure from being underrated, waiting with saintly patience for just the right moment to deploy Occam's razor or Wittgenstein's ruler. It could perhaps have been said of him that he exhibited Zen-like traits without any of the oriental baggage. None of his obituarists captured that facet of his personality; nor another, superficially contradictory one, his tendency to confuse talking with conversation. Not that Sebastian was innocent of that failing.

The windshield wipers slapped back and forth, white noise on a mouse-grey morning as they tailgated an unhurrying Massey Ferguson. Then came the inevitable road works. What must it be like standing in all weathers with a giant lollipop in your grip telling pissed-off motorists to either stop or go while your hole-digging mates lean on long-handled shovels admiring their handiwork? Presumably, if you're of misanthropic bent, you get a mighty buzz holding up the red one for as long as possible. He had often wondered if the lollipop men in their hi-vis jackets ever became muddled and instead of a red and green showing in sync there were two greens. Now, that would be a jam and a half: no way forward, no way back. Better still, imagine you are either hungover or terminally bored and decide to subvert the system just for the hell of it, like a malevolent deity. Such a job is on a par with being a parking warden or a traffic cop, albeit without the power-conferring uniform and all-important peaked hat. Getting paid to bring misery to people you don't know is surely some compensation for standing like a badly dressed Gallowglass in the unremitting rain. But what, if anything, did these roadmen talk about at home after work with their nearest and dearest, having spent the best part of the day holding a pole and gawping at frustrated drivers in their idling cars? No wonder so many people were addicted to soaps and reality TV, desperate to escape the daily grind, the crushing pointlessness of life. Sebastian could just imagine George taking exception to that last conjecture. "Ah ha! Elitism combined with presumption. The original sin of the chattering classes. What, my dear Sebastian, if your unheeding lollipop man were using those tedious pole-wielding hours to contemplate some of philosophy's toughest questions thereby transmuting drudgery into an opportunity for mindfulness of the highest order? And let me remind you, to take but two examples at random, that your hero Ludwig Wittgenstein was a fan of cowboy movies and AJ Ayer a Spurs supporter. We must be careful not to typecast or default to a presumption of ignorance in the case of our fellow man. Without wishing to gainsay Bertrand Russell, I don't think we can conclude that all plebs are docile sheep. Or to put it otherwise, one man's couch potato is another's Plato.'

Carla noticed Sebastian smiling to himself, though not for any reason she might have imagined. A clerihew was taking shape: 'Jackson Pollock / hired a trollop / who agreed to strip / drip by drip.' He and George had often exchanged doggerel, a practice dating from their Trinity days. Trying to keep up with his friend, who possessed an enviable facility for wit, could prove dispiriting at times but it helped sharpen his edge. He'd step into the ring with George, spar and emerge bruised but better equipped for the next session. One limerick in particular, the very first one by George, had stuck in his mind over the decades. 'There once was a young man called Simon / who became infatuated with a pieman. / Overwhelmed with lust / he bit off his crust / which tasted much better than hymen.' Its stickability had less to do with its sophomoric silliness than the fact that he had had to look up the meaning of hymen: sex education was a thing of the future in nineteen sixties Castletownmorris. Might still be, for all he knew.

There'd be little point trying to explain the finer points of such bawdy nonsense to Carla and, in any case, he hadn't a clue how to translate clerihew into Spanish: it'd most likely require paraphrasing. By Tullamore, a comfort break was in order. 'Toilets' read the sign. Sebastian favoured public convenience over toilet. It said all that needed to be said but with delicate obliqueness. If that made him a fogey, so be it. Above the stainless-steel urinal that doubled as an ashtray someone had written 'Mick sucks dick' and underneath it another wit had added 'Dick sucks Mick.' Off to one side, in scrawly green letters, a cultural variant on the fellatio theme: 'Muslims suck.' It would be covered over by day's end. There was no place for that sort of thing in the New Ireland, not even in a reeking Offaly latrine.

# METRO MAN

A brisk ten-minute walk took them from the hotel to HEX's offices, just off elegant Fitzwilliam Square. Their visit was unscheduled, the aim being to catch the shysters on the hop. 'Conyers. Dr Sebastian Conyers. Here to see Reginald Davis.' The receptionist, framed with brushed chrome and glass, seemed nonplussed. Individual customers did not usually turn up at corporate HQ, much less customers without an appointment. Still, the combination of the tailored suit and clipped tone persuaded Donna to pick up the phone after momentary hesitation. It at once became clear that Mr Davis, who since his early teens had disavowed the expanded version of his given name, would prefer to remain untroubled at his desk on the fifth floor. Which left the young lady unsure how to proceed. 'If I may,' said Sebastian, relieving her of the slender handpiece and stating to the voice at the other end in what could only be termed peremptory fashion that if he didn't come down sharpish, then his visitor would be coming up. Carla noticed Donna fidgeting with her lanyard, and sensing the young woman's anxiety, flashed a reassuring girls-together smile. 'So sorry,' breathed Sebastian as he handed back the phone with consummate politeness, 'but sometimes one simply has to take matters into one's own hands.' A couple of minutes later, and somewhat to his surprise, a trainee managerial type in a non-iron shirt and pointy-toed brown leather shoes appeared. 'Hello. I'm Reg Davis. How can I help you, Mr...?' 'Conyers. Dr Conyers, owner of the eponymous hotel in Rathboffin for which your company has provided cover.' Neither extended the other a hand. Sebastian, however, retained conversational advantage. 'Given that your email system seems to have an inexplicable aversion to messages sent by either myself or my general manager, we thought it best if we personally delivered the documents you claim, on multiple occasions, not to have received. This way there can be no ambiguity, no further confusion.' With that, he shoved a sheaf of papers into Reg's unsuspecting grasp while Carla, as planned, pulled out her phone and took a photo of the hand-off. 'Now, Mr Davis, we have visual proof that you are indeed in possession of the documents that have heretofore eluded you and your colleagues.' To anyone watching it would have looked as if a writ was being served in time-honoured fashion; comedic but effective. And with that the cameo concluded, leaving the HEXers bemused.

A quarter of an hour later Carla was exploring some of the less appreciated treasures of the National Gallery and Sebastian making purposeful way to the plush Liffyside offices of Fay & Florin. Donna, in her defence, had not at any point been less than personable in her interactions with the out-of-towners. Which could not be said of her opposite number in Docklands. Here at the curvaceous reception desk, he again encountered the Botox-ed twentysomething blessed with the people skills of a Soviet era shop assistant. What lay beneath the carapace of makeup? Gavin greeted him with warmth, placing a consoling hand on his shoulder 'Good to see you. Terrible business altogether. The scrummage at the event was horrifying enough but the arson, well that was unconscionable. Have they found the perpetrators? Has all the makings of a terrorist attack, if you ask me, though, of course, you can't say that sort of think any more without being branded a racist or some such. You know, Sebastian, in our rebellious youth we kind of looked up to the guards, feared them, you might even say. Step out of line and you'd get a good kick up the arse or a clout over the head with a truncheon. We all knew the difference between right and wrong and they didn't mess about or worry about what our parents might say. Now their hands are tied, and they spend most of time filling out forms and trying not to upset anyone.' It was coming off like a well-rehearsed stump speech. He throttled back. 'But enough of all that; what about yourself? I trust *your* life is not in imminent danger. Do you still have police protection?'

Once Gavin's questions had exhausted themselves, Sebastic provided an update, including his latest interview with the investigating authorities, before moving on to the real business of the day: succession management. In the light of what had happened he had every right to wash his hands of the Parnell. 'Your friend George,' Gavin assured him, 'would without a shadow of a doubt have insisted that you distance yourself as far as humanly possible from the prize at this point. Once the dust has settled, we can find someone else to take the reins, thereby ensuring that the spirt of the bequest is honoured in full. Perhaps some of the people you know in the literary world might be able to come up with names. The coffers are healthy enough to provide not unattractive remuneration for what is, after all, a part-time position. If it was rugby we were talking about, I might well be able to help out, but high-brow literature has never been my thing. I'll be honest with you, Sebastian. I tried reading *The Callous Crescent* after what happened but didn't get beyond the first chapter. On the other hand, my wife read it from cover to cover and could not grasp what all the fuss was about. She enjoyed it. Do you think those protesters actually read the book? You do have to wonder, don't you?' Sebastian promised Gavin that he'd get back to him with some names once he'd been in touch with Annabel Hyde, an influential publisher with whom he had worked when establishing the Parnell.

# SCREEN TIME

A state-he-art workstation sat atop the Connemara marble island, a half-empty bottle of Sauvignon Blanc off to one side. Sebastian shuffled his buttocks on the curved-back counter stool, and with clenching anticipation clicked on the light blue icon. Although they had texted back and forth, this would be their first Skype call since the 'incident,' Sebastian's term-of-art for the totality of events leading up to and occurring both during and after the awarding of the prize. Annabel looked exactly as she had during their brief liaison in London, so too her top-floor office. The antique banker's desk remained the room's centre of gravity, a fondly remembered site of sexual calisthenics. 'I want to hear everything, absolutely everything, from beginning to end,' she insisted with a giddy, childlike petulance, not that technicolour accounts of the evening hadn't already reached her from multiple sources. Amelia, only to be expected, had provided a blow-by-blow description of the fiasco for her long-time publisher, not least the part played by the despicable Nic Langdale. Mention of her knee trembler with Sebastian in the broom cupboard prior to the ceremony was, understandably, redacted from the account. Both ladies believed themselves to have established a unique rapport with the amiable hotelier, one about which it would have been unseemly to boast; friendship demanded no less. That fornication might have been a common denominator occurred to neither one. Perhaps it was impermissible in female literary circles for fact to be stranger than fiction.

From her eyrie in Bloomsbury a freshly coiffed Annabel could see beyond the open-plan kitchen to the living area with its panoramic window. She imagined the distant Atlantic's languid swell, memories of her summer visit to Ballyhannah rising of their own accord.

Sebastian, in a navy-blue crew neck sweater, seemed so close she felt she could reach out and touch him. The urge was on her, as they might say in McTigue's. It was a little after six and she was the only one still at Constitution Press. 'Thank God it's Friday' had infected the tony world of publishing as it had almost everywhere else: come four, her colleagues scattered to the pubs of Fitzrovia. She fingered a tumbler of what he took to be Scotch, a refill in fact. The conversation at once assumed the character of a baseline rally at Roland Garros. Both served up reams of questions; hers mainly about what had happened; his mostly about what to do next. Back and forth it went, moments of high seriousness interlaced with passages of sustained hilarity. They'd cut one another off, drive the conversation in a new direction, then scramble back to fill in gaps, fact check. So much catching up to do, so many loose ends to be pulled together. She could tell that he'd be dining out on the story for years to come. And why shouldn't he? It would be small recompense for all the tribulations he had endured. 'You know, Sebastian, I wish I had been with you when the faecal matter hit the fan.' He knew she meant it but wasn't sure whether it was because she had missed his company or had missed out on all the excitement. In publishing circles, the Parnell inaugural would attain near mythic status, on a par with JFK's assassination, the Cuban missile standoff or, if you're Karl Ove Knausgård, the shooting of Olof Palme. 'Were you in Rathboffin when…?' quickly became the most asked question at literary events that year.

'You're quitting?' She sounded surprised at first, swiftly corrected herself. 'I suppose I shouldn't be. Why *would* you want to continue in the role after that? Why would anyone, come to think of it?' 'Well, that's where you come in,' he interjected. 'Can you think of someone who might take my place? Half-time position, decent remuneration, no shortage of cultural capital. You get to meet some nice and, well, some not so nice people. Better than a quango; more autonomy, better pay. And you're pretty much your own boss. By the way, did you know that Ireland has more than 800 quangos? Bureaucracy gone bonkers.' 'Steady on, Sebastian, or I'll be throwing my own hat into the ring.' Her smile seemed to span the top half of the eighteen-inch screen, while her cleavage filled the bottom. His eyes toggled between teeth and teats. He shifted position on the stool to relieve the pressure on his most private part. She didn't need to read his mind: his body language was unambiguous. After a few seconds fiddling with garments, it was down to business. She leaned back under fixed gaze of Joseph Addison, slid her right hand down inside her M&S knickers and began to finger herself, light strokes at first. With the left she fondled an exposed breast. Sebastian half sitting, half standing, had tugged out his penis, baby pink and blue-veined, cute as a new-born manatee. Securely re-positioned on his stool, trousers marooned around his thighs, it was less a case of 'with ravish'd soul, and looks amaz'd, upon her beauteous face he gaz'd' than a frenzied self-milking, eyes fixated on her right breast. Moans, faked or otherwise, emanated from Bloomsbury Square, contrapuntal grunts from Ireland's coast. 'Sebastian, holy fuck I'm coming, I'm coming.' She was rocking in her incongruous Hermann Miller chair. Five hundred and fifty miles west his wearying hand continued to move like a well-greased piston, ever faster. Climax was seconds away. A knock, then a slightly louder one. 'Christ! Someone's at the door!' He jabbed manically at the keyboard as if trying to squash a pesky fruit fly. Annabel vanished from the screen. In came Carla with the papers he had asked her to bring over. He'd clean forgotten they were going to the pub at seven. The fumbling continued, but the bloody thing refused go back where it belonged. His penis really did seem to have a mind of its own—the old autonomic nervous system up to its tricks once again. Carla was standing no more than ten feet away. He crouched down behind the island, like a naughty schoolboy, the grunts now born of frustration, not pleasure. His visitor, mortified and backing off, put two and two together. Computer porn. She'd just caught her boss with his pants down, literally. Not a crime, of course. Perfectly understandable. A single man, after all. No law against masturbation in the privacy of one's home, as far as she knew. If there was, then she'd be guilty of multiple infractions herself, the one difference being that she relied on private fantasy rather than extraneous stimuli. Yet, this was the same man for whom she had feelings, a man she admired. Sebastian was terrified she'd put two and two together and come up with five. Bad enough if she thought she had caught him viewing porn but what if she imagined he had been engaging in screen sex; worse, screen sex with someone he knew, worse still, someone they both knew?

In situations such as this there really is only one option and that is for both parties to act as if absolutely nothing has happened. Which, of course, is even harder to do if you are, like Sebastian, prone to blushing and, if like Carla, you have a sense of decorum that is easily offended—not to imply that she was a prude. He thought of laughing the matter off, of making a joke at his own expense, but feared it would backfire. Her instinct was to offer profuse apologies; after all, she had entered his house without hearing the words 'Come in!' He had told her there was no need to knock. Better safe than sorry, though. She should have waited. His house, after all. Basic good manners. He had just lived through a very difficult period, needed to de-stress. Why shouldn't he be permitted some pleasure? It's human nature after all. We shouldn't stigmatize people. Pornography isn't necessarily bad; indeed, it may even have some therapeutic benefits. Didn't some leading feminists maintain that it was liberating rather than degrading, emancipatory rather than objectifying? In any case, since she had transgressed, it was she who ought to apologize. She had violated his personal space, causing him to experience excruciating embarrassment. Should this adversely affect their relationship, then she would have to accept some if not all the blame. If anything, he deserved to be viewed as a victim of poor decision making on her part. Had Sebastian been aware of what the well-mannered *señorita* with piercing green eyes was thinking, he might have felt compelled to give her an on-the-spot tutorial on gaslighting and the Stockholm syndrome. But at that precise moment he was preoccupied with stuffing a recalcitrant penis back into his briefs, a task not easily accomplished when one is bent in a near foetal position between a stool and a kitchen island and the elastic of one's Calvin Kleins is caught up in an uncooperative zip.

By evening's end, the awkwardness had dissipated, both by then having consumed more alcohol than normal. Directing the conversation to the subject of her mother and possible ways in which the first steps towards a rapprochement might be taken had proved an effective diversionary tactic, so much so that on parting she hugged him in a manner that was at once warm and unselfconscious. Despite that reassuring signal, he endured a restless night, reviewing the ghastly episode over and over, with each re-run seeing, or imagining, yet another overlooked detail. It would be one of those ineradicable memories that travels through life with you like a stray dog that won't be shaken off. For possibly the first time in his middle years he experienced a feeling of self-loathing. Masturbation, he knew, was a perfectly natural, indeed healthy act, safe, pleasurable and stress-relieving. If it were a pill, it'd be even more of a blockbuster than Prozac. Shame need not enter the frame. Men and women self-pleasure, as do animals, routinely and effortlessly. Yet, we tend to either steer conversation clear of the subject or snigger at the thought of it, resorting more often than not to euphemisms and circumlocutions. It's almost as natural as talking a pee or a dump yet remains taboo in polite circles. In another bed, a mere hundred yards away, Carla also lay awake, unable to achieve comfort and plumping her pillow as if suffering from obsessive compulsive disorder, one minute thinking of her mother and what might be, the next of Sebastian and what had been. She slipped her hand down her ever so slightly convex belly and over her mons pubis, heading unerringly for the clitoris, exhibiting a deftness of touch that Sebastian could only have dreamed of achieving. She moaned, cooed almost. Here she was, doing what he had been doing only a few hours earlier. That realization made it seem less shocking to her. If, for the sake of argument, he had been looking at photos of her on the screen and masturbating to them, then would that be really be so very different from what she was doing at that moment? Carla relied upon her imagination to conjure up erotic images, while he used video clips of professional pornographers—outsourcing in B-school terminology. Their approaches may have differed, but not the outcome. No harm was done, no injuries sustained, other perhaps than to his *amour propre*. Imagine, she chided herself, how *he* might have felt had he stumbled unwittingly into her room just as she was stroking to orgasm? By the time the first slivers of morning could be seen in the east she had slipped into a welcome sleep.

# CLEAR THE DECKS

By late July, the stubborn fog of uncertainty had lifted enough for Sebastian to start to think about what might come next. Following the insurance settlement, a spring had returned to his step. Although appreciably less than what would be required to build a perfect replica of The Conyers from the ground up, the pay-out could not in fairness be described as derisory. On the plus side, never again would he have to interact with the ghastly Reg Davis and his fellow HEXers. And as is sometimes the way, good news begat good news. Thanks to a referral from Brendan Byrne, he succeeded in selling the hotel (freehold and insurance award, plus good will) to Richard O'Dougherty, an enterprising scrap merchant from the Midlands, one of a handful of bottom-feeders who had made a pretty penny in the wake of the property market collapse. Sebastian grew to almost like the rubicund cove with the crushing handshake. 'Call-me-Dick' was planning to launch a chain of mid-size, reasonably priced hotels. In less than eighteen months, The Conyers would morph into the Traveller's Nest, and bear the imprint of the developer's wife, Sharon, a mother of five with a passion for interior decorating. Above the fireplace, where St Sebastian had once reigned supreme, she planned to install a custom-made, polychrome Lotus flower mandala, with smaller wooden versions, pink or purple, gracing each of the bedrooms. Guest feedback would lead her to set up her own mandala-manufacturing company using the latest laser technology. In time, she'd become a familiar face on morning TV and a role model for Traveller women all over Ireland, expatiating on the subjects of motherhood and entrepreneurship.

They met in Lurch's premises to conclude the formalities of the sale. Call-me-Dick took a shine to liver-spotted Mrs Dooley and wasted no time in dispensing his roguish charm. He had a repertoire of one-liners for every social occasion, for every audience. The laughter was approaching near illegal levels when Lurch emerged from his office with the stealth of a surfacing submarine. They duly crammed into the manilla file mausoleum. Lurch droned; Call-me-Dick cracked a knuckle or two; Sebastian closed his eyes and tried to imagine Annabel stretched out naked on the desk in front of him; Carla contemplated her boss's jawline and incipiently bulbous nose. Later the trio enjoyed a celebratory drink in Keenan's, Lurch using an afternoon courthouse appearance as his excuse—Mrs Dooley, attired that day in a lookalike Chanel two-piece, would willingly have acted as alternate had she but been invited. Call-me-Dick, a pint of rusty-red Smithwick's and a glinting ball of malt in front of him, quickly warmed to the now redundant chief operating officer of The Conyers. His gannet eyes locked on Carla. At some point he'd need to staff up the new business. What better than an experienced hand on the tiller? 'It'll be a grand wee hotel, all mod cons. Stylish, too, what with the missus looking after the décor and that. There'll be no skimping, no cutting corners, I can promise you. It won't be a bland budget joint or one of those posh, up-their-own-arses establishments you see in the glossies. I want the Traveller's Nest to become the hotel of choice for punters who expect high standards but at a fair price.' Sebastian listened but could not have cared less about Call-me-Dick's plans, punters or price points. 'Gotta hit the road.' O'Dougherty, rising, hitched his trousers with his left hand while with the other slipped Carla his business card. 'Let's stay in touch. Exciting times ahead.' A medley of hugs, backslaps and handshakes followed. 'You know what they say. A Rolling Stone gathers no Kate Moss.' With a meaty belly laugh he was gone.

  A month after his aborted Skype session with Annabel, Sebastian flew to London to pick her brains. Online sex couldn't compete with intimacy *in vivo*. Slathering bodily fluids across a computer screen was no match for the immediacy, the heady aromatic delights of fleshy, sweaty coitus. They slobbered, sucked and shagged, healthy mid-lifers, unencumbered by spouses or partners, parents or offspring. What could beat transactional sex, stripped of complication, recrimination or expectation? Each explored every square inch of the other's compliant body; fingers, tongues and toes were all called into service, probing crevices and cavities with gleeful impunity. If there'd been a memento T-shirt, it would have been emblazoned with the words 'Coyness is for kids.' Neither gave any thought to the idea of a long-term relationship; neither possessed nor professed romantic feelings for the other: carefree carnality summed it up.

Armed with three recommendations, Sebastian returned to Ireland, even more bounce in his step. It would prove to be their very last meeting, for reasons that never became clear to Annabel, not that she would bear any kind of grudge or experience any lasting sadness. A penis in a pair of red trousers was not exactly a rarity in her world. For every Sebastian there waited in the wings a troupe of well-spoken Hugos or Julians. Sebastian's life, though, was about to take a turn that even he could not have envisaged and, as a result, Annabel Hyde would be reduced to just another statistic, another notch on the bedpost. Were *A Trifecta of Tribulations* ever to be written, his shapely fuck buddy would warrant a couple of pages: without the Skype episodes perhaps less. Mediation added a modicum of novelty to a subject that had been covered exhaustively in literature. When it came to sex, standing out in the wordsmithing crowd posed a challenge. Not in a million years could he have written 'how a change of semen can make a woman bloom!' or thought to refer to himself as 'going about with his tube from one woman to another.' For good reason did the likes of Henry Miller and James Joyce stop readers in their tracks; their singular, convention-flouting prose demanded attention, induced equal measures of admiration and envy in aspirants. Sebastian couldn't write for peanuts, recognized the fact. His guiding principle remained unchanged: If you're not JP Donleavy or Edna O'Brien, push aside the typewriter and stick to scribbling graffiti on loo walls. To his way of thinking, lack of self-awareness was among the most egregious of adulthood's sins. Did dinner party bores never hear themselves? Did fat people never look in the mirror? Did politicians never imagine the public despised them? He at least was aware of his failings, even if he couldn't rectify them.

# FLIGHT OF FANCY

By mid-June, Petronella Brabazon, recently retired from her position as senior commissioning editor with a major publisher, agreed to take on the role of director, having met, successively, with Sebastian, Gavin Florin and Brendan Byrne. Daughter of a brigadier and educated at Cheltenham and Durham, the fifty-five-year-old, pince-nez-wearing spinster was forthright in manner and speech. She rather reminded Sebastian of Clarissa Dickson Wright, though he had no idea whether she could cook or ride sidecar. Petronella—addressed by a select few as Pet—knew Annabel well but had no inkling that her good friend and the Conyers chap were, or had been, close. 'We'll show the blackguards,' she honked when discussion turned to the subject of the riot and subsequent arson. 'Damn cowards, that lot. Just let them stick their noses into our affairs again, and we'll give them what for.' Listening to her he wondered if perhaps it were she rather than her father who had held the rank of brigadier. Over the course of a vinous weekend in Bristol, her birthplace, Sebastian laid out the short history of the prize and its remit. They discussed vintage claret—he from the perspective of one increasingly priced out of the market and she from that of a summer intern and trainee with an old school wine merchant in the city—before moving on to matters of finance, jury composition and schedule. He reeled her in like an unresistant rainbow trout. That he resembled her older brother, a society portrait painter, may have played a part. She, of course, might wish to change the venue or tweak certain procedural aspects, but those were issues to run by Gavin. Thereafter, everything proceeded with military efficiency and in less than a month Sebastian's association with the prize established by his late friend had come to a formal conclusion. The Parnell was now in the safest of establishment hands. George could have no tenable grounds for complaint, unless the idea of an upper middle class English lady of stentorian voice and uncertain sexuality overseeing a prize for Irish writing constituted an issue.

The brawling Islamicists, having appeared in court and been found guilty, were awaiting sentencing—a token slap on minority wrists most likely. In the interim, a member of the group had inadvertently let slip the identity of the arsonist. The craven fellow had, however, fled to his homeland in the Maghreb. In due course, he would be the subject of a failed extradition request, the long arm of the law once again proving too short when it came to international terrorism. As far as the ructions in and around the town hall were concerned, Rathboffin's Warholian moment had passed. Three months after the destruction of The Conyers came news of the Boston marathon bombing, the carnage there proving incomparably worse than anything the tiny west of Ireland town had experienced since its founding. Terrorist attacks made for gripping media headlines: the larger the body count, the bolder the font size—the cynical calculus of callousness, George once called it. But such attacks were like icebergs; the dead being the visible tip. The wounded, the maimed and the permanently traumatized were the seven eighths that remained largely out of sight, many suffering injuries that may have made them wish they had been killed outright. At some point, The Conyers would reopen, as good (or nearly as good) as new, the scars plastered and painted over. Not so for several of those forced to flee the premises on the night in question. Their scars might not be physical in nature, but the psychological after-effects of the attack would prove long-lasting. And all because someone took exception to a work of imagination.

Sebastian was a free agent, Carla technically unemployed. By now, he no longer felt a need for police protection. Time to move on, even if justice had yet to be served in comprehensive fashion. He took her to *Chez Claude* to celebrate both the handover to Petronella and the contract signing with Call-me-Dick. Claude, true to form, fluttered around their table like a peacock performing a mating dance, a forgivable if hardly endearing idiocy. When the curtain came down and the *patron* took his act elsewhere, Sebastian raised a glass to his companion. 'Thank you for everything,' he said, leaning forward and resting his hand on hers for a couple of seconds. She smiled, a smile of distracted appreciation, trying not to forget her lines. She'd rehearsed her remarks earlier that day. Common decency required that she say something, sooner rather than later. 'Sebastian, it's time for me to find a job now that everything has been sorted out. I cannot depend on you any longer. It's not right. Really, you have been so generous., but I need to find a place of my own.' He had anticipated the moment and butted in like an offended stag, this time parking his palm on the back of her fanned fingers. 'A job I understand, but the barn is yours for as long as you would like, job or no job. I mean it. Since I occupied the barn rent-free, I don't see why you shouldn't. It's what George would have wanted, I'm sure of it. Anyway, who'd go to the pub with me if you moved back to Rathboffin?' Having been deflected from her script, she was working out what to say next when he pulled an envelope from his inside jacket pocket and handed it to her. 'What's this? Tickets? To Madrid? I don't understand.' He had *his* lines off pat. 'Don't you think we've earned a little break? We're going to Salamanca' Bewilderment washed through her features. 'But Salamanca? That's...' 'That's the idea,' he said, completing her sentence. 'Maybe you'll be inspired to contact her, maybe not. Either way, we can have a well-deserved break, and you'll have an opportunity to brush up on your Spanish. As for contacting your mother, you don't need to decide right now. No pressure whatsoever. Maybe just being there will help sort out your thoughts. I hope you don't think I've over-stepped the mark and, of course, you are under no obligation to accept. But let me tell you, I am going, one way or the other, and I certainly could use an interpreter.'

Carla padded about her living room, peering out into the pitch of night towards the distant lighthouse, her mood one of feathery nervousness. The rotating beam skimmed the sea's surface with the delicacy of a blade bestowing knighthoods. It never varied, never faltered in its task. Loop followed loop, every sixty or so seconds. In such predictability does reassurance reside. Her agitated fingers played with the surprise ticket. She looked at it multiple times half expecting it to say something or maybe dissolve in her hands. July 10th, Dublin->Madrid. July 16th, Madrid >Dublin. Business class. She held it aloft under the standing lamp, scrutinized the details: same name, same dates, same itinerary. She folded it in the middle, then again and yet again without thought or intention, an accidental origamist. The 'what if?' questions pullulated. What if she encountered her in the street? What if she made contact and later regretted it? Then came perhaps the most obvious question of all: what on earth had prompted Sebastian to make such a gesture? Not once had he alluded to the idea of a trip. An impulse? Just the sort of thing that would appeal to the charmingly unpredictable Irishman, she concluded, her anxiety reading returning to normal. To spurn a week in her native land with a man for whom she had a special if ill-advised fondness would seem to make little sense. She collapsed into sleep, dreamt in Spanish.

In a king-sized bed not far away, Sebastian, woozy and wakeful, stared ceilingward. No point in resisting. He'd be released to sleep when mind and body, operating in concert, determined the time was right, not a moment sooner. For now, he had the luxury of reflecting on his impulse. Exactly what had impelled him to book an overseas holiday? He'd never subscribed fully to Gide's notion of the *acte gratuit*. A nifty novelistic conceit, but not the stuff of reality. Causality underpinned the empirical world; decisions like events had triggers, overt or masked, acknowledged or unperceived. Utterly unmotivated behaviour? It simply didn't make sense. For every effect, every outcome there existed a cause. That was a simple, irrefutable, non-negotiable fact. A one-hundred percent gratuitous gesture? Impossible, unless one is talking about the random actions of a lunatic and even then, there'd be a bio-chemical-level explanation. Inevitably, there's an explanation to be found. All it requires is some committed grubbing about in the thickets of sloppy thinking and the recesses of memory. Abiogenesis may explain how human life evolved on planet Earth, but the notion that thoughts formed themselves out of nothing? That was drifting off into the more fanciful realms of artificial intelligence. Deep down he had booked those tickets for a reason, and he owed it to himself—his rational self, the very same self that had spent many a happy hour debating heavyweight philosophical topics with George—to come up with the answer. His decision may have been whimsical in nature, but whimsy lacked explanatory power. So, why Salamanca? Did he really care so much about Carla that he was prepared to invest time and money in a long-shot effort to engineer a rapprochement between estranged parent and child? What made him feel he had a right to meddle in her private affairs? He could just as easily have booked a holiday in Barcelona; better still, her hometown of Santiago de Compostela. So, he *was* trying to ingratiate himself with her, insinuate himself in her personal life. But why? Just then, he started to harden. Who says men don't think with their dicks?

# PART VI

# FLYING THE FLAG

Even before checking in, Sebastian was transported. In the distance he could see the distinctive red, white and yellow livery blazoned across the fuselage and tailfin: the colours of the Spanish flag, vibrant and proud. The sight returned him to Madrid, to an information systems conference early on in his career. For reasons beyond articulation, he had clammed up part way through his presentation, one for which he had rehearsed every natural-seeming pause and tonal inflection in front of a full-length mirror: manufactured spontaneity, method acting for dons, he christened the approach. Absolutely nothing would be left to chance. And on the day, all had indeed been proceeding according to plan until, without warning or ostensible cause, the wheels came off. No one present seemed to realize it was a panic attack of sorts. The nagging little voice of self-doubt that he would come to know only too well over the course of his truncated career knocked him for six. The words ceased to flow; a numbness enveloped him. It was something more than imposter syndrome, a form of expressive aphasia. He once described the sensation to George as comparable to slow-motion drowning, without the flailing around.

Since experienced academics didn't suffer from stage fright, the audience simply assumed he had a frog in his throat or was suffering from a very minor upset: jetlag or a localized variant of Montezuma's revenge, something inconsequential at any rate. Nothing in his demeanour suggested either a transient ischemic attack or coronary. He wasn't clasping his chest, clutching the dais or crumpling like a ragdoll at the knees. Consuelo, a fellow panellist blessed with a sixth sense, came to his aid, without fluster or melodrama, bearing a glass of water. For ten or so seconds, she stood by his side at the podium until he gave a nod signalling all was well. The discombobulating voice retreated before her smile, like a vampire confronted by a crucifix. Equilibrium restored; he resumed his remarks almost as if nothing had happened. The potency of pulchritude, he'd later think. From the respectful applause at session's end, he concluded that the half-way hiccup had already been forgotten, had in no way detracted from his talk. Six hours later, a freshly showered and shirted Sebastian was seated next to his ministering angel at the concluding dinner. Magical moments have a way of happening at international meetings, as if engineered by an unseen hand. Veterans of the conference world learn to go with the flow, not to over-think the possibilities; newbies over-imagine the possibilities, overplay their hands. In the main, social niceties are observed while normative boundaries are stretched, the Chatham House Rule applying. On an early summer evening, one hundred and fifty information systems specialists from all over had funnelled into a venerable restaurant next to the Plaza Mayor, the merry group occupying a function suite on the upper floor. Sangria flowed and Flamenco rattled the century-old floorboards. It was the kind of wrap-up dinner that occurs multiple times daily across the globe, as academic caravans roll from one choice location to the next, leaving empty wine carafes and congealed condoms in their wake. Nice work if you can get it, and what honest attendee could disagree? He attacked the roast suckling pig like a trencherman and drank with a liberality the locals had come to associate with his nationality. Consuelo was neither surprised nor disapproving. The more he consumed, the funnier he became, though at no time descending into boorishness of either speech or action. There followed the moon-lit meander through the city's sometimes raucous, sometimes hushed old streets down to the Palacio Royal with its view out over the gardens and park; the playful, bilingual back-and-forth; the tentative entwining of fingers; the decorous cheek-kiss; the near wordless arm-in-arm stroll back to the hotel. Only the ending deviated from the time-honoured script: Consuelo, he discovered in the foyer, had recently become engaged to a cultural anthropologist. The gods of the symposium had their little laugh. He never saw her again.

A contretemps at check-in interrupted his jaunt down memory lane. The airport was busy: peak holiday time. The attire and demeanour of the couple ahead of him shrieked not just economy but Benidorm or Magaluf. The husband, a diminutive buzz-cut plug of man had plumped for beige cargo shorts, ideal for showcasing his blue-inked calves and sheathing his tightly furled copy of *The Sun*. The wife's gruffness was not endearing her to the woman behind the desk. 'As I said, this is for business class passengers only. I'm afraid you'll have to join the economy queue.' Polite and clear though the instruction was, it engendered churlish resistance. For some people, belligerence is a default setting. It had been for Elaine Claffey since early adolescence. A holy terror, the nuns called her; others had flowerier monikers for the termagant. Every time Mrs Claffey raised her voice or gesticulated, her mottled underarm flesh wobbled like the belly of a scuttling old tabby. Things were about to escalate in all-too familiar fashion. Hefty heels were being dug in; preparations being made on both sides of the desk for a war of attrition. Obduracy, however, is not a trait that flies well in airports. As a rule, one's fellow passengers favour dispute resolution over delay-inducing confrontation, whatever the rights and wrongs of the situation. Sebastian understood the agent's position and would have been no less dogmatic had he been in her shoes. But he had a flight to catch, and Finglas's finest were not going to get in the way. 'Enough! Why don't you do as the young lady says and step aside? This line is for business class passengers only and *that*,' he said pointing,' is economy class.' The accent did it. 'What the fuck's it gotta do with you, you English git?' Eddie Claffey surprised not only his wife but himself with this burst of bravado. The agent blanched. Sebastian experienced intestinal tightening. He'd take the runt out in no time. There'd be no backing down. 'Aw, leave it, Eddie.' Seeing her husband man up in such unexpected fashion had come as a shock, albeit a most agreeable one. 'Leave it, Love. This fecking egit isn't worth it. And as for that cow.' Sebastian's and Eddie's eyes unlocked. The agent exhaled, shot a glance at Sebastian. With a rallentando of muttered expletives, the Claffeys dragged their Disney-themed roller bags towards the back of the snaking economy queue.

# TURBULENCE

Well before boarding time, a line had started to form at the gate. Rather than sit, lounge or snooze, people preferred to stand, as if the plane might leave without them or some blighter would nick their confirmed seat. It puzzled Sebastian, made no sense whatsoever. As soon as the first plonker took up position, others followed, like sheep. It said something about humankind and the ability of a minority to influence a majority: herd behaviour and all that. Why would anyone want to spend a minute more than necessary in a cramped seat in an over-heated aircraft if they could help it? He had a game that he played whenever he flew: aim to be the very last passenger on board; wait for the final boarding call; better still, wait until your name is called for the first time over the public address system with the attendant threat of having your bags removed from the aircraft. Of course, if your checked bags are already buried in the hold, there's really no need to worry; you'll still make it with time to spare. A frivolous if harmless diversion, it added a little spice to the travails of travel post 9/11. Anyway, someone had to be last on, so why not him, strolling relaxedly along the empty jetway, through the cabin entry door and straight down the uncrowded aisle to his seat? No hanging around as bumblers played musical chairs, lassoed errant children or struggled to stash their luggage in the overhead bins.

Had Carla been with him she would, he knew, have been puzzled by his little game. He still could not believe that she had upped anchor. The keys to both the barn and Audi had been slipped through his letterbox along with a handwritten note thanking him for all that he had done for her. No warning, no explanation. 'It is best if I leave now,' was all he had to work with. Leave? For where? Why? The out-of-character abruptness of her departure made him think that the reason, or reasons, had nothing to do with either their professional or personal relationship. Which meant he wasn't at fault. Which is what mattered. Good thing, too, that she hadn't walked out when managing the hotel. That really would have messed things up. Yes, he'd miss his green-eyed *amiga*, but heartbroken…?

The purser, a graceful woman in her mid-thirties with tied-back, lustrous black hair and chili red lipstick welcomed him on board with a Carla-like smile. Her male colleague, the spitting image of El Cordobés in his youth, right down to the dark flop of hair and cuspids, greeted him a respectful nod of the head and relieved him of his hand luggage. Both flight attendants could have been professional models hired to showcase the carrier's stylish uniforms. What must cabin crew make of slobs like the Claffeys who consider beachwear appropriate for air travel? They surely had nicknames for the different types of passengers: the phobic, the complainer, the busybody, the poseur. The purser made the standard bilingual announcements and then El Cordobés rattled through the safety rigmarole, a matador of the skies reduced to faffing about mid-aisle with a demo seat belt and plastic oxygen mask for the benefit of people who, in the improbable event of an emergency water landing, would not remember a word he said. More to the point, it was an open secret in the industry that following a crash, no one would be walking or swimming away. But asses had to be covered, hence the palaver. Sebastian would, naturally, have paid rapt attention had it been the purser performing the safety demo. Trolley dollies, he reckoned, could distinguish in an instant between those who were genuinely interested in seeing and hearing what to do in case of an emergency and those systematically undressing them with their eyes. He'd been found out more than once.

The pilot introduced himself and his female co-pilot, the seat belt sign came on, the cabin door clunked into locked position, the massive engines whined into life and with a judder or two the plane taxied slowly away from the apron. Six minutes later, the gleaming Iberian Airbus thundered down a strip of ramrod-straight asphalt and concrete, lifted its nosecone and with a familiar grinding sound retracted the landing gear. The angle of attack pushed Sebastian and the Madrilenian MILF next to him back in their seats. Overhead bins rattled like castanets. The thrill never faded. Dublin bay, grey green and corrugated, opened up beneath them as the plane banked steeply to the right before barrelling up into a blanket of buffeting cloud. As soon as cruising altitude was reached, the attendants unstrapped from their jump seats and set to work, first drawing the all-important curtain that separated the worlds of business and economy, a line not for crossing. Sebastian watched the *pas de deux* unfold in the cramped forward galley. This Iberian dream team exhibited faultless choreography, each mindful of the other's steps: heedful interaction at its finest. The tasks being performed may have been mundane, but the manner of their execution was a thing of no little beauty: '*Multum in Parvo*' would have been an apt title for the mile-high performance, reckoned Sebastian.

A spumy Cava prepped his palate for a restaurant-worthy *pollo a limón*, accompanied by a crisp, dry white Rioja. Measured top-ups came without asking; for dessert a scrumptious *Pastel de chocolate y des almandras*. To Sebastian's chagrin, El Cordobés, not the dark-haired purser, attended to their side of the aisle. Nothing seemed too much trouble for the steward, who found ready favour with the stylish woman seated to his left. At each naturally occurring opportunity the pair chirped in Spanish, weaving in and out of one another's unfinished sentences, all much too fast-paced for Sebastian to catch more than the occasional word. Instead, he dipped in and out of a charity-shop copy of Somerset Maugham's *Fernando* he had bought the week before. Here, thirty-three thousand feet up over continental Europe, he remembered the super-animated Carla that few people in the English-speaking world ever encountered. Speaking in her native tongue, she'd roll her Rs, flex her full complement of facial muscles in a way she rarely if ever did when speaking English and gesture with an arabesque fluency that left Sebastian mesmerized. He felt a slight twinge of sadness, then glanced at the MILF with whom he had exchanged not a word. Why couldn't the fang-faced fucker get back into the galley, stow the dishes, tidy up the trash or whatever Iberia paid him to do? It wasn't his job to schmooze with female passengers. Not that Sebastian, a normative egoist when it suited his purposes, would have acted any differently had he been in the bullfighter's shoes.

Five rows back, Eddie and Elaine Claffey's antics had not endeared them to those in their immediate vicinity, nor to the hard-pressed flight attendants responsible for the packed economy section. Empty San Miguel tins littered the pair's tray tables. Their most recent request for *una cerveza mas*—an expression Elaine had found in a phrase book borrowed from her teenage daughter—had been met with a firm shake of the head, not because her Spanish was execrable but because she and her husband were. Matters had not been helped by Eddie's knocking back the two miniatures of Smirnoff that he had secreted in his hand luggage. Loudmouths are rarely agreeable company; within the tubular confines of a commercial aircraft, they guarantee collective misery. Needing to pee, a sozzled Eddie shifted his detritus to his wife's tray-table before pulling himself up by holding on to the back of the seat in front of him. In so doing, he accidentally tugged the unsuspecting passenger's hair. Her muted shriek caused him to stumble back into Elaine's territory. Cans tumbled every which way. With a porcine grunt and a determined shove from the missus, Eddie was returned to vertical. Staggering out into the aisle, he bumped against the passenger seated directly across from him, knocking over yet more drink. Oblivious, he blundered towards the front of the plane, yanking aside the dividing curtain as if it should not have been there in the first place. Was not freedom of movement one of the foundational principles underpinning the European Union? At that same moment, three rows ahead, Sebastian was also feeling a need to relieve himself. Just as he rose from his aisle seat, Eddie Claffey bulldozed into him, whether with intent or not, only he knew. 'I beg your pardon. What the hell do you think you're doing?' He recognized the pugnacious chin, could smell the alcohol. 'This is for business class passengers. You have no right to be here. Use the facilities in your own bloody area.' It was red-rag-to-a-bull time. 'Ya fuckin' ponce,' hissed Eddie. 'What, what did you just call me?' came the well-spoken but minatory reply. The vodka and beer had by now washed away any scintilla of rationality or proportionality Eddie might have possessed. Off balance and consumed by anger, he released a scything punch that sailed past its intended target only to strike the MILF. The matador sprang into instinctive action, grabbed wee Eddie by the scruff of his neck and frog-marched him back to his seat, earning a flurry of applause for his unhesitating intervention. It was a white-handkerchiefs-worthy performance. 'You have just committed a criminal offence. Do you realize the consequences?' Elaine looked bewildered at first but was not so intoxicated that she failed to appreciate the potential gravity of the situation. Her apologies on her husband's behalf would prove ineffectual. Air rage places everyone in an intolerable situation. Eddie shrivelled into his seat, before releasing an audible and protracted belch. Back in business class, the solicitous purser was applying ice to the poor woman's head while doing her level best to discourage vigilante justice. 'I assure you, Sir, the police will take care of this. Please try to forget him.' Once they had arrived at Barajas and taxied to the gate, the pilot made a calm and courteous announcement requesting that all passengers remain in place with their seat belts fastened. Shortly thereafter, two armed *Guardia Civil* officers boarded the aircraft and, following consultation with both the captain and purser, strode down the aisle. Before long, they reappeared with a handcuffed Eddie whose face resembled a Francis Bacon self-portrait. His slatternly wife, flushed and furious, trailed behind, pulling the pair's carry-on bags. Her expression was one of unadulterated hatred. 'Enjoy your stay,' Sebastian called after her. Mickey Mouse's smile never wavered.

As Eddie Claffey stewed in a sweltering Spanish gaol, Elaine strove to spur the British consulate into action. Their plight, however, elicited zero sympathy from authorities on either side. The Claffeys were as much an embarrassment to their own country as they were an affront to the host nation. Once upon a time, they and their ilk sought little more than the annual two weeks in Bray or Bundoran; if encumbered with children, where better than Butlin's Mosney camp with its breezy Redcoats? Grim it may have been in the eyes of cosmopolites, but such was life in socially stratified Ireland. International travel remained the preserve of the few: the affluent, the culturally sophisticated types who knew that espresso didn't have an x, that you didn't call the Parisian waiter *'Garçon!'*, that Mario Lanza wasn't an Italian sportscar.

In a matter of a generation or so, fishing villages like Benidorm had devolved into dystopian playpens for boozing Brits and Paddys bloated of belly and pink of skin. As the package holiday industry mushroomed, the great unwashed spread their wings, flapping into parts of the civilized world heretofore untainted. How many times had George listened to Sebastian railing against the iniquities of cheap travel? 'What's the point of going all the way to Spain to eat fish and chips and knock back pints of Guinness in an Irish pub alongside ex-pats? Why not stay at home and use the savings to drink twice as much in your local or wherever?' Foreign travel, in his eyes, did not constitute a right, something to which every citizen had automatic entitlement; rather, it should be earned. 'If you can't be bothered to read up on the history, culture and traditions of other countries and feel no inclination to acquire at least a smattering of the language, why on earth should you be granted admission? The issuance of a passport ought to come with certain expectations, if not indeed requirements. The pleasures of reflective travel are being sacrificed at the altar of populism.' He had phrased it in exactly those words to George one evening in McTigue's. Such unapologetic elitism guaranteed either amusement or offence. George saw past the rodomontade. 'You know,

Sebastian, not only is snobbery an inherently distasteful trait, but one that, I suspect, masks underlying insecurities in a person. The need to denigrate others in sweepingly dismissive fashion points to a lurking fear that one may oneself be not all that different from those whom one purports to despise. Snobbery, I would contend, is ultimately, a form of bullying, charmless and cowardly, provoked by a deep-seated sense of inadequacy. Peek behind the curtain of bluster and what you'll find more often than not is self-loathing.' That took the wind out of Sebastian's puffed-up sails.

By early afternoon he was speeding northwest through the parmesan-coloured Castilian countryside in a rental car. He suffered no after-effects from the in-flight brouhaha and had quickly put the incident behind him, something the wretched Claffeys would be unable to do. He made a short stop in Ávila, with 'its reserve, its taciturnity and its ceremonial stiffness'—Maugham's assessment predated the tourism plague. And it wasn't Ávila's walls or Romanesque churches that Sebastian had learned about at school. For his generation, the place was synonymous with Saint Teresa and her raptures, levitation and extreme asceticism. The story goes she'd ask other Carmelites to hold her down lest she floated up and away like a hot air balloon. That was the kind of claptrap he and his fellow pupils were fed in the nineteen-fifties. She should have been bloody well sectioned. Then, the miraculous was part and parcel of everyday life: turning water into wine, raising people from the dead, healing the terminally ill. The Bible made *Harry Potter* seem anodyne. Jesus had more tricks up his sleeve than Houdini and Uri Geller combined. There were multitudes of miracles. And not just the golden oldies from the Bible. Every saint seemed to have a special party trick: St Blaise saving the life of a young boy choking on a chicken bone, St Francis healing the leper, pacifying the big bad wolf. Hundreds of saints apparently channelling divine power to good earthly effect, in the process subverting the established laws of physics, chemistry and biology. Even today, the nonsense continues with Lourdes and Fátima,

Knock and Medjugorje, the Blessed Virgin Mother popping up all over the place and grown men in red socks and silly hats urging their flocks to take it all literally. Amazing how belief makes the unbelievable credible. Had Carla come with him she might well have informed him that that Franco slept with the revered saint's stolen hand by his side. But his Girl Friday had performed her own vanishing trick and it would take more than a miracle to bring her back.

# THE SQUARE FELLOW

Salamanca announced itself from afar, a muster of honey-coloured buildings shimmering in the intense, early-evening light. *La Dorado* was the ancient city's nickname according to the guidebook. He could see why. From the moment he pulled up outside the hotel, a converted convent, it was as if he had entered a slower-paced, softer-hued world. Rathboffin bore as much resemblance to Salamanca as a cheap Timex did to a top-of-the-range Patek Philippe. By eight the Plaza Mayor was thronged, pulsing with multi-generational life and rippling laughter. The twin sounds of belligerent voices and shattering glass that would have been inevitable on such an evening in Ireland were not to be heard. Here, people drank with moderation, conversation not intoxication being what mattered. It was like being housed inside a Brobdingnagian beehive, the buzzing loud but benign. Rathboffin had nothing remotely comparable. Outside dining in the west of Ireland demanded a hardiness of spirit that few possessed: an exquisite form of penitential pleasure might be the best way to describe the experience, just the kind of thing that would appeal to a mortifying Opus Dei member. Seated beneath a medallion of Philip II, he knocked back a glass of the local red. Wasn't it a miracle how setting could transform one's oenological impressions? For people watchers this was paradise on earth. Sebastian's eyes traced the outline of every passing female with the discernment of a buyer in a sales paddock. The incessant parade of youthful and not-so-youthful good looks at once lifted and cast down his spirit. *Tempus fugit.* Too bloody true. *Carpe diem.* Wise words. All of life condensed in a Latin phrase or two. He scanned the square. *Diem* staring him straight in the face, brimming with vitality and optimism, but out of reach. *In vino veritas.* He drained another glass. Carla had, of course, been aware of his fondness for the female form and tried not to take it personally when his gaze wandered. Not that he lacked self-awareness. The occasional sheepish look she would take as an apology. And not that he had ignored her; far from it. He could be a master of attentiveness, amusing and engaging, when he set his mind to it. It certainly didn't require much effort when seated next to an attractive thirty-something-year-old Spaniard. He knew which side his bread was buttered on, but almost overnight his slice had vanished.

As he drifted towards the outer banks of melancholy, a group of strolling musicians attired in minstrel costumes hooved into view. A sash-bedecked fellow strumming a lute-like instrument parked himself in front of Sebastian, while his mates formed a semi-circle around the table. All eyes locked onto the ensemble, escape being impossible. There could be no turning away of the head or dismissive hand gesture. Good manners as much as custom dictated polite if not enthusiastic attentiveness for the duration. The tempo increased, clapping from nearby tables kicked in. If Carla had been there, she'd no doubt have swirled and twirled with the bearded troubadour. In a half-hearted effort to play along, Sebastian drummed the table-top with his fingers, served up an undercooked smile. Public exhibitionism had never been his thing. Almost as soon as he deposited a ten Euro note in the tambourine player's collecting cap, the black-caped musicians set off in search of the next sucker. Another drink was called for. '*Tunos*, we call them,' the waitress volunteered with amiable indifference.

By nine, nagging hunger and light-headedness necessitated a change of scenery. He weaved along a cobweb of side streets and secured a table in a family-run establishment. There, the waistcoated waiter—the stereotype of a Flamenco guitarist—switched at once to English. Sebastian sat, a fair head in a chattering forest of brown and black, unnoticed, happy to be able to appreciate the local talent. He watched himself watching the watched. He missed Carla, and yet he didn't. It was as if he had been released back into the wide world. The dent in his *amour propre*, which the wine had highlighted rather than masked, would no doubt be fixed in due course. As he zig-zagged homewards, the occasional clang of a church bell reinforced the sense of antiquity, of time passing and past. A long and strange day drew to its close. Within minutes, he was out for the count in a bed that would have been an affront to St Teresa. Between spells of REM sleep, he made several trips to the bathroom.

Breakfast was served on the elevated terrace. From under a cantilever patio umbrella, taut as an acrobat's abs, he stared out at a dizzying patchwork of terracotta tiles. The waitress was no oil painting—a phrase beloved of his father—but she did remind him a little of William Orpen's saucer eyed-Spanish woman, minus the headgear. Fading fragments of a multiplex dream surfaced: a gypsy wrestling with a bloodied matador, a green-eyed flight attendant levitating in a darkened square. Various elements of the previous day were there but recast in the manner of Dalí. If dreaming was the brain's way of processing events, tidying up loose ends and storing information for future use, why all the quixotic, madcap stuff? How did that help us sort through the issues and fears we shied away from in our waking hours? It never ceased to amaze him how different his dreamworld was from his waking life—the difference between Surrealism and Precisionism, between near madness and meticulousness. As he mulled it over, the images from the night before gradually etiolated and the orderly present reasserted control. Polyglot voices rose and fell in the still fresh morning air. Nearby, the American contingent, marked out by their copies of *Fodor's* and baseball caps, prepared to sally forth, bucket lists memorized, fanny packs replete with survival essentials. The handful of Spanish guests jabbered incessantly, causing him to wonder how they ever found the time to masticate. The proverbial Irishman might be able to talk the hind leg off a donkey, but a wound-up Spaniard would surely leave the poor creature legless. At the far end, a couple of middle-aged Germans, heavily bespectacled, hunched over a large-scale map of the town planning their day, while a British couple on the cusp of senility attempted conversation with a venturesome New Zealander. In terms of awfulness, how could one possibly choose between the Antipodean and Ulster-Scots accents? More than once, George had accused his friend of superficiality, of being too quick to dismiss individuals based on externalities. All languages and dialects may be equal in the eyes of sociolinguists, but when it came to pronunciation, even more to accent, Sebastian was not for turning. Nordies and Kiwis butchered the English language. Simple as that. A matter of taste not class, he'd argue.

Before long, he had the place to himself. After a cursory exchange in Spanglish with the waitress, he got up to leave. Better not fritter away the day. So much to be seen. A thorough brushing of the teeth, a parting pee and he was off, pocket map tucked into his back pocket. The receptionist had given it to him along with an extravagant smile. She must belong to the glass half full brigade, another Carla. He rather envied such people, but a sunny disposition probably had less to do with one's philosophy or approach to life than serotonin levels. He didn't deny that mindfulness, spirituality and religion could sometimes help folk get through the day or deal with personal crises, but, ultimately, chemistry was king. That's why neuroscience must be anathema to poets and romanticists. If all it takes to alter our mood is an electric shock, a jab or a pill, then surely that strips the mystery and magic out of existence. Or as he once put it to George: 'If the book of life is the Periodic Table, what does that mean for poor old Proust?'

Residents and students moved through the city with ease, slaloming around groups of camera-toting tourists, nipping past the gawpers. From on high, humans weaving hither and tither must resemble a giant colony of ants: an apparently chaotic yet wondrously self-regulating system, just the sort of phenomenon that might once have engaged Sebastian intellectually. He ambled, alone and anonymous, through the maze of streets with no destination or purpose in mind other than to savour the moment, every so often doubling back on himself. Damned if he was going to pull out the map in public and announce to the world that he was a tourist—as if the world would be paying the slightest attention. How could so many buildings centuries old still be in such good repair? The effect, ever so mildly unsettling, was like walking around a gigantic set on an MGM lot in Hollywood built for a blockbuster historical movie of some kind. Come to think of it, hadn't both Hernan Cortés and Christopher Columbus spent time in Salamanca; hadn't both lived epic lives? As much as the architecture, the animation and the bustle of the place appealed to him. Churches, courtyards, museums and the like could wait. For now, he needed to feel, to inhale, to give himself over to the place. Serious cultural engagement was for another day. He'd let his eyes, ears and nose do the work, a case of sensing rather than thinking. In a haberdashery shop that viewed modernity with suspicion, he purchased a banded Panama hat. It complemented his linen suit. Irish skulls were not designed with Spanish summers in mind, and he knew enough about skin cancer to know that the price of a Panama was a price worth paying.

# SAINTS ALIVE!

On a street that led off the main square he came across an antique shop. *Antigüedades Casillas* had been around for a while, that much was clear from the hand-painted gold lettering on the glass shop sign: almost certainly a family-run enterprise. The intelligent, uncluttered window display held his attention. A small oil painting, roughly eighteen by twenty inches, occupied pride of place. Illuminated by a single overhead light, it packed a punch. What were the odds? He'd come all this way and almost the first thing he sees is a portrait of St Sebastian. Even if his namesake hadn't been in the window, he would have gone inside. The shop extended farther back than he imagined, allowing Sr Casillas to showcase his carefully curated stock: rustic furniture, devotional items, blue Grenadian bowls, eighteenth and nineteenth-century landscapes, brightly coloured Majolica and Talavera. The premises were well lit but far from clinically bright. Every item had a price tag. Nothing worse than having to ask. That gave the vendor an opportunity to set prices according to his estimation of your net worth: dynamic pricing, Sebastian called it. He would browse before taking a closer look at the picture. No need to flag interest unnecessarily early. The notion of a fixed price was, he also knew, alien to the trade. If he was tempted, he'd negotiate. The owner would expect no less. For ten or so minutes, he had the run of the place. He could have walked off with a few choice pieces, had he felt inclined. No sign of security cameras anywhere.

As he leaned in behind the window, trying to get a closer look at the picture, he heard a female voice. She was wearing a lightweight two-piece suit with a fitted three-button jacket and a skirt that covered her knees. A small gold cross hung from a filigree chain around her lightly wrinkled neck. Neither attractive nor unattractive, she looked like a woman of sixty little familiar with either economic hardship or debauchery. A jellyfish-purple birthmark beneath her right eye provided a note of distinctiveness she could have done without. Something about her, not the blemish, made him stare longer than would be deemed polite. 'Good day. Can I help you?' she asked—or so he presumed—in quickfire Spanish. For an instant, he thought he was listening to Carla. Maybe all Spanish women of a certain caste sounded the same. He responded with a fluent-ish *'Perdon, pero no hablo español.'* Each then proceeded to maul the other's native tongue but as often happens in such situations managed to achieve rudimentary understanding. Language rarely acted as a bulwark when it came to trade or barter. Like water, money found a way around barriers, physical or legal. He pointed at the ebony-framed picture, pronouncing the saint's name the way he had heard Carla do. With that, Sra Casillas—assuming it was she—extracted the piece from the window, handed it to him and withdrew; hovering constituted a cardinal sin in the business. The painting, oil on canvas, recently surface-cleaned he reckoned, was unsigned. A faded dealer's label carried a hard-to-decipher gallery name and a date that could have been 1794, as well as an auction lot number. The backing board and tiny, rusted nails looked original to the piece. The saint might not have stepped outside his frame in more than two centuries. When it came to Irish art, Sebastian knew his way around, but his knowledge of late eighteenth-century Spanish oil paintings matched his knowledge of the Spanish subjective tense. It was, he could see, a well-executed study with the youthful martyr strapped to a tree trunk. You didn't need to be a connoisseur to appreciate the draughtsmanship. Six arrows punctured the martyr's nacreous flesh, not enough to wipe the beatific smile from his face. In truth, he looked more like a chap who had just had a blowjob rather than one exhaling his last. *'Quanto es?'* he asked, knowing full well that the tag said €3,250.

With that, the baton passed to Esteban Casillas. He emerged from an office at the rear wearing a light-weight beige cardigan over a pale blue shirt. Pressed slacks and burgundy leather loafers completed the default wardrobe of *El Mundo*-reading males over the age of fifty. Peeking out of a side pocket, a soft pack of *Ducados*. A bookish fellow thought Sebastian, seeing the high-domed head and thinning, slightly mad-scientist hair. The tortoise shell glasses dangling on a strap reinforced the impression. Sr Casillas introduced himself with an economical smile. He spoke in serviceable if slightly stilted English—honed during the year that he apprenticed with a major auction house in London—and proceeded to answer Sebastian's questions. The name of the artist remained indeterminate, though the work had been attributed by a museum director friend, tentatively, to a quite well-known Italian painter with an unpronounceable and easily forgotten name. Esteban could tell from the cut of Sebastian's gib—an archaic turn of phrase he had encountered when in England and never forgotten—that he was likely both a serious and quite possibly knowledgeable customer. Neither would be wasting the other's time. Sra Casillas had summoned her husband discretely from his lair. When it came to matters of price and provenance, she deferred to him. Esteban had inherited not only a good eye but also the business from his father, whose own father had established it before the Civil War. He knew the ins and outs of the antiques world, the exhilarating highs and crushing lows, but had yet to appreciate the future strategic importance of the Internet and online trading to bricks and mortar businesses such as his own. Gentle goading from his wife to create a website had been met with resistance typical of his generation. *Antigüedades Casillas* had been trading with some success for almost nine decades and, thus, to his mind, there seemed little need to rush into unfamiliar territory. 'Remember,' he would say with affectionate teasing to his spouse, 'the story of the Gardarene swine?' Of course, she did. Didn't they, every single day of their lives, read selected passages from the Good Book? They lived for and rejoiced in the Lord, tithed their income to the Order. After a respectful back and forth, a price of €2,900 was agreed upon, at which point the two males shook hands. Sra Casillas then bubble-wrapped the piece before slipping it into a royal blue carrier bag on which the entwined initials AC were printed in gold above the words *Fondada en 1923*.

The realization struck him with epiphanic force as headed towards the *Gran Via*. It had been staring him in the face, like a caged chimp in a municipal zoo. Hadn't Carla told him only a couple of weeks before that her mother was now married to an antique dealer? Hadn't he almost immediately noticed the similarity between Sra Casillas's speaking voice and Carla's? And the clincher: Sr Casillas had twice referred to the woman as Fernanda, Carla's mother's name. Triangulation, the intelligence analyst's dream. Perfect evidentiary alignment and yet, somehow, he had missed it. What a brace of coincidences: first, stumbling upon St Sebastian and, second, Carla's estranged mother. Had he set out with systematic intent to find her, it might have taken days, weeks even. If only he had connected the dots. But supposing he had, what exactly would he have done? After all, it was Carla's not his business. And Carla was no longer his business.

Desperate for a pee, he was barrelling along the street towards the hotel, carrier bag flapping by his side. Mad dogs and Englishmen thought more than one bemused local. Stepping smartly out onto the pedestrian crossing, he looked neither right nor left, failed to spot a dark blue Seat Ibiza bearing down on him, at the wheel a dark-skinned young man. Muhammad and Akeem, handpicked for the task, had been stalking the Parnell Prize director since his arrival in the country, all the way from the airport to Salamanca. Except when in bed, he hadn't been alone the entire time. The car screeched to a halt. From the open rear window Akeem pointed a compact sub-machine gun at the transfixed figure less than six feet away. A fusillade of bullets tore into Sebastian's torso. The Panama spiralled backwards; the elegant bag with the bubble-wrapped martyr dropped with a clunk onto the road. In a matter of seconds, the hijacked vehicle was careening down the street, only just avoiding a collision with a delivery truck. Blood oozed from multiple parts of the cruciform body, staining shirt and suit. Shrieks of horror and disbelief from distraught bystanders drowned out the agonized moans. In the escaping Seat jubilant cries of *'Allahu akbar!'* counterpointed the first of the wailing sirens. Justice had been served.